GREATER LOVE

GREATER LOVE

DEVYN BAKEWELL

NEW DEGREE PRESS

COPYRIGHT © 2020 DEVYN BAKEWELL

GREATER LOVE

ISBN   978-1-63676-540-2   *Paperback*

           978-1-63676-093-3   *Kindle Ebook*

           978-1-63676-094-0   *Ebook*

To my biggest supporters,
My best friends,
My greatest loves,
My sisters,
Taelor and Bryce.
I love you.

TABLE OF CONTENTS

———

AUTHOR'S NOTE 9

PROLOGUE 11

CHAPTER 1 13

CHAPTER 2 19

CHAPTER 3 23

CHAPTER 4 33

CHAPTER 5 39

CHAPTER 6 55

CHAPTER 7 65

CHAPTER 8 75

CHAPTER 9 83

CHAPTER 10 95

CHAPTER 11 111

CHAPTER 12 131

CHAPTER 13 149

CHAPTER 14 161

CHAPTER 15 175

CHAPTER 16 185

CHAPTER 17 199

CHAPTER 18 215

CHAPTER 19 221

CHAPTER 20   235

CHAPTER 21   251

CHAPTER 22   265

CHAPTER 23   275

CHAPTER 24   289

CHAPTER 25   301

ACKNOWLEDGMENTS   307

ABOUT THE AUTHOR   311

AUTHOR'S NOTE

———

Why aren't more black female voices in literature? For centuries, black women have been role models, influencers, and dynamic representations of strong womanhood. We are known to be trendsetters, loyal partners, hardworking businesswomen, and so much more. But despite this, our representation in literary canon is barely existent. Especially in today's society, if a black woman loves to read and wants to find knowledge about women like her for black women like her, she must engage in a hard battle.

I learned to love reading way before I ever learned to love myself as a black woman, or even as an individual. Growing up, I read a lot of romance books centered around women who did not look like me, did not relate to me, and did not understand what I was going through. I'd hear about black women getting shot by police for doing nothing, kidnapped without government action for months, or beat up at political rallies for fighting for what they believed in. We'd even created new inventions, started businesses, and made worldwide discoveries while giving back to our own communities and ones even less fortunate. Black women were constantly fighting to maintain their voices, and with these amazing, sometimes heartbreaking experiences, we still find it hard to tell our stories. This is what led me to write this book.

Like many black women, Ryan is a girl in the shadows. She is young, brilliant, hardworking, and defeating the odds placed against her from a young age. She sees better for herself and does not ask for help. She fights her battles with her own two hands and does not back down. She wants her life to change and will do anything to achieve the goals she's set for herself. But anything is hard to accomplish completely on your own, and she learns to lean on others and to let people support and love you.

We must accept the love and support that we ache for. Black women have been failed by a society that does not pay us nearly enough attention or give us our due diligence, but that does not mean other people won't. And when we create stable bonds and safe spaces where black women can feel supported and loved and safe, communities will be made. Strong communities enable black women to find their voice, discover what makes them so great, and go out into the world and achieve anything. When you know you are supported, the heights one can reach are beyond imagination. True growth starts with the individual, but you need others to learn about yourself and love what you bring to the table.

This book is for young black girls just trying to find their way. Keep hoping, keep aspiring to be better than what's around you, and keep loving. We'll all find our way, together.

PROLOGUE

Never in a million years did I think I'd fall in love with her.
From our first conversation during freshman move-in,
she seemed to hate everything about me. My friends, my
sport, my personality. My compliments couldn't put a smile
on her face, and a simple gesture like walking her home
wasn't enough.

I tried not to care. Told myself she didn't know me and
her opinion didn't matter. But with every conversation, she
captivated me. She told it like it was. She was stubborn and
difficult while being kind and loving and selfless all at the
same time.

We'd spent our entire lives at the same schools. She lived
twelve houses from mine in the same shitty neighborhood
but was bound to escape it. She was smart, brilliant, and
beautiful, and I'm sad it took so long for me to notice. In
high school, she kept to herself and maybe had two friends.
You couldn't find her at a game and definitely not at a party.
She was the definition of a fly on the wall.

She could've gone anywhere—Yale, Princeton, Harvard—
so I couldn't help but be surprised when I found out she was
the only other person from G-Heights, California, to pack

her things and head to a historically black university in New York City—completely on the other side of the country. I didn't expect for my one true love to be her. Our path was never easy, but we were meant to walk it together.

My dad taught me that God makes soul mates for everyone, but I always thought, *If that was true, why did he give men so many beautiful options?* I thought finding one woman to spend your life with was impossible. I could barely keep a girl for a couple of months. I got bored, or a girl proved herself to be way too complicated, so I moved on to the next best thing. My own mom left before I even started thinking about girls. Growing up, the first thing I learned about women was how selfish they could be. I believed that on top of complaining too much and almost always depending on their man to do everything, they usually ended up leaving when life got too hard.

Falling in love with Ryan let me know I had things completely wrong.

CHAPTER 1

RYAN

I wonder if anyone will notice I'm the only incoming freshman without a parent helping them move in.

My heart races and I start to sweat, seeing other girls getting out of their cars, hands full of boxes. Parents are dressed in TRUTH DAD or TRUTH MOM T-shirts with huge "I'm so proud my child's going to college" smiles, pushing mini fridges and microwaves in large moving carts. Meanwhile, here I am watching a stranger pull my three suitcases out of a taxi that I had to scrounge coins together just to hire to get here.

Javon's probably right. I'm almost three thousand miles away from home with no friends, no family, and no job to support me. My own father wasn't about to give me the little cash he had. How am I supposed to survive in big, bad New York?

"D'you plan on getting out the car anytime soon?" said the taxi driver as he sets my last bag on the curb in front of his red Toyota Prius. "You're wasting my gas." He pauses, adding, "Not to mention my time."

I pull myself out of my thoughts and get out of the car, painfully handing him the fifty-two dollars it took to get here from the airport. The man rolls his eyes, snatches the money from my hand, jumps in the car without ever acknowledging my thank-you, and zooms down the street before I can even grab my bag.

Thanks for the welcome.

"Excuse me!"

I turn around to see a completely bald, golden-skinned woman running toward me with a clipboard.

"You're a freshman, right?"

"Yeah," I say, forcing a smile.

"Great!" she exclaims, "I'm De'Onna Brown . . . senior bio major from Dallas." She reaches her hand out for me to shake, and I politely do. "I'm going to bring someone over with a cart to take your stuff up. Are your parents still looking for parking? I know it's kind of crazy around here."

"No. This is all I have." Her words slap the fake smile off my face. It hasn't been five minutes since I got here and she's already hit me in the softest spot of my heart today. "I'll carry my own stuff."

"Girl, no!" She giggles. "We've got some big, strong guys from the football team ready to help you." She turns around and motions one over. I grab my bags so I can bolt to the lobby without being disturbed, but a guy's already running our way. "Can you help her with her bags?"

"Yeah, of course." His voice is too familiar, and with every heavy step I recognize another part of him—his large, muscular body, round gut, sepia, almost copper-colored skin, and high cheekbones. He takes my bag, which looks miniature in his big, chubby hands, looking at me. Almond-shaped eyes grow into circles the second our eyes lock. "Ryan?"

"You two know each other?"

In seconds, I've managed to lose more than 50 percent of my money and run into the exact type of person I'm trying to run away from. Here's another nigga from my toxic little neighborhood. He was one of the star lineman on a football team full of men known for breaking hearts and hymens, adding to the list of black men who are solely worried about themselves. And he's the first man I'm meeting in college? Just my fucking luck.

We weren't friends then and weren't going to be now. I'd escaped California to leave all that shit behind me. "Sorry. Do I know you?"

His eyes shift, and he almost looks sad. Or maybe it's shock. "I've probably just seen you on GroupMe or something. You're from Cali too, right?"

I nod, kicking myself for having no idea what GroupMe is. "Yeah, I am."

"I'll let you two get to it," De'Onna says. "Nice meeting you, Ryan. I'll see you later, D." She skips off to bother the next family before either of us can respond.

He's already placed my bags in a large blue cart when I turn around to face him. They look pitiful, only furthering my embarrassment. "I'll carry my own bags. You can spend your time helping someone with more stuff."

"No can do. Coach is watching," Devyn Baker, who I'm guessing now goes by D, nods across the street, where a three hundred-pound bald man with a swollen belly stares at us. He smiles and waves.

"You're stuck with me," Devyn says.

I roll my eyes and let him follow me to Harriet Hall, my new home. "Why didn't you want De'Onna to know we know each other?"

Devyn's lived maybe twelve houses down from me since I was three years old. Fifteen years and we've probably exchanged fewer than five words. Girls in G-Heights tend to be outspoken, ready to fight when needed, and always ready to party. If this isn't you, then you get passed by. That's what happened to me while athletes like Devyn were supported in their endeavors to rise out of our own little version of hell. I hate any man who's a part of that stupid mind-set.

"I don't know." I shrug. "We just went to the same school. I don't really know you."

"We grew up near each other, Ryan. I've known you since we were kids."

All these years "knowing" each other, and he's never even looked my way. I force another smile onto my face, ready to do anything to get rid of him. "I guess you're right, huh? My bad. I never thought of it that way."

I walk into the lobby to check into my dorm, ignoring Devyn as he tries to stir up a conversation with the front desk lady. I would be living on the fourth floor in the oldest and cheapest dorm on campus. Another example of my luck today. I was even excited to get a roommate, but then the lady tells me that Harriet Hall has so many vacant rooms, everyone will get their own. So it'll be twice as hard to make friends. Even better!

Devyn and I walk into the slow-ass elevator, extending my time with him. "This place is almost as bad as the athletic dorm."

"Athletes? In shitty dorms? No one can convince me of that."

"They're apartments, so we have a kitchen and stuff, but shit barely works. Plus they're ugly," he says, making me laugh. "I didn't think it was possible to put a smile on your face."

The elevator opens at the perfect time, allowing me to get out of the compacted space. I unlock my door to see a room even uglier than I expected. White walls are chipped from floor to ceiling. An old desk stands against the wall between two twin XL beds with raggedy blue mattresses, and the navy carpet had obviously not been cleaned in years. Broken blinds hang loosely from the small window.

"Home," Devyn jokes, walking into the room. He takes my things out of the cart.

"Let me help you."

"I got it." He laughs, setting the bags next to my desk. "Need help with anything else?"

I just want him to get out, but part of me is afraid to be alone. This place is hideous and dingy . . . not to mention dark. "I'm good, thanks."

Nodding, Devyn grabs the cart and heads out of my room. "Hey." He stops. "Why didn't your dad help you move in?"

Once my dad found out where I was going to college, his hatred for me only increased. The man has never helped me or given me money for lunch or a single piece of clothing, but when I begged him to help me a little with my college expenses, he refused. He's all I have, and I can't rely on him.

"I was gonna miss my flight waiting for him, so I left," I half joke. Ironically, Devyn's father had taken me to the airport after catching me walking down our street with my bags at three o'clock this morning. I don't know if Devyn knows, but if he does, I'll act stupid right along with him. "Thanks again for helping out. I should start unpacking."

"I'll see you around?" Devyn asks. The slight look of pity that comes across his face only infuriates me. I give him one more of my award-winning fake smiles, slamming the door in his face.

After an hour of unpacking, I start to feel like I'm getting my life together. All I have to decorate my room is an orange-and-pink tribal print comforter, a small desk lamp, and a matching rug. Two pictures of my best friends from back home, Hope and Diana, adorn the desktop, and I hang the painting of Ava DuVernay, living idol and filmmaker, that they gave me as a going-away present. They're the only part of home I'll miss.

CHAPTER 2

I spend the rest of the afternoon going over my class schedule. My goal is to maintain a 4.0 on top of fully supporting myself so I can prove to my father that I'm going to succeed no matter what. I don't need him. My dreams of becoming the biggest black female screenwriter and producer isn't optional. I have to make it.

At ten o'clock I have my first floor meeting, giving me a chance to mingle with all of my floormates. Unlike other colleges, Truth has a "no-freshman-weekend-parties" rule. Rumor is that last year almost fifteen kids were sent to the hospital with alcohol poisoning. I'm relieved, though, mainly because I've never been to a party before and don't want to be alone in this scary dorm if I choose not to go.

Jordan, our RA, goes over housing rules, visitations, and the "family dinners" he'd be hosting for us once a week. I'm surprised to find out only five other people are on my floor. Nico, a poli sci major and the only other girl on the floor, is the first to spark up a conversation when she invites us all to hang out in her room after the meeting.

She kicks the door open, her large, bleach-blonde Afro swaying side to side as she prances into the room. "Make yourself at home, guys!" Her room is flamboyantly decorated with tapestries and lights on every wall. A red love seat sits in the corner and a DJ booth closed off by curtains is in another. She quickly made Harriet Hall her home, which I both envied and admired.

My other two floormates, Troy and Jakaida (Jay), and I all follow in behind her, amazed by what she's done with the place. We listen carefully as she shows us around her dorm and plays one of her DJ mixes. We all get comfortable between her bed and the love seat, taking turns asking the group questions.

"What's a random thing you've never done before?" Troy, a jazz major from northern California, asks us as he leans back on the fuzzy body pillows on Nico's bed. "I've never gone surfing."

I laughed. "I can second that one."

"You can't steal his, though! You'd think all Cali people are practically born on a surfboard," Nico jokes, making me laugh. If only she knew. "I've never straightened my hair."

"Ever?" Jay, the definition of a huge teddy bear, asks in his thick Texas accent.

"Nope!" Nico shakes her head as she leans back next to Troy. "I've dyed it. But no heat will ever touch this head." She's different than anyone I've ever met, with her pale, ivory skin, pouty lips, and round black eyes. "When I want something different, I just go to my aunt's braiding shop in Queens. She gets me right every time!"

"Okay, I've never . . ." Jay takes a minute to think of his answer. "Broken a bone."

"I've never tried alcohol before," I blurt out next, and I'm shocked when all of their heads turn to me.

"What?" Troy laughs. "Ever?"

I shake my head.

"You've never had like some of your mom's wine or something?" Nico asks, and I shake my head again. "This is about to be the best night ever!" She jumps off the bed and skips to her mini fridge, pulling out a bottle of Everclear and orange juice.

Troy leaps up from Nico's bed and goes over to her. "Yo, you're lit! Ryan, this is your official college initiation! We gotta do some shots!"

I get a little nervous thinking about getting drunk around people I just met, but part of me is aching to let my hair down just a little. So far, my floormates seem really cool. "Doesn't this go against the whole no parties thing?"

I look at Jay, who's sitting next to me. He shrugs. "I'll do it if you do."

Nico comes over to us, bottle in hand, and squeezes in between me and Jay. "Ryan, don't worry, I got you. We're the only girls here, so we're practically sisters now." She pauses, adding, "But you're also the only person who likes men in this room, which damn near makes me one of the boys."

"Is that so?" I laugh.

"Yes!" Nico gets up, dances toward a cabinet, and pulls out some cups. "Guys, we are a little family! We're going to be in this trap house for the whole year; that calls for a toast!"

"You gotta be high." Jay laughs for the first time since we all met.

"I'm excited! I'm finally out of the confined space of my adolescence!" She starts pouring the liquor in the cups. "You guys are going to love this. I'm practically a bartender." She hands Troy a drink to bring me, and then raises her cup in the air. "Fam . . . here's to what looks like the start of a good-ass freshman year!"

Here's to college.

CHAPTER 3

———

Sunlight blinds my eyes, forcing me to close them again. My stomach feels like it's on fire, and I take a minute to register I'm in my new dorm room, which I don't remember returning to at all. Last time I checked, Nico's room was spinning from too much dancing, shades of violet, orange, and gold from the tapestries around the room all bleeding together.

It's just past eleven thirty, which only upsets me. I was supposed to get up early to prepare for a job interview. I'd completely miscalculated last night, and I didn't have time for mistakes.

But last night was fun. I'd danced and laughed and had fun with these new people. Making new friends felt freeing, bonding in ways I couldn't with my girls back home. It was exactly what I wanted and needed. Despite my fears, everything would be okay, and surprisingly, I didn't get too sick and embarrass myself in front of my new floormates. Regardless, I shake off the uneasiness of my first hangover and start the day.

A knock interrupts me as I grab my robe. I'll let Troy, who's passed out on my extra bed, sleep for now and change in the bathroom. This will be my first time using a communal bathroom, and I'm a little scared about it.

Someone knocks at the door again, and I walk over to find it unlocked.

"Hey." I smile at Jay. He holds three cups of Starbucks coffee.

"Coffee delivery," he says, his accent especially thick this morning. I can't get enough of it. "It'll help whatever way you're feeling this morning."

I thank him, taking a long sip and then invite him in.

"Ryan, I see why you don't drink." Jay chuckles. "You're a fish. I don't know how many cups you went through last night."

"Really?" I whisper. "I didn't make a fool of myself, right?"

"Nah . . . we had a good time. Plus, that one," he says, nodding toward Troy, "drank more than anyone, so who knows when he'll wake up." He sets Troy's coffee on the desk.

"He's gotta get out of here soon," I reply. "I have to meet this guy about a job in like an hour."

"That's no fun."

"At all," I say, "but I need money. I'm about to hop in the shower."

Jay nods. "Well, don't let me keep you. Go ahead, and I'll get Troy out of here by the time you're out."

The thought of Jay trying to wake Troy's knocked-out ass up makes me laugh. The snoring was the only indication he wasn't dead. "You're the best, you know that?" My words put a smile on his face. "And thanks for the coffee." I slip on my shower shoes and hurry out of the room.

When I return after my shower, hair straightened and with lip gloss and a little mascara on, I'm happy to see Jay lived up to his promise. I'm feeling nervous about my interview, but I've been talking to the owner of a Mexican restaurant about a waitressing job and he told me to just come by when I got to town. I just have to get a simple job that can work around my class schedule.

New York is a professional place, but this isn't the kind of job that requires me to wear a business suit. Instead, I wear a fitted skirt that comes down right above my knee and an old white tank top to let the owner know I'm a struggling college student desperate for a job. Since I'm not aggressive or super outgoing like most New Yorkers I've come to know, hopefully my charm and politeness can land me the job.

Mi Cocina Mexicana is a ten-minute walk from campus. A small, round Mexican woman with long, curly hair is playing on her phone at the hostess table as I enter. She smiles when she sees me. "¡Hola! Just one?"

"I'm here to interview for the server position. I've been in contact with the owner, and he told me to just stop by and apply for the job."

"I am the owner," she says, her accent thick. "But you've been in contact with my husband. We've talked about you. Come have a seat . . . let's chat." She calls to someone in the back in Spanish, and a man walks out. "This is my husband, Antonio. Antonio, this is the girl you've been talking to from California."

I extend my hand to him. "Ryan," I say as he shakes my hand. "It's nice to finally meet you, sir."

Antonio, who's handsome for a man almost certainly thirty years my senior, laughs. "Call me Tony. It's nice to meet you, *mi amor*. Let's talk before the lunch crowd comes in."

We spend the next hour going over my class schedule and discussing pay, which is more than I thought I'd be getting. Tony and his wife, Maria, are nice, but they obviously care about their business. I'd be working five days a week. It's a lot, but New York's an expensive city, and I want to be comfortable and able to buy anything I want or need. I agree to start this week, giving me a day to get myself settled. The job seems like a perfect fit. When I get back to campus, I'm starving, so I text Nico and we agree to try out the café on campus. She's sitting on a bench in front of the building in some black workout shorts and a matching tank top with Nike running shoes. Large sunglasses hide half her face, letting me know she's indeed hungover.

"I don't know how you're awake," she says. "I could barely open my eyes to read your text."

"I'm sorry. You didn't have to come." I laugh.

"No, I'm starving," she replies. "My fridge only has alcohol and pudding."

"We should go shopping later." Since I got a new job that pays me well, I can use my leftover cash to get some stuff for my dorm.

"Later tonight?" she asks as we walk in and hand a woman our student IDs to swipe. "I'm going to need another nap after this."

"No problem." We grab our food—sushi for her, mac and cheese for me—and find a booth in the corner of the room. The dining hall is filled with students bantering and talking. You can distinguish the freshmen from other students because they have their IDs on lanyards. I keep mine in my wallet, not wanting to be obvious.

"How far did you live from school? Since you're from New York," I ask, trying to start the conversation. I really want Nico to like me. I think we could be close friends.

Nico picks up her sushi with chopsticks before responding. "A little less than an hour, depending on traffic. Just far enough for my parents to not come out here often."

"You want to keep them away?"

"Definitely. Truth's a little too . . . urban for them," she replies. "I'm from upstate New York, and my parents run this huge high society church over there. They expected me to go to Columbia or NYU, but I love it here. Plus, I love my girlfriend, so . . ." She shrugs and eats another piece of sushi. Nico's girlfriend, Sasha, is a sophomore at Truth. "Do they know you're gay?"

She nods, chewing her food. "Yeah, and they're not happy about it, but it's the twenty-first century. They'll get over it."

"Does that get to you?"

"Nah. My life's good, you know? Like, I'm in a good relationship and I'm happy. I used to only date assholes before I came out. Guys always treated me like shit. I had to decide to worry about me first. If my parents don't change, then they can't be a part of my life. If they do, they will. I can't be unhappy just because they don't accept who I am."

"I like that," I reply. "That's a great take to have on life."

"Think so?" Nico laughs. "I just think people shouldn't walk around being hurt because of what other people are doing. Life's better when you mind your own business."

"You know, I see why people always ask you if you're high," I say, making us both laugh. "You're too philosophical."

"Most of the time I am." She chuckles. "Hey, being high really helps a hangover. Plus, I'm woke as fuck. No one can tell me otherwise."

"You've got a point there, girl." I laugh.

"Just wait till you meet my girlfriend." Nico picks the last of her shrimp tempura roll up with her hands and throws it in her mouth. "She's worse than me. But what about you? You're quiet, but I can tell you've got a wild side. We saw some of it last night."

"What about me?"

"Anything. Mom? Dad? Brothers and sisters?"

"I never knew my mom. It's just me and my dad. We've never been close." And thank God for that. "I kind of grew up on my own. I don't have any siblings, but I'm almost sure I've got some somewhere in the world."

Nico nods. "That had to have its ups and downs. What's the craziest thing you ever did in high school?"

"Honestly, I didn't even do much in high school except work. I just focused on school so I could get the fuck out of there."

Nico chuckles. "We're gonna change that!"

I shake my head, laughing.

"Seriously!" she insists. "If I don't manage your crazy, when you finally decide to, you'll go overboard! This is your first time in New York. You could end up in all types of shit. Drugs . . . holing up with nasty guys . . . selling yourself for money."

"That has to be the biggest stereotype of New York I've ever heard." I laugh. "And you're from here! All that can happen anywhere."

"I know, but I don't want that happening to you," she jokes. "You're a sweet girl. Pimps eat that shit up."

"Do you know any pimps?"

"My brother's a pimp."

My eyes go wide. Her parents are probably the most disappointed preachers in the whole world. Nico bursts out in laughter.

"You Cali people are too gullible. No, I don't know any fucking pimps!" She gets up. "Hold up. I gotta get some fries . . . and some mac and cheese. I love fish as much as the next lesbian, but this sushi is not hitting."

***

Even in its scorching summer humidity, New York is still crazy beautiful. The sun shines on huge green trees and piles of freshly cut green grass in the courtyard. Flowers bloom brighter and bigger, and the heat puts smiles on everyone's face in a way only sunshine can.

After lunch with Nico, I take some time to get more acquainted with campus. The mood is filled with Sunday quietness and peace as people sit on benches or on blankets in the grass, playing games and chatting with friends. The East Coast is known for its brutal winters, and since that'd be new, I make a point to not take the sun's warmth for granted. How lucky am I to live here? To be in the school of my dreams? My attraction to Truth was its distance from California, but I'm excited to embrace the HBCU experience and see where it'll take my career. I want to make shows that inspire the black community, show the diversity in our culture, and touch on black issues. I've written some stuff, but I'm really hoping to get on someone's film crew to learn what working in the field is like.

I notice three guys in football practice uniforms coming my way and instantly get a little intimidated. In high school, my initial instinct would be to run from these guys, but I remind myself I'm trying to change my life.

"Hey, beautiful," the one in the middle says. He's small for a football player, but broad with muscular shoulders. His skin's the color of dark wood, and glistening from sweat. Freshly done cornrows and waxed eyebrows tell me he knows he's cute and used to having eyes on him.

"Hi." I smile at them.

"What's your name?" The guys on each side of him just stand there with smirks on their faces . . . weird.

"Ryan. How about you?"

"I'm Avery. This is Justin and Davis. We saw you walking and thought we'd come introduce ourselves. What year are you?"

"Freshman." Avery's cute but a little short for my taste, about an inch taller than me. I can't imagine myself being attracted to him. I can already tell he's a hoe. "And you are . . . ?"

"Oh, you a baby." Avery laughs, broadcasting an award-winning smile of pearly white teeth. "We're sophomores. Davis is a junior."

"Ave, we're gonna head back. See you at the crib, man," says Justin.

"I'll catch y'all later," Avery says as they walk away.

"You could've gone with them if you wanted," I say.

His face turns up. "Nah . . . I'm tryna talk to you. Where you headed?"

"Nowhere." I chuckle. "I was just walking around, getting used to campus, but I'm done."

"Can I walk with you?"

I nod. "Feel free." A slight breeze begins as we walk down the courtyard. "So, you're on the football team?"

"I am." He nods. "Second string QB."

"Why aren't you the first?" I joke.

Avery rubs the top of his head, laughing. "First strings are usually seniors. I get good play time, though, so no problem. You gon' come to my games?"

"Maybe a couple." Truth doesn't have the best football team, but I heard they've gotten better the past couple years. Before they had a zero-winning streak.

"Not all of them?"

I chuckle. "No can do . . . gotta work."

"How'd you already find a job?"

I shrug. "I don't like being told no."

We spend the next few minutes going over Truth intros—every student's way of asking you to tell them about yourself—and talking about where we're from. Avery makes any and every attempt to flirt with me, from asking if I know the school's stereotype on Cali girls (which I still don't, since he told me I'd have to wait and find out) to encouraging me to go to more parties so we can get "loose together." The closer we get to my dorm, the more I want to get away from him.

"Thanks for walking me, but I should go," I say as we get to the entrance of my building.

"I enjoyed our talk," Avery replies. "I'll text you. Maybe we can link tonight."

That's definitely not happening. Hit me up tomorrow, buddy. "Yeah, let me know."

"Bet." He pulls me into a hug, and as I let go, he pinches my butt and plants a kiss at the corner of my mouth. "See you later."

"Bye." I rush inside.

What the fuck? With absolutely no dating experience, I'm still pretty sure a guy should wait more than thirty minutes after meeting to kiss you. Does he do this to every girl he talks to? He and his lips need to stay the hell away from me.

CHAPTER 4

———

I quickly learn just how tightly Maria and Tony run their ship. Their expectations are high. I spend most shifts on my feet serving, hosting, and washing dishes after closing. And with homework, my nights are long, and study or bonding sessions with my floormates have made them even longer. Between managing work and school, my schedule is packed the first couple of days of the semester. But I remind myself to be thankful for the opportunities.

On the first weekend of the semester, all I'm looking forward to is getting some much-needed sleep. Even though I have work, I plan to get in bed as soon as I clock out tonight. But first, I have a meeting with the football coach for a tutoring job. The extra cash will give me enough to wash clothes and have a little extra food money to spend on groceries and at restaurants. I've only been here for a few days, but the dining halls are already getting old.

I walk into the school's auditorium to see the football coach sitting at a table with stacks of paper.

"Good afternoon," I say, reaching out my hand for him to shake. "I'm here to apply for the tutoring job."

"Hey." He's a kind, chocolate bald man with a warm smile covered by a goatee. "Have a seat."

I hand him a copy of my resume and high school transcripts before I sit. "I have a couple of questions. First—I already have a job, so I was wondering, what are the hours I'll be working?"

Coach takes a long look at my resume. "You pick your own hours. I'm going to ask you some questions, and we'll match you with a player based on your strengths and their tutoring needs. You'll meet for two hours three times a week. If you guys meet more, fine, but I highly doubt any of my players will agree to that. Just make sure you record on the sign-in sheet whenever you do."

"Okay, sounds good." I nod. Picking my own hours makes things so much easier.

"I've turned down a lot of women for this position, but because of your work experience, your GPA, where you're from, and the fact that you already have a job, I know you're hardworking. A lot of girls apply for this position to get close to the players, and I'll tell you now that you *will* be replaced if we don't see improvements in their grades. Some of these boys are not as bright in the classroom as they are on the field. That's why we've put them in a directed study where they can get the attention they need—"

"No offense, sir, but I doubt I'll be hooking up with any of them. I need the money. That's my only purpose for applying for this job."

"Good. I'm glad we got that out of the way."

"How do you know where I'm from?"

The coach smiles. "Your resume. We're bred from the same place."

Even after leaving home, it still haunts me. "Really? You're from G-Heights?"

He nods. "Really. I understand why you work so hard. That's not the best place to come from, and not the place to stay."

I agree.

The rest of the time we spend discussing my current place of employment and talking more about expectations. He asks me a few more questions about the subjects I am best at.

"We'll have everyone partnered up by tomorrow night, and after that, you can set up your first meeting," the coach tells me. "You are a well-rounded student, and I trust that you won't let me down. If you don't think the job will be too much with school on top of your waitress job, you're hired."

I can't help but smile.

"Thank you so much, sir." I get up to shake his hand.

"Call me Coach K." He laughs, taking my hand. "We'll talk soon." He hands me a sheet of paper. "These are the instructions for what you need to do before your first meeting. You need to set some rules, and when you meet up, you can talk about what you both expect for the semester."

"Great," I reply. "Thank you again."

"You too, Ryan. See you soon." I leave the auditorium feeling proud of myself.

***

Remember me?

I'm annoyed to see Avery's text as I walk home from work four days later. It's almost one o'clock in the morning, and as scary and dangerous as this is, I find the quiet, light-covered city to be calming. Even though Truth is about an hour and a half from the chaos of New York City, you can see it from a distance, which I always find fascinating. LA doesn't light up like this.

None of my floormates are around when I get to the dorms, which relieves me. I need to avoid all distractions tonight and get done with all my homework by three at the latest. But I have a little time to text Avery.

Avery: Did you save my number? It's Avery.

Me: My bad, I forgot. What's up?

Avery: WYD? Was gonna ask you to come over . . .

I laugh at Avery's text and myself for entertaining him. Of course he'd try to hook up. I don't talk to guys often, but I know when I'm being summoned for a booty call.

I decide to just respond in the morning. He's obviously a player, and I don't expect much from him. *At least take a girl out before you try to fuck her.* Also, taking four days to text a girl post-meeting isn't going to make her want you.

I work through my homework a lot quicker than I thought, and I'm exhausted by the time I'm finished. I get in bed and under the covers before checking my email. Coach K's email is at the top of the list.

Ryan,

Are you available to meet sometime in the morning? Let me know. Since you are willing to work around your current work and school, I will make sure the player is on your schedule.

Thanks,

Coach K
Head Defensive and Offensive Lineman Coach
Truth University

As great as that sounds, it's the postscript that upsets me.

PS. You've been paired with Devyn Baker. Figured two LA natives would get along.

CHAPTER 5

___

DEVYN

Football players are excused from classes the Friday before our first game, so I don't need to be up before noon. But shout-out to Ryan for scheduling a nine o'clock meeting the first day I'd be able to get some extra sleep since I moved out here in May.

Coach has to be playing a sick game with me. I begged him not to pair me with her. She hated me on move-in day, and I'm not trying to deal with her weird attitude for the whole year. But he just says it'll be a good fit. I don't know about all that shit.

I'm just trying to focus on football, but my grades in high school almost stopped me from being able to play at all. They definitely held me back from going to a school with a better team, but I've dwelled on that enough. Even on this dumbass team, it's time to ball out. That way I can make it to the NFL and get out of here. I'll put more effort into school. I promised myself and my dad that I'll work harder.

Ryan's not about to go easy on me. No girl's ever shown such a dislike for me, and I'm tired of going back and forth on why. I don't know what I did to piss her off so bad, but after moving her into that crack house Truth called a dorm, I couldn't be bothered. She barely said thank you, acted like she didn't know me, and then damn near slammed the door in my face. What's the point of being a bitch for no reason?

I take my time walking to Carver Deli, the coffee shop behind the admissions building where she told me to meet her. I'm unsurprised to see her already there. I have to admit, she looks cute in a short orange dress that hugs her body, a vast difference from the baggy, all-covering clothes I usually saw her wear in California.

I take the seat across from her. "Hey."

She doesn't bother to smile. "Good morning." Her eyes are low, and she looks tired in her seat. "Do you need a coffee or something, or can we get started?"

I don't drink coffee, but I knew she wouldn't care if I told her. "Nah," I replied. "I'm good."

Reaching in her backpack, Ryan pulls out two sheets of paper. "Okay, let's start by discussing which classes you need help in. Coach K didn't mention it in the email."

I hand her my schedule. I know the fact that it's crumbled probably makes her hate me more. Good. It's time to give her the same energy she gives me.

She takes a second to look at it, pulling out a highlighter, and begins marking up the page. "Okay, you have an English class, a math lecture, psych, and African studies . . . which ones are easiest?"

"Math."

Ryan nods. "Okay, so we'll spend most of our time together working on English. My Greek lit professor's the same as your African lit. Does she give weekly essays?"

I nod.

"Have you written yours?"

"No. It's due Monday."

"Did you start the book?"

I just look at her. No, I didn't read the fuckin' book!

"You can write a six-page essay on a book you haven't read?" Her satirical personality only pisses me off. She sighs. "Okay, we're going to start tutoring as soon as possible. Are you free tomorrow?"

"I've got a game."

"Home or away?"

"Away, but we don't leave till the morning since it's close."

"I get off at eleven tonight. Is that too late?"

Players in directed study can't go to any pregame bonding events, so I might as well get some homework done. "That's fine."

"Good," she replies. "Um . . . we can meet at my job if you want. I know the library closes early on weekends."

"We can meet at my place. Everyone will be at the hotel tonight, and I have a kitchen table we can work on."

She hesitates. "Okay . . . I take Intro to Psych, too, so we'll start with that and African studies. Can we meet on Saturday and Sunday, too, so we can finish your essay?"

"My game," I remind her.

"I have work until two both days, so we can do it in the evening."

I planned on going out after my game, but I'm scared she'll tell my coach if I don't cooperate. I'm starting on the defensive line tomorrow and won't do anything to jeopardize it.

I nod. "Okay, I'll let you know when we're on our way back."

A hint of a smile touches her lips. Was she happy I was doing whatever she said? I'm the easiest guy in the world. She's the difficult one. "Sounds good." She looks down at her sheet of paper. "Okay, now let's talk about my list of expectations."

"Expectations?"

"Yeah," she replies. "So, you know I work crazy hours, so you'll have to be lenient with me. I know we have to meet three times a week, but if you can't for two hours, I'm willing to work more days a week for an hour. We just have to plan to make sure it fits both of our schedules. Also, start taking notes. That way I know what you're learning in class. You could record your lectures, but it's easier on both of us if you just pay attention."

What makes her think I don't listen in class? "I'll do both?"

"Good idea," she says.

"Am I allowed to tell you *my* list of expectations?"

A confused expression comes across her face.

"You've made your list of demands. We can't meet halfway?"

"Go ahead. Let's talk about it."

"I need at least a 3.0 to keep my starting position. You cover academics and I cover the football, so—"

"You expect me to do your work for you?" She laughs. "What would I gain from that?"

I already hate being interrupted, but her assumption upsets me.

"I didn't say that," I continue. "I need help. I wasn't put in tutoring for no reason. I'll be there. I won't miss a session. I'll make good grades. All I expect from you, other than to fix your attitude, is to help me."

"Excuse me?"

"You don't like me; that's fine. I'm not a fan of you, either, so let's get this shit done and over with." I'm tired of how she keeps stereotyping me as some dumb athlete. I'm trying to turn over a new leaf. "You know, you volunteered to do this. You can always quit."

"No, I can't just quit," she flares. "I don't have the money to just quit. I need this job as much as I need the other one." She opens her mouth to say something else, but instead packs up her things. "Look, I have things to do before work. Here's my number. Text me and I'll let you know when I'm coming." She gets up from the table and storms out.

Fuck. Now I feel bad.

***

RYAN

I'm still upset with Devyn when I walk into his dorm later that night. Because I got off at eleven, our tutoring session doesn't have to be as late as I thought. He meets me in the lobby dressed in gray sweatpants and a black Truth Football T-shirt. His stupid-ass face only makes me angrier, but I try to shake it off. There's work to be done . . . and fast.

"Hey," Devyn says, looking happier than he did earlier. "Ready to put me to work?"

"I guess."

"That sounded kind of weird once I said it." We walk over to the security guard and Devyn checks me in.

"Make it a quick one," the guard says to Devyn. "You got a game tomorrow."

Devyn laughs. "I already know, man."

The fucking nerve of these guys. Where do they get off making sexual jokes like I'm not even here?

Devyn leads the way down the hall and up two flights of stairs. Cook Hall, where he lives, doesn't look much better than Harriet other than its larger size. I follow him to the last room at the end of the second floor to see a nice setup with a full kitchen and attached living room. A big TV hangs on the wall and two Xboxes sit on a table underneath.

"How many people live here?" I ask.

Devyn grabs his backpack off the couch and brings it to the table. "Three of us—me and two other linemen."

"Did you pick your roommates?"

He nods. "Yeah. We moved in about a month before everyone else, so the coaches let us pick." I sit at the table and pull out my planner, pencil bag, and laptop. "I know you just got off work, so I made a pizza. You're welcome to it."

His hospitality is surprising. As much as I want to deny his offer, I'm starving. "Thanks, that's really nice." This time, I receive an actual smile as he walks into the kitchen, putting two slices of pizza on a plate and three on the other. He takes two cans of Sprite out of the refrigerator.

"Bon appétit." Devyn places the food in front of me and takes the seat next to mine.

"This doesn't count as part of our two hours."

"I'll read and eat at the same time." He takes a copy of *The Color Purple* from his bag. "Since I don't need help reading, what are you going to do?"

"Eat. But I have some homework too." I reach over him for my pencil bag and pull out a highlighter and pen. "Annotate."

"Annotate what?"

He's never taken notes in a book before?

"The book," I chuckle. "Highlight important things and circle words you don't know. We can discuss every couple chapters you read to figure out what you want to write about."

Devyn gets straight to work as I finish my dinner. I misjudged him, assuming he couldn't work hard, and I wonder if his attitude was all an act. If so, why does he feel the need to do it? After eating, I work on some English homework while Devyn continues reading. We work diligently for half an hour longer than expected. Once Devyn gets to work, he's focused and solemn. I wonder why he didn't make better grades in high school.

Before I knew it, it's almost two o'clock and way past time for me to go home.

"Thank you," Devyn tells me as we clean up our things. "You don't have to do this, but it really helps that you are."

The words surprise me and make me blush. "You did good. At the rate you're going, we'll finish this essay quick."

Devyn smiles shyly. "I'll, um, let you know when we're on our way back tomorrow. It shouldn't be later than six."

"Cool."

"Let me grab you a jacket. It's cold outside." Devyn disappears into the room next to the kitchen before I can decline. I felt too confident in my tight orange dress to change before work.

My eyes feel heavy as Devyn comes out with a black Truth Football crewneck in his hand. I take the jacket from him against my own will, not wanting to be rude. "I'm ready when you are."

We walk back to the lobby in silence, where the guard is busily watching something on his smartphone. Devyn nods at him, and he looks me up and down, shaking his head in disgust. It must be the sweatshirt.

"See you later," I say as Devyn opens the door for me. He follows me out of the building. "What are you doing?"

"You think I'm going to let you walk back alone?"

He doesn't have to be so chivalrous. "I live three buildings away."

"Exactly. The least I can do is make sure you get home safe after our sessions." He laughs. "That's another one of *my rules*. Come on. It's cold and we both need some sleep."

I'd completely forgotten about my early shift tomorrow! Instead of continuing to argue for no reason, I nod and let him lead the way to my dorm.

***

I arrive to work the next morning in the worst mood ever. Despite barely being able to open my eyes, the check I'll be receiving later is enough motivation to wake my ass up.

"*¡Buenos días, princesa!*" Tony chirps as I walk into the kitchen to clock in. "You look tired."

I look at my reflection in a big pot hanging on the wall. The heavy bags under my eyes are a complete giveaway.

I spend the morning wiping down and setting tables for the early lunch crowd. My shift starts two hours before the restaurant opens, but so much work must be done before. Nine or ten families are waiting at the door and rush in as soon as we open. I'm the only waitress working the early shift, so I find myself counting down the seconds till I can go.

During my break, Tony lets me rest in his office. I spend the time watching the Truth versus Rutgers game on some branch ESPN channel and scarfing down a couple of cheese enchiladas. Sadly, Truth is losing zero to twenty-eight in the second quarter, and I doubt they'll make a comeback. But

Devyn plays the entire thirty minutes of my break. I remember seeing his number, 29, from his football bag.

I convince Tony to let me put the game on a TV in the dining room so I can finish watching while I work but can't pay close attention once the lunch rush gets too hectic. The game ends zero to sixty-three, and I feel bad for Devyn and his teammates.

"Ryan!" Maria calls as I finish picking up the check from a booth in the back. I look to see they left no tip. I hate serving fucking teenagers. "Here you go, *mija*." She hands me an envelope. "Go home. Take the day off tomorrow; you've had a long first week."

"Really?" She nods. *Thank God!*

"You've more than proved yourself around here," she tells me. "You're doing amazing. See you Tuesday." I am so happy to go home that I almost run out of there with my smock still on.

I rush to the bank, go to Target, and spend the rest of the evening decorating my room with Troy keeping me company. Nico strolls into the room in a pink lingerie slip and clear sparkly jellies as I wait for Devyn to get back from his game.

"Friends!" She runs and plants a kiss on Troy's cheek. "I feel like I haven't seen anyone in forever! Especially you, Ry. They've been working you like a slave in that Mexican woman's kitchen!"

I laugh. "It's called *My Mexican Kitchen*. I'm not someone's maid."

"Oh," Nico replies, "That's definitely good to know because I was really about to talk to you about other ways to get money." She rummages through my food cabinet and grabs a sleeve of Chips Ahoy! cookies before taking a seat next to Troy on the spare bed.

"What are those other ways to get money?" I ask her.

She shoves a cookie in her mouth, then says, "You could become a party promoter."

"Or a drug dealer," Troy adds.

"Or do hair or makeup or nails. You know, everything is a hustle at this school. I'll put you in the Truth Quicksell GroupMe to give you some inspiration."

I laugh. "What is that?"

"You know Ryan lives under a rock," Troy tells Nico, laughing. "It's where people sell things—clothes, shoes, drugs, themselves . . ."

"Themselves?"

"He means their talents," Nico interrupts. "Like, if you can style, cut, and put in a weave, you put pictures of your clients, and then if people like it, they'll pay you to do their hair."

"Really?" I'd gotten my first weave before I left California but didn't like how it came out. My neighbor did it, and she rushed through the whole thing. "Do you know anyone that can do my hair?"

"I'll do it!" Nico perks up. "I've been waiting to get my hands on that head."

"How much?"

Nico shrugs. "For free as long as I can take pictures of your hair and makeup for a look book I'm doing. I'm trying to be more professional so I can get more clients doing hair for parties, dates, and big events."

I was starting to love this school and the people in it more every day.

"Okay, but can we take pictures tomorrow? I have to tutor tonight."

"You got the tutoring athletes job?" Troy laughs and I nod. "I went out with this girl the other night, and she told me they only gave one girl the job. I should've known it was you."

How could they only hire one female tutor?

"Coach told me they were interviewing girls harder because a lot of them were hooking up with players instead of working."

"How sexist!" Nico exclaims.

I laugh. "You're right, but it's not that we aren't allowed to hook up or date them. They just expect the guys to finish their work too."

"Who're you tutoring?"

I accidently groan. "Devyn Baker. We basically grew up going to all the same schools. He's your typical dumb athlete with a cute smile." Our tutoring session went well last night, but I still had my doubts about him.

"You know . . ." Troy lingers dramatically. "My mom used to hate my dad when he played college ball. Her heart softened with time."

"Gross!" I laugh. "That's definitely not happening . . . not in a million years. Devyn's not even my type."

"Yeah, yeah." Nico rolls her eyes. "Grab your chair, Ry. It won't take me long to fix your hair before tutoring. Is your hair washed?"

"It is," I tell her.

"Let me grab my stuff. You're about to look so good. This is definitely a date!" She zips out of the room before I can correct her.

***

If I hate one thing in this world, it's being on a man's time. I feel pathetic as I wait for Devyn to text that he's back from his game. Putting the final touches on my room gives me a good distraction. I still want to get some kind of couch in here, like the one Nico has, but the added blankets and throw pillows I'd put on the spare bed work as a good compromise.

I get up and go to the mirror. One good thing to come out of today is my little makeover from Nico. I look like a different person! That girl has a gift. Despite how itchy and tight my head feels, my hair looks amazing. Nico ended up taking my weave out and giving me a completely new sew in, switching my part from the side to the middle, which makes me look a little older. We even discussed dying it but figured that was a job for another day. For the first time in my life, I'm feeling sexy . . . it's a good change.

At eight, I text Devyn that I'm about to head over and jump out of bed to grab my stuff. Why do I feel excited to see him all of a sudden? I take a second to remind myself this isn't a date.

> **Devyn:** You can't come here. My roommates are having people over . . . not good for tutoring.

His text instantly ruins my mood.

> **Me:** Well, where else are we supposed to go?

He's the one who needs my help, so he's got to figure this one out on his own.

Devyn: Come check me in. I'm here.

Part of me wants to just cancel tutoring, only so he can't get the signature for next week's game, but I know that won't help either of us. It means a lot to me that I was the only female hire, and I know the coaches expect a lot more from me. Coach K picked me for a reason, and I don't want to disappoint him.

I take the stairs, purposely making Devyn wait. When I get to the lobby, he's moping on one of the couches, looking beat down. I wonder if it's because of the game.

"Devyn," I say. He looks up when he hears my voice. "Come on."

We walk to the elevator in silence, which is painfully awkward. I feel bad for him if he's this sad about his game. I don't know what to say to him other than something stupid like, *You ready to work hard?* But why is he taking this so seriously? Truth didn't have the best football record, plus Devyn's a lineman, so it's not like he makes touchdowns. I guess it's a team effort thing I don't understand.

The elevator finally makes it to the fourth floor after what feels like fifteen minutes, and Devyn mutely follows me to my room. Luckily, none of my floormates are here to harass us or endlessly barge into the room to make sure we're studying.

"You can sit wherever," I tell him. He makes himself comfortable on my bed instead of the spare one. He has to be trying to irritate me, but I won't let him. "Are you hungry? I don't have, like, dinner food, but I have snacks, or we can order something." I could use a little break from the dining halls anyway.

"I'm good. Let's just finish."

"Okay." I nod. "Let's just continue how we did last night."
I grab my pencil bag off the table Troy had built me and hand
it to him. "Let me know when you're ready to discuss."

"Do you mind if I listen to music?"

I shake my head. "No. As long as it doesn't distract you."
I'm starting to sound like his mom or something. *Shut the
fuck up and just let the boy do what he wants.*

Devyn grabs his backpack and pulls out a small speaker.
"I'll play it low to not distract you." A slow Wale song softly
wafts through the room. Devyn hands me his phone, not
saying a word, and then hops back on my bed to start reading.

I can instantly tell Devyn's distracted, but I figure he just
needs time to warm up and get his head in the game. But
after thirty minutes, he's yet to turn one page in his book,
and I decide to see what's up.

"How's it going?" I finish the last of the sandwich I made
to avoid spending more money. I close my laptop to hide the
intense Facebook scrolling I've been doing . . . so much for
either of us getting work done.

Devyn's eyes go from mine to his copy of *The Color Purple.*
"I'm sorry . . . guess I'm not into this today." He tells me, "You
want to reschedule?"

I lean back in my seat. "Let's take a little break," I say.
"It's still early."

He groans.

He has more than half the book to finish and a whole
essay. We don't have time to reschedule. "What's wrong?"

Laughter escapes his lips. "Do you even care?"

"I wouldn't ask if I didn't." I cross my hands over my chest.
"Look, I get that we're not the best of friends . . . or even
friends, but it's better for you to voice whatever you're going
through now so we can get back to work . . . or start the work."

"This shit's just annoying . . . having to do this."

I don't feel bad for him if his only problem is not wanting to do homework. "Well, whose fault is that?" I laugh.

Devyn points at me. "That attitude doesn't make this any easier. What's your fuckin' problem with me?"

He continues to use my attitude toward him as a way to tear me down when it only pisses me off. If he was at arm's length instead of across the room, I'd slap the shit out of him. "I get that you're upset about working a little harder because *you* didn't care about your grades in high school, or maybe because of your game, but you're not going to take that out on me." I get up from the table, trying hard not to yell. No man should ever have the audacity to curse at a woman who's done nothing to him. That is one of the things that pisses me off about my father. Men know how to speak to a woman correctly. Anything he fails to do is intentional. "You're right . . . we shouldn't do this tonight."

Devyn slides off the bed, taking all my covers off with him, and throws his things into his bag. "Here," he says, taking out another crumpled piece of paper and holding it out to me. "Sign it."

I bark out a bitter laugh. He has some nerve. "Fuck off, Devyn." I never cuss at people, but he was really starting to get to me.

"Why do you even have this job?" Devyn yells. "Like you said, you have a job. I'm sick of all this being on *your* schedule thing when you're doing none of the work, so . . ."

"Get out!" I yank the door open and push him out. "I'll talk to Coach K tomorrow about finding you a replacement tutor." I slam the door before he can say another fucking word to me. Good or bad—I don't want to hear a thing he has to say.

CHAPTER 6

DEVYN

Ryan knows just how to irk the shit out of a man.

Two hours later and I still don't know what that girl's problem is. I manage to get under her skin more than anyone else in this world, and I can't figure out why. Every time I see her around campus, she's smiling, radiant even, and never looks sad or upset. But when she's around me, all that changes. She's always uptight, too serious, and just unenjoyable. Last night was the first time she's been calm and, honestly, cool to be around. She even looked sexy, sitting there working beside me, discussing the book. I should've known it was too good to be true.

She shuts down so quickly, which I hate. I don't get her. Sure, I wasn't my best tonight, but I didn't expect her to snap the way she did. I saw a fire and rage in her tonight I've never seen before, so I know I took it too far and sent her over the edge. But right when I think she'll voice some part of her secret life, or why she hates me so much, she shuts down faster than ever and literally pushes me out the door. Sometimes I really fucking hate women.

I go home, smoke two blunts with my roommates, and still can't shake off the anger I'm feeling. I figure my dad can talk me down. I just hope he can't tell how high I am. He answers on the second ring. "Son!"

"Hey, Dad." It feels good to hear his voice. My dad depends on me going to college and making it big. When my mom left, he stood by me and my little brother and sister our whole lives. His injuries from a car accident he'd gotten into when I was sixteen causes his body to tear down a little quicker than most forty-year-old men. His body can't take his factory job, and sooner than later, I'll have to support my family. "How are you?"

"I'm good. We miss you around here." He laughs. "No one's around for me to yell at."

His cheerfulness and the thought of my angelic siblings brightens my mood. I need to call more often so they don't forget me. "I miss you guys."

"I watched the game," he says. "Tough loss, but it's just a rough start. I saw a lot of potential."

"Coach said we got cocky too fast." It probably didn't help that the quarterback and the entire offensive line decided to get wasted the night before. I wasn't going to tell my dad that, though. I just need to get NFL recruiters to look my way so I can get called to enter the draft. "Listen, I've got a question for you."

"What's up?"

"You know Ryan McKnight?"

"Javon's daughter?"

"I don't know him," I sigh. "But his daughter goes here and somehow got paired to be my tutor. She's constantly bitching at me . . . it's driving me fuckin' insane."

"Hold on, hold on. Be nice." My dad laughs. "I raised you better than that. She doesn't come from the best home situation. She's probably just got her guard up."

"None of us do."

"But you have a dad who loves and cares about you. Her mom's not around and her dad's not the best . . . sells drugs and a few other things too."

"Like what?"

"Mostly girls. Sometimes cars or jewelry. Whatever he can get his hands on, for real."

"He's a pimp?"

The background noise grows distant, so he's probably going to his room to avoid my nosey little sister. "I don't know everything, but the police have stood outside of his house maybe a dozen times in the past year, and they've picked him up a couple times too. He used to always have girls running in and out of his place, but since Ryan's left, it's like a party every night over there."

"If her dad has all this money, why does she work, like, two or three jobs?" Most dealers I know had a good amount of cash.

"I don't know, son. But last time I saw him, he was high as a kite. The last time I saw Ryan was the day she left, crying in the street about how her dad was supposed to take her to the airport and never came home the night before."

I feel bad for Ryan and feel even worse for the things I said earlier. But how was I supposed to know? She doesn't talk about herself, and the one time I brought up home, she acted like she had no idea what I was talking about. "She told you that? What'd you do?"

"I dropped her off on my way to work," he tells me. "She's obviously going through a lot, so maybe she has a reason to be angry, D. Take it easy on her."

"She doesn't fuck with me at all, Dad. Especially after tonight, she may never speak to me again."

"I'm sure you were a dick too. You've never taken being disliked well."

I laugh. He definitely has a point there.

"She seems like a smart girl. Just be patient with her. She can probably help you out with school, and she's cute . . . so that should help."

I sigh. "I'll call her and apologize."

"There you go," he says. "Do it in person; girls like that. Let me know how it goes. I love you."

"I love you too, Pops. I'll call tomorrow." We hang up.

I know that waiting until tomorrow to fix things won't help, so I put on my sweatshirt and make my way to Harriet Hall to apologize.

My high has me feeling like I'm on that elevator for half an hour. When it opens, two guys and a girl are talking in the hallway. They all look surprised to see me.

"Who are you?" a girl with a blonde Afro asks. I ignore her and the guy with dreads who speaks after. I'm not here for them. I'm only here so tutoring can stop being so awful. I walk past them and knock on Ryan's door.

"Come in!" she yells. Her facial expression goes from calm to unreadable when she sees me at the door. "What the hell are you doing here?" She jumps out of bed and rushes past me, closing the door behind us. "How did you even get up here?"

"I'm so sorry about earlier," I tell her. "I was upset about the game, but I had no reason to say the things I said. I get that you're doing me a favor, and I do enjoy our tutoring sessions."

She looks at me for, like, twenty seconds before respond-ing. "How long did it take you to come up with that line?"

"It's not a line. I mean what I'm saying."

Ryan looks at me as if I'm not making any sense, and honestly, maybe I'm not. "Look, I know that we're not getting through to each other. Maybe you do need a new tutor."

"That's not true." I take a step toward her and she steps backward. "We have this bond; I saw it yesterday. I just want the chance to make things right between us. I really need your help."

She keeps her hands on her hips, and her angry glare disappears into a deep sigh. "Fine . . . I'll continue tutoring you, but we need to establish some rules."

More rules?

"You're kind of bossy, you know that?" I laugh.

Surprisingly, she laughs with me. "I'm just . . . finding my voice. It's nice to finally have one after all this time." This is the most she's ever talked to me since we met. I can't get the thought of her dad being a pimp out of my head, but I don't want to ask and upset her.

"Can we be friends? Like, actual friends? I'm really a nice guy."

Her mouth curves into a little smile, and I have to admit she's gorgeous.

"I don't know about all that . . . but I'm willing to give it a try for the sake of your grades."

I want to hug her but won't cross a line. "Now . . . my rules," she continues.

"I'm all ears," I say, walking over to her bed to take a seat. She sits next to me. She smells good, like brown sugar and another sweet scent I can't think of.

"You have to focus during our meetings, and if something's wrong . . . ask for help. I get that it's upsetting to lose games, but we could have just taken a minute, talked through it, and then you'd be almost done with *The Color Purple* by now," she says. "And you can't just speak to me rudely. I'm not going to tolerate it. I don't care how upset you are."

"But what about the way you treat me?"

She huffs. "I'll try to calm my attitude." I don't have the energy to press her about why she doesn't like me.

"So, tomorrow you need to finish the book so we can finish your essay. What time is practice over?"

"Eight."

"Okay, so just come any time after that . . . no rush." She leans back against the wall. "Also, thanks for apologizing. I underestimated you."

"What do you mean?" The bed starts to feel like a cloud under me.

Ryan shrugs. "It's not important." We lock eyes, and she raises an eyebrow. "Are you high?"

I laugh. "I won't lie . . . I am."

Ryan chuckles, shaking her head.

"I was so mad after I left and needed to calm down. This come-down is hitting me kind of hard, though."

"How do you get high before an early morning practice? Isn't it hard to wake up?"

"You've never been high before?"

She shakes her head. "Nope . . . never will, either. Don't you get drug tested?"

"At the end of the month. I usually don't smoke, but . . ." I shrug, not knowing what else to say. "I don't think I can muster up the energy to head back. This might be weird to ask, but do you mind if I take a little nap before I leave?"

"Well . . ." Her slow response has my eyes starting to close.
"I guess. If you need to."

"For real?" I'm surprised. I was sure she'd have me trekking back to my apartment just for asking.

Ryan gets up. "Yeah, can't have you getting lost on your way home." She laughs. "I have a spare bed, so you can take it. Extra pillows and blankets are there, so knock yourself out." I get up and pull her into my arms. "I'm so happy we're friends."

"I think *no touching* should also be one of our rules." I laugh, letting her go. "Friends hug." Ryan's so tense all the time; she should get high and relax for once. "You look good today." I say it without thinking but mean every word. Her hair's different, the black tank top she's wearing make her boobs look bigger, and her skinny jeans hug her waist in all the right places.

"Thanks." She crosses her arms over her chest. I can tell I said the wrong thing, so I shuffle to the bed and get comfortable before she can change her mind. Man, am I excited to lie down. This bed isn't as nice as Ryan's, but it'll do.

***

RYAN

Devyn falls asleep as soon as his head hits the pillow.

I've spent way too many nights alone, so I don't mind when people spend the night. It means a lot to me that Devyn came back to apologize. Even I felt uneasy about our fight. At the end of the day, I know Devyn really needs my help with school, and I want to give it to him. He's proving to be different from your average jock, but I can't pinpoint exactly how. They all have that charming personality and are good at talking to girls, but something particular about him interests me.

I take off my jeans and grab my shower caddy to wash off the day. Predictably, Nico's waiting for me in her room, the door wide open. She practically flies off the couch as soon as I open my door.

"That's him?" she asks enthusiastically.

"Shh . . ." I close the door behind me to not disturb him, but I'm sure Devyn won't be waking up any time soon. "Yeah, that's Devyn—the guy I tutor."

"Since when do tutees come over for late night sessions?" I laugh. "He's knocked out." I crack the door open for her to see. "No studying or hooking up will be happening tonight." Or ever . . . not between me and Devyn.

Nico leans against the doorframe. "Do you want to hook up with him? I don't blame you . . . he's a cutie."

"He's a player," I correct her. "In more ways than one. It's written all over his face . . . plus I doubt he's looking for a serious relationship."

"And you are?"

I take a minute to think about it before responding. After all I've been through in my life, I don't need anything unstable. "Yeah, random hookups seem to always come with someone getting attached and hurt. I'm not going to put myself in that situation."

Nico nods. "Understandable." She sighs. "Well I'll let you go. Sasha's on her way from some party."

"You didn't want to go?"

She shakes her head. "Not tonight. I just wanted to relax and cuddle up to my boo, but I guess I can't always have it my way."

Nico and her girlfriend obviously weren't in the best place these days, but she'll never say that. I just hope she knows I'm here if she needs me. "You'll see her tonight!" I say, trying to cheer her up. "You'll be alright. I gotta wash up so I can keep an eye on my guest."

"Have fun." Nico laughs as I walk away. "Oh, Ry!" I turn around to see a hint of a smile on her face. "You never said you didn't want to hook up with him. Does that mean you want something a little more?"

"No." I chuckle. "We're not headed in that direction."

"I think you should switch courses. If you ask me, you guys would be pretty cute."

CHAPTER 7

RYAN

Between school and two jobs, my busy schedule starts to get to me. By Thursday, I'm exhausted, both physically and mentally. I spend my break lying on Tony's big brown couch, working on homework so that Devyn and I can start on the massive amount of work he has due this week. He even surprised me by buying an agenda where he can record all of his work for me to see. We haven't had a tutoring session since Monday, mainly because of timing conflicts between my job and his practices.

I'll admit, now that all the beef's settled, I'm genuinely starting to enjoy my tutoring sessions with Devyn. It surprised me to find him gone when I woke up after our little sleepover Saturday night. However, he did text me, thanking me for letting him stay, which was sweet of him. Maybe we can have a healthy friendship, but I doubt we'll ever hang out outside of our tutoring sessions.

While working on sociology homework, I get a call from a number with a Los Angeles area code. I'd Skyped Hope and Diana just the night before and was almost positive it wasn't one of them.

"Hello?"

"Annie!" My stomach turns at the awful nickname. Only two people in this world call me that, and I hate them both. This'll be the first time I've heard from him since I got to New York, and I haven't missed him. "You forget you have a dad?" He's the last person I want to talk to. After he flaked on driving me to the airport, I vowed never to speak to him again. Whose phone is he calling me from?

"No." I should ask if he's okay or if he's taking care of himself. I want to know who's prying him off the kitchen table after one of his many late nights or poker games with customers he calls *coworkers.* "What do you need?"

"You really think I need something?" His laughter makes me tense. This man has hurt me in more ways than one. We've never had, and will never have, one of those father-daughter bonds. We'll never laugh together or hug, and he'll never walk me down the aisle. "I know you need some money, and I got a way to get you some."

"I'm not coming home," I retort.

"I didn't fucking ask you to!" he yells. He must know I'm about to hang up, because he quickly adds, "Ivan said he'll bring you some money."

Knots instantly grow in my stomach at the mention of my dad's sick bastard of a partner. They spend their time running the streets, coming in and out of my deceased grandmother's home with hundreds of drunken men and drugged women to entertain them. Ivan and my father are the worst kind of men in this world.

"That's not happening."

"All he's asking is that you spend a couple of days with him, Annie. That's nothing you haven't done before, and I'll give you three grand. He's going out there anyway to pick up these twins that want to work for me."

"No. Tell Ivan to stay the hell away from me—"

"No point getting upset," my father cuts me off, laughing. "You know that's a lot more than I pay—"

"It's not happening!" I yell over the phone just as Tony pokes his head into the room. I stare at him, embarrassed that he's heard my outburst.

He closes the door behind him. "Your break ended five minutes ago. I'd give you some more time, but we're getting busy in there."

I hang up the phone without saying another word to my father. "I'm sorry, it won't happen again."

"No problem," Tony tells me. "Everything okay?"

"Of course," I say, walking past him. "Thanks for asking."

I leave his office vowing to never answer a call from an unrecognizable number again.

***

DEVYN

The restaurant Ryan works at is the hardest place to find in all of New York. I've been going up and down the same street for damn near twenty minutes when I see her taking someone's order in the window. But seeing her makes my icy mood go away. Ryan's a good friend to have now that she's let down that wall a little bit.

Honestly, she's kind of funny and cool.

She looks up at me as I enter. "Hey," she says with a smile that isn't exactly hers. I've seen her real laugh, and it's not like the polite smile she's giving me right now. She looks at the Chinese couple she's serving. "Your meal should be coming out very soon. Can I get you something while you wait?" They tell her no, and she comes over to me. I think she's going to hug me, but she just stands right in front of me.

"I'm ready to work."

"That's good," she replies kindly. "Pick a booth; I'll be done in a minute. Are you hungry?"

I can't lie. "I'm starving."

Her cheeks flush as she tries to hide her smile. "What do you want? I'll have them cook us something."

"What's good here?"

"Everything," she replies. "But the cheese enchiladas are my favorite."

I laugh. "Make mine beef and we got a deal."

She heads to the kitchen.

I grab the round booth across from the Chinese couple. They're the only other people in here, and it seems like everyone's starting to clean up. It's a little after ten, so they just closed. I wonder if it bothers Ryan when people come in so close to closing hours. It would definitely irritate the hell out of me.

I'm feeling exhausted after a hard practice followed by a long meeting with my coaches, but something about Ryan motivates me to work hard and impress her. I want her to think of me as more than just some dumb football player. I take my homework out and get to work before Ryan gets on my case. Lord knows she's often looking for a reason.

"Here you go." Twenty minutes later, Ryan comes to the table and sets the plate in front of me. My mouth waters as the scent of the three enchiladas surrounded by beans and rice hit my nose. She sets her own food on the table and sits across from me. She's taken off her apron and is wearing light blue skinny jeans and a black sweater that hangs loosely off her shoulders. Her style's changing from how it was in high school—she's starting to show off her smooth skin and curves.

I thank her and take my first bite, more than satisfied with the taste. I thought this was a nice, friendly dinner, but Ryan doesn't seem in the mood to talk. She sits even quieter than usual, picking at her food with her eyes glued to her plate.

"You finish all your homework?" I ask after ten minutes of no conversation. I'm almost done with my food, and her plate's full.

She shakes her head, not looking at me. "I have a few things to get done. How's *The White Man's Burden* going?"

Why can't she look at me?

"It's not my favorite, but I'm almost done with the week's reading."

She nods.

"Ryan, what's wrong?"

She looks at me with red eyes, worry lines on her forehead, and a deeply curved frown. "I'm fine. Thanks for asking."

I shift in my seat, feeling anxious. Why can't she talk to me? "You don't usually act like this. Even when you're mad at me, you're not this quiet."

She opens her mouth to speak, but tears fall instead. I move my things aside to get closer to her. "Are you homesick or something?"

"Not at all," she cries. I pull her closer, not caring about her *no touching* rule. "I'm sorry . . . I can't do this today. I'll sign your sheet; I'm so sorry."

"Don't worry about it." As much as I need her help, I can manage to do homework alone. "Tell me what's wrong."

Ryan wipes away her tears. "Just a lot of stuff going on with my dad," she tells me. "I don't know what I'm going to do."

"You can tell me, if you want." I need to know what's going on and how I can help.

More tears fall down her face as the walls come down. "You probably already know he's not the best guy . . ."

I nod, keeping quiet so she continues to speak.

"He's *so* awful. I mean, he uses everyone around him while destroying anyone in his way. I thought moving out here meant I'd get away from all that shit, but his partner is coming out here for the weekend and he wants to see me. I said no, but I'm scared he'll show up on campus." She hiccups from all the crying, burying her face in her hands. "I don't know what I'm going to do if he does."

"Why are you so scared of him?"

She shakes her head, and I know I've asked too many questions. Her walls rise, blocking her emotions. "Can we leave?"

I nod. "Let's finish at my place." I have to know the full story.

Ryan cleans up our plates as I call an Uber and comes back right as it pulls up. I pull her inside, and her hand remains in mine the entire ride to campus and as we walk into my dorm.

"Woah . . . hey." Avery, the worst quarterback on the team, whistles as he comes out of his apartment next to mine.

"Hi, Avery," Ryan says. She doesn't bother to fake a smile.

"What're you two doing this late?"

Ryan looks up at me, asking for help. He definitely wouldn't leave us alone if we told him we were going to study. He is the nosiest motherfucker on the planet.

"This is my girl," I reply the only thing I can think to say.

Ryan's eyes go wide.

Avery looks shocked. Was something going on between the two of them? He brought three different girls to his apartment *today*.

"For real?"

"Yup." I open my door and pull Ryan in. "We'll see you later, man." This way, if they have something going on, it's shut down. Ryan deserves better than him.

Two of my roommates are sitting on the couch, playing video games. They don't even notice us walk in. I let go of Ryan's hand and let her follow me to my bedroom.

My room's the smallest of the three bedrooms in my suite, but it has a nice full-sized bed, desk, and TV to occupy my time. It's a chill little spot, so I spend as much time in here as I can. Other than the picture of my little brother and sister that my dad gave me after he'd helped move me in, the decor is Spartan.

"Home sweet home," I say, throwing my backpack on the floor. "Please . . . make yourself comfortable." I watch Ryan take off her backpack and sit on my desk chair before I collapse at the foot of the bed. I kick off my shoes, scooting them against the wall, then I sit on the floor beside her.

Ryan turns to me as she takes off her boots. "I've never told anyone this . . . not even my best friends back home." She's basically whispering, and all I can do is thank God my roommates aren't being loud so I can hear her.

"When I was fourteen, I woke up in the middle of the night to this yelling . . . or maybe fighting. My . . . the room was right next to the kitchen, so I could hear everything they were saying. My dad . . . he dabbles in a lot of things—women, gambling, drugs, alcohol. He was either high or trying to get high. I can't exactly remember, but he was begging this guy for something." She pauses as tears stream down her face again. "And then a few minutes later, this man came into my room."

The words make a loud sob escape her lips. We're inches apart, and I want to reach over and hold her. But I don't know if that's right.

"It was my first time. I screamed for my dad to help me, to protect me, but he never came, so I just laid there. I didn't fight back or . . . or do anything. Didn't go to the police or a teacher, and I guess that made my dad think it was okay, because he made that man his business partner, and let him rape me until the second I left for college."

I need to help her. She's suffering, and all I can do is reach over, pick her up, and hold her. She shakes in my arms, seeming so fragile I think I might break her.

"My dad called me today and offered me three thousand dollars to spend the weekend with his partner," she cries. "I know my dad's never cared about me, but he's taken things to a whole new level. I can't do this. Ivan will be in New York, and he's going to come here and find me."

I pull her closer. "He won't."

"Don't make promises you can't keep, Devyn." She's terrified, and I don't know what else to do to calm her down. "I have no clue what to do."

"Ryan," I pull back and hold her face in my hands. "I'll be here all weekend, so I'm going to help you. We'll figure this out. You don't have to solve this all on your own anymore."

"I'm so scared," she whispers, her eyes glued to mine.

"Trust me. Everything will be okay." I know that's the hardest thing I can ask her to do right now.

***

RYAN

I wake up hot. I open my eyes. Darkness still reigns outside, and I'm thankful that I'm able to get a little more sleep before class. Would it really hurt to skip one day? I take a moment to register I'm in someone else's bed, wrapped in someone's arms. Did I really open the deepest, darkest parts of myself to *Devyn Baker*? As much as I want to punish myself for trusting someone so new to my life, it felt good to tell someone. This was a secret between me and my father, always making me feel like a victim. Things weren't like that anymore.

Devyn turns to his side, letting me go, which saddens me. I like the feeling of being in his arms. It's comfortable, safe even. He's thick and muscular, and I can't help but welcome his strong hold. He's the first person to ever hold me like that.

He looks back, now awake. "You okay?"

How long did I spend crying in his arms?

"Yeah, I'm okay."

Devyn turns to face me and pulls me back into him.

"I can leave if you want your bed to yourself."

"You're good." I can hear the smile in his voice. "This bed's too big for one person, anyway. But you *do* owe me a tutoring session."

I snicker. He's enforcing rules now? "I know."

"Are you comfortable? Do you need anything?"

I'd love to change out of these jeans, but I keep quiet.

Devyn's fingers slide up and down my back as he quietly hums. It's the sweetest gesture anyone has ever shown me. I wonder if he hums often, or sings. I nuzzle my face into his neck, taking note of how our legs wrap around each other's. "I'll protect you, Ry," he whispers, and then kisses the top of my head.

I get as close to him as I can, letting myself relax for the first time in what feels like years. For now, I'll wrap myself in this moment and completely into him. Life's struggles can wait for a couple hours.

CHAPTER 8

RYAN

Devyn's not next to me when I wake up later that morning. I'm tightly wrapped into his dark blue comforter, and I know he's the one who did this. I never move in my sleep. The guard took my school ID when Devyn checked me in, so I can't even leave if I wanted to. It doesn't help that if I did leave, everyone would know I was leaving the football side of the athletic dorms. I grab my phone to call him, but the ringer goes off somewhere nearby. Did he really forget his phone?

Seconds later, the door opens slowly and in comes Devyn. He looks and smells fresh out of the shower, the delicious and strong scent of his soap, lotion, and cologne filling the room.

"You're calling?"

"I thought you left."

"I did. I had practice."

"You should've woken me up before you left. I could've gone back to my room."

Devyn laughs, showing off a huge smile with pearly white teeth. His beard looks trimmed and his hair's freshly cut and glistening. He looks almost too good for it to be so early.

"At four-thirty? You were knocked out."

"I'm going to be so late for class." I groan and dramatically fall on the bed.

"It's okay to miss class sometimes," he says as he takes the seat next to me.

I look at him, shocked. "No, it's not! And you should be going to class too!"

"Not till twelve."

"I don't even have time to change."

"Wear something of mine." He shrugs.

He's got an answer for everything, doesn't he?

"I know I'm a bigger girl," I tell him. "But I doubt we're the same size."

Devyn chuckles. "I know, but take a shirt or something." He goes to his closet and pulls out a dark gray sweater. "This might work." He throws it, almost knocking me over.

The sweater doesn't look too bad. It's loose and fits like a dress. I take my jeans off and cuff the long sleeves before slipping my boots, socks, and coat back on. I use the baby wipes on Devyn's dresser to wipe off what's left of my makeup, and I run my fingers through my hair, tucking one side behind the ear. I'm definitely pulling off a messy look, but it'll have to do.

When I walk out of Devyn's room, he's drinking a large jar of applesauce, making me laugh. He looks at me, puts the jar down, and wipes his mouth with the back of his hand.

"Are you laughing at me?"

"Need a spoon?"

Devyn laughs. "It's more fun this way." He screws the lid back on the jar and puts it in the fridge. "You look good."

I barely resist smiling at the compliment.

"I told you you'd pull it off."

"Thanks?" I blush, not knowing how to answer.

"Ready?" he asks. "Or are you ditching class?"

"No skipping class for me."

"Figured." Devyn grabs his phone and leads the way out. "So, you still want to do tutoring tonight?"

I nod. "I have work, but I can come after? Or you can come to my dorm. It's up to you."

We walk in silence, Devyn contemplating. "Come here. Do you mind studying in my room?"

I shake my head.

"Bet. It's a date."

Date? Is he serious? I'm too afraid to ask him to clarify, so I just nod like an idiot.

I can't wrap my head around the fact that this isn't awkward. After last night, this just feels different. Like we've reached a new page, but we're both carrying on like things are normal. He knows my biggest secret and promised to protect me from my worst nightmare. Were those heat-of-the-moment promises?

"I'll see you tonight then," he says.

"You will." To address the elephant in the room, I wrap my arms around his neck and hug him. "Thank you for everything."

A second passes, then he hugs me back. Devyn nuzzles his face in my neck, just like I'd done to him this morning.

"I enjoy spending time with you," he whispers. "We'll talk later, okay?"

I nod, letting him go before I start crying. I haven't thought about Ivan all morning and don't want to start. "Have a good day. Let me know if you need anything."

"I will." Devyn lets me go, and even though I don't want to leave him, I head to class.

I don't want to admit how much I'm starting to like Devyn. He's sweet and comforting, and he's promised to protect me—something no one's ever done. I don't know why he's so willing, but for the first time in my life, I'll admit I need protection from Ivan.

I'm not about to give up my independence for a guy. I need to continue to put myself first and can't get wrapped up in Devyn. However, I am curious about this "plan" of his.

Instead of thinking too much and forcing myself to put my guard up against someone who could really be there for me, I'm going to try to trust Devyn until he gives me a reason not to. I can be careful to avoid getting my heart broken, but does he even want a relationship?

My teacher doesn't notice my tardiness, so I spend the last forty minutes distracted, praying Ivan doesn't show up in New York. If he comes tonight, I'll be at work where I'm safe. The best thing to do is stay around people I feel safe with.

After class, I run home to change into work clothes. My shower ends up being quick, mainly because the water's freezing. When I return, Nico's on my bed and Jay's at the table eating a sandwich.

"Hey, guys!" I'm excited they've come to hang out. Jay nods at me while eating.

"Hey, ghost."

"I've been here!" I laugh. "You know I work crazy hours."

"What days do you have off?" Nico asks. "We've got to have another floormate bonding session."

"Sundays and Mondays." Once Devyn's tutoring and my course load increased, I had to slow down.

"Alright, I'll plan something since our RA's gone MIA since our first floor meeting. What happened to our family dinners?"

"Who knows?" Jay laughs. I dig in my closet to find something to wear. "So, Ryan. Nico tells me you didn't come home last night, and that you must've been up to something *juicy*. *Juicy* is her word, not mine."

I smile. Jay's so adorable. He looks like a little pumpkin. "That's because Nico's queen gossip!" I giggle and Nico sticks her tongue out at me. "You really want to hear about boy drama, Jay?"

"I knew you were with a guy!" Nico jumps in excitement as I wait for Jay's answer.

He shrugs. "I'm already here, so might as well."

I pull on a pair of black leggings. "I was at Devyn's."

"I told you they were hooking up!" Nico says to Jay.

"You just said Ryan was fucking someone. I didn't know who."

"We did no fucking," I reply. "I fell asleep during tutoring, but I don't know. It feels like something's going on."

"What don't you know?" Nico asks.

I shrug, slipping on a dark green long-sleeve shirt. I notice Jay keeps his eyes on my sandwich as I'm changing, and it makes me appreciate him even more. "I just feel like he gets around. You know how athletes are."

"In a room full of niggas that ain't shit, one nigga always is," Nico says, making me and Jay laugh. "Seriously! I mean, he seems cool, and he was all frantic to talk to you after you guys got in that fight."

"How do you know about that?"

Nico shrugs. "These walls are thin as hell."

I look at Jay who's taking his last bite of food. "What do you think?"

"I mean, I haven't seen you two to really know, but you're tutoring him, so you're stuck with him regardless."

"That's terrible advice," Nico states.

Jay smiles. "I watch people, so I'll be able to tell once I see. Bring him by, and I'll be able to tell immediately."

I get in the bed with Nico, feeling tired even after sleeping so well in Devyn's arms. "I can set that up. Do you guys have any plans for the weekend?"

"Just a party tomorrow. You want to come?" Nico responds as I pull my fleece blanket over us.

"Maybe . . . I should go to a party one of these days," I say.

"What about tonight?"

"I'm making Troy take me on a date. We were going to see if you wanted to join us."

I try my best to look like I'm not excited to spend time with Devyn rather than Troy and Nico. "I have to tutor. How about you, Jay?"

"I'm hitting up this spoken word event with a couple friends in my creative writing class. Then we're gonna go eat," Jay says. "I'm thinking of performing soon."

"Please let me know when!" I exclaim. "I'll even take off work. I didn't know you do spoken word."

"No one does. But I'll let you know if I decide."

My roommates are so amazing and talented. "What time is work?"

The digits 11:53 a.m. shine across my phone.

"One." I look at Nico. "Take a nap with me? I miss you."

Nico's become my best friend here. I even like her a little more than my friends back home.

"I could use a little sister time."

Jay gets up. "That's my cue." He envelops us in a group hug, then promptly leaves.

"I love him." I chuckle. "He could've stayed if he wanted."

"Me too, but his advice fucking sucked," she replies.

We lie down. "So, what's going on with you and Sasha?"

Nico sighs. "I don't even know. She's been acting weird."

"Why do you say that?"

"I've barely seen her since we got here, and when I do, she only comes in the middle of the night when she's drunk after a party or poetry reading or something," Nico says. "I was here almost every weekend last year. She begged me to go to Truth. But now it's like we're just fucking around instead of in an actual relationship."

I hate seeing Nico as anything other than her vibrant self. "Have you talked to her about it?"

She shakes her head. "No, I've been too scared to hear what she's going to say. If she'll want to break up or whatever. She's always been good at reading me . . . she should know something's wrong."

We go back and forth about if she should schedule a talk with Sasha. She doesn't want to sound needy, but she should at least give her girlfriend the opportunity to fix what's wrong. She's approaching this situation completely opposite of the way she does with her parents with the same thing. No one in your life should make you so unhappy.

When I finally get her to text Sasha to hang out tonight and talk, I decide to confess something I've been going back and forth about all day. "I think I like Devyn."

Nico chuckles. "You think?"

"I just don't know. I'm really not trying to get hurt."

"Well, I'm sure he knows you're not the kind of girl that just wants to fuck. He cares about you." She laughs. "That nigga ran through here like someone had attacked you *just* to apologize."

"He was just high." I laugh.

"Don't matter. He likes you."

"He knows so much about me . . . more than anyone," I tell her. "So, we have this connection, and it probably drives my feelings toward him and my strong need to trust him. But I don't know how to deal with these feelings. I've never done random hookups, but can I even trust that he—"

"Ryan!" Nico interrupts. "You're thinking way too hard!"

I groan. "I'm crazy, right?"

"You're not," she says. "Just take it one step at a time. See if you two are on the same page, but remember you're just hanging out right now. Let things flow and see where it goes."

"Okay, I'm going to talk to him."

"It's going to be okay. Let me know how it goes."

Ironically, I'm able to get Nico to talk to Sasha but can't even find the strength to talk to Devyn.

CHAPTER 9

RYAN

Work goes by super fast today, so I'm in a great mood by 10:45 p.m. when I'm getting ready to walk out the door.

"Ryan!" Maria yells from the front. "Someone's here for you!"

My heart stops. How did Ivan already figure out where I work? My chest and heart collide rapidly as I try to figure out who could've told him where to find me.

"Ryan!" Maria yells again after I wait a couple minutes too long.

I take a deep breath and try to get myself together. I'm in a safe environment where everyone can hear my screams. I grab my bag, head to the front of the restaurant, and am more than relieved to see Devyn in the lobby talking to Maria.

He smiles when he sees me. "Hey."

All the muscles in my face relax, and a look of concern comes across his.

"Hey," I reply. Maria leaves the lobby, shooting me a wink on her way to the kitchen. Devyn walks over and pulls me into a hug. I wrap my arms around him as he finds his new favorite spot at the nape of my neck. "What are you doing here?"

"I didn't want you walking to campus this late by yourself," he murmurs. "What's wrong?"

I shake my head. "I thought you were someone else."

Devyn lets me go and grabs my hand. "Ready?" I ask.

He nods, leading me out of the restaurant.

Devyn pulls a set of keys out of his pocket and unlocks a large red truck. "It's my roommate's car," he says, answering my unasked question. "He's letting me borrow it for the night." I release his hand to get in.

He turns on the heat, then plays with his phone to put on music. A soft Frank Ocean song fills the car's speakers, and we're off. We're less than five minutes from school, and I'm sad when the drive ends. I've forgotten how nice it is to sit and relax in the car for a while.

In the familiar space of Devyn's apartment, tons of people crowd the common area and kitchen. Devyn takes my hand and pulls me into him. "My roommates decided to throw a party last minute. Follow me." Devyn slaps hands with different guys on the way to the kitchen and grabs a small container of some type of pasta from the refrigerator. He takes my hand again and pulls me into his room.

"The noise won't distract you?" I ask.

Devyn takes my bag off my shoulders, sets it on his bed, and then goes to the microwave to heat up his food. "I'll drown them out. I'm almost done with the reading too."

"Really?"

Devyn laughs. "Yeah. I'll get started on the essay tomorrow so you can look at it."

I nod, excited to see the progress he's making in his classes. "It's just this math packet I need help with."

"I'll look at it while you read."

Devyn hands me the container. "Here you go."

I laugh. "For me?"

Devyn nods. "I ate most of it earlier." He then hands me a fork. "I promise it's good."

"You made it?"

He nods. "I can cook, girl. My dad works late, so I usually made dinner for my little brother and sister." He's not lying. I take my first bite, and it's delicious. "Told you. I'm damn near a chef." He reaches over me to grab his book and then plops down in the middle of the bed. "Make yourself comfortable, Ry."

I grin. "Since when did we start using nicknames?"

Devyn opens his book. "I heard one of your floormates call you Ry once and I liked it," he tells me. "I thought all your friends called you that."

"We *are* friends now, huh?"

Devyn smiles. "I'm starting to think we're a little more than that." Nervousness pricks the back of my neck and I decide not to push the subject any further. What are we? Cuddle buddies?

"Do your homework."

Hours pass and the party only gets louder. I don't know how Devyn's able to get so much work done with all the noise. He seems content, being here with me when he could be out there drinking or smoking or doing whatever people do at parties. Also how did the team party at night and play in the morning? No wonder we suck . . .

I can't concentrate with the noise, but somehow, we're able to work through Devyn's math homework. He doesn't ask too many questions, so I sit there looking at clothes online and stalking Nico's Instagram, which is filled with pictures of her girlfriend and creatively edited selfies. I wonder if she's worked things out with Sasha.

A loud sigh takes me away from my social media distraction. I look up to find Devyn looking at me. "I'm getting tired."

"You done for the night?"

"Let's finish this tomorrow." He moves his work aside to get closer to me. "How're you feeling?"

"I'm as good as someone could be in my predicament." I shrug. "Can I ask you a question?"

"Am I in trouble?"

I chuckle. "I don't think so."

"Then talk to me. But first—" He pauses, taking my hand and pulling me into him. "You lay with me all last night, and now you don't want to be near me. I showered right before I picked you up, so I know I don't smell."

I giggle. "It's not that." The problem is he makes me *so* nervous.

"What do you want to talk about?"

I look at him. "Okay, having a voice is important, and right now I feel like I'm suppressing mine. When I took this job, Coach K told me a lot of girls would just apply to get close to the players, and that was never and would never be my intention."

"And . . . ?"

I sigh. Spit it out already! "I don't want to make things awkward, and if they get awkward, I'm sorry, but I really like you. I tried to hold it in, but just with everything going on, I've just figured out that I like you more than I thought I did . . . more than a friend." I'm rambling, and he's saying nothing. "I'm sorry if things are weird now, or if you want a new tutor. I just thought you should know."

"I know you like me," he responds.

"It's that obvious?"

Devyn laughs. "I mean, I wasn't sure until about twenty-four hours ago you were feeling me. But I saw how you were warming up to me as a friend."

I nod.

"Ryan, look at me."

I do.

"Do you really think I'd put this much effort and time and care into a girl I didn't like?"

"What?"

"It's obvious I'm feeling the same way."

"It is?"

He laughs. "I thought so. I just don't want to rush you into anything. You've been through a lot."

"Yeah." I sigh. "So, if you're just trying to hook up . . . that's not going to work."

"What makes you think I want that?" He laughs.

I shrug. "You know. Reputations and stuff . . ."

"Don't believe that." Devyn smiles. "Isn't that what made you hate me when we first met? I'm not interested in anyone other than you."

"Good." I try hard not to smile and desperately fail.

"Let's just take things one day at a time and see where they go," Devyn proposes. "I don't want to overwhelm you."

He's being reasonable. Has he always been like this? Maybe I'm the crazy one . . .

"I'd like that."

"Come here." Devyn grabs my waist, picking me up to straddle his lap. "Is this okay?"

I nod.

"Let me hold you."

I wrap my arms around his neck and hold on, resting my nose in his neck and inhaling his scent.

"This is my favorite thing to do."

I laugh. "Yeah?"

"For now, at least."

I lean back to look at him. We're closer than we've ever been before, our noses barely touching. "What do you mean?"

"I'm waiting for you to kiss me."

A hint of a smile comes across my face. "You don't have to ask. You nervous?"

Devyn's lips curve, a cocky grin on his face. "I don't get nervous about things like that, baby."

The pet name makes my heart pound. Figuring Devyn's more nervous than he lets on, I lean in and touch my lips to his. A soft moan escapes his mouth before he makes the kiss more intense. His hands move to the small of my back as he pulls me closer. Kissing Devyn feels like all my problems don't exist. The charge I get from his affection makes me forget everything else.

"Am I hurting you?" I ask, letting my low self-esteem get in the way of my first kiss.

Devyn laughs at my question, and then goes right back to kissing me.

"You're so cute." Devyn grabs my waist and scoots me back. "What do you want?"

"What do you mean?"

He rests his hand on my thigh, breathless from all the kissing. "I've found things go easier when we both lay out on the table what we want and don't want and what we like and don't like."

I'm not sure what he's asking. "You go first."

Devyn leans against the headboard behind him. "You have to understand that football comes first for me; I want to go to the NFL and I won't let anyone or anything jeopardize that."

"I wouldn't ask you to compromise football to do whatever we're doing. You'll still have to do your homework too. That doesn't end. My job's just as important."

"But football doesn't mean you're not important," he tells me, "because you are; it's just time management. Sometimes it's hard to balance, but you're my tutor so I have to make time to see you."

Someone from the living room bangs on Devyn's door, making me jump. "Just ignore it; the door's locked."

"What else?"

"I don't want you talking to other niggas. I can be territorial."

I don't know if I like him thinking I belong to him.

"That's the last thing I want to worry about. So whatever you have going on with Avery . . . it's done."

I have to ask. "What do I have going on with Avery?"

He responds with a shrug.

"He walked me home from the yard once, and we never hung out again. He kissed me the first time we met, and then asked me to come over in the wee hours of the night. And you know that didn't happen." I pause for a moment to gather my thoughts. "Wait . . . that's why you told him I was your girl?"

"You are now." Devyn scratches his head, nervous. "Your turn."

"Well, I'm *really* not ready to have sex yet." My stomach cramps as I talk. "I know it's a huge part of being in a relationship, so if you need that frequently, that might be a problem."

"I'm not going to try you," he tells me. "We can take things like that on your terms."

I nod. "I'm shy."

"You open up," Devyn says. "So, is this, like, your first relationship?"

I nod, avoiding eye contact. "How about you?"

"Nothing like this," he says. "Our connection seems deeper than anything I've ever had with another girl. I don't know if it's 'cause we come from the same place or what."

I love how much he understands why I hate where we grew up.

"I'm never going back there."

Devyn nods. "I want you to feel protected with me. You can stay here, or I can come to your place while your dad's partner is in New York. I don't want you scared walking around campus and wouldn't mind you being glued to my hip for the next couple of days."

"I have work."

Devyn frowns. "I was kind of hoping you'd come to my game tomorrow."

"I'll have to miss the first half, but I'll come after?"

"Uber there. Don't walk back to campus alone. I'll give you my account info."

Part of me enjoys his protectiveness. "You don't have to."

Devyn pulls me back into him and kisses me. "Let me do this, okay?"

I nod, unable to say no to him. I don't want to take his money, though. "What days don't you work?"

"Sunday and Monday."

"That's a lot of hours."

"I need a lot of money." I chuckle. "You play football seven days a week. *That's* a lot of hours."

"I guess." My work wouldn't change. I'm not sacrificing having money just to be with him.

"So, your plan to keep Ivan away from me is to glue me to you?"

"It's the only way I'll know you're safe," he says. "You're safest with me. I can tell. You thought it was him at the restaurant."

I nod. "You should've texted me you were coming."

"I was being spontaneous," Devyn admits. "That was my bad. I should've known better."

"It was a nice surprise," I say as another person bangs on the door, interrupting our moment.

"You want to go to your place? I'm sure you need clothes for work."

I chuckle. "I brought some . . . just in case."

A smirk comes across Devyn's face. "Good." He nuzzles his face into my neck. "I'm too lazy to walk all the way to your dorm."

"When will everyone leave?" I ask. "How're you supposed to play tomorrow if everyone's hungover?"

"I don't know." He groans. "I don't get it either."

I chuckle. "As long as you play well, then that's all that matters."

"I can't hold the team as a lineman," he says. "What time is it?" Devyn checks my phone. "You have a missed call . . . sorry. I shouldn't have looked."

Why would he think that? I doubt it's anyone important. I look. The same LA number my dad called from.

"What's wrong, baby?"

I sigh. "It's my dad . . . or Ivan. It's the same number he called me from yesterday." Why were the problems I ran away from coming back to haunt me? I delete the call, pushing it far from my mind. I'm not in the mood for this tonight.

"He's really going to try to see you?"

I press my lips together. "He thinks he owns me. He's probably the reason my dad didn't want me moving to New York." Ivan told me many times I was his while inside of me. I refused to pretend I liked the things he did, hoping he'd eventually get sick of me. "Can we talk about something else? I just want to be here with you."

"You are with me." Devyn smiles.

"Then let's be in the moment." I kiss him again and try to forget my past. I just want to live my life. The last couple days have been too fucking great.

Devyn kisses me back, his happiness contagious. "I should go to bed soon."

"How will you sleep with all this noise?"

"I guess I'm used to it." Devyn's rubs up and down my back in the best way. No one has ever touched me with as much care as he does. "I'll play music if it'll help you sleep."

I agree and get up to change, pretending not to notice Devyn take off his shirt. I only packed work clothes. "Devyn . . ." I turn around. He's eyeing me. "Can I borrow some pajamas?"

I know he wants to make fun of me, but instead he throws me the shirt in his hand. I strip off my clothes and put on the oversized T-shirt that hits the middle of my thighs. "It looks good on you," Devyn says. I turn off the lights and tiptoe to him.

I get under the covers and cuddle up, resting my face on his chest, my hands around his waist. "I love this," I admit.

Devyn's body vibrates against mine as he laughs. "What do you love about it?"

"Being close to you." For some reason I feel like I can say anything to him. "It feels safe."

He kisses my forehead. His hands move under my ass and he pulls my legs between his. "I'm happy you're here."

"Me too," I confess. The room goes silent as I focus on just us. "You think you'll be able to handle me? I come with a lot of baggage."

Devyn brings his lips to mine, kissing me. "Definitely. You're worth it."

CHAPTER 10

DEVYN

I wake up before my seven-fifteen alarm with Ryan tightly wrapped around my waist, her hair sprawled over her face and her mouth open. She looks so peaceful; I don't want to wake her. She has to be tired with everything going on.

Her phone buzzes on my desk for the hundredth time since we went to sleep. I want to reach over and check if it's the same number from earlier—tell whoever it is to leave Ryan alone. But it would just make her anxious, and I want to settle her fears so she doesn't have to worry about shit like that. But we both know Ivan will likely come looking for her if he's not here already.

My dad scared me out of ever talking to drug dealers from my neighborhood, threatening that he would find out and beat my ass. I didn't smoke often, but if I did, I made sure to get it from the white kids at school just to be sure he'd have no idea. But the men in G-Heights are loyal. No way in hell can I ask around about Ivan and it not backfire. All I know is I better not see him or Ryan's dad, because I don't think I'll be able to stop myself from killing them both for abusing her. With everything Ryan's been through, she deserves to live in peace.

How do I keep her safe from him? Is her dad here too? I can't be with her in class or at work. How long will Ivan be here, and what will he do with Ryan if he gets to her?

Last night, I called my dad for advice. I know Ryan doesn't want anyone to know about her past, so I gave him little information and just said I didn't know why she was afraid of Ivan, but she cried about him during tutoring. He'd said to just stay with her to ease her worries. His lack of questions and clarification makes me think he knows more about Ryan than he lets on.

On game days, I usually wake up late, eat a good breakfast, and get into the zone to win. It'd be different doing all that with Ryan here, but I don't mind the company.

My alarm goes off, making Ryan jump and then stir in my arms. "Turn it off." She groans, ducking under the covers.

"I'd let you sleep, but you'll be late for work."

She clings to me. "I don't want to go," she whines. "Let's lie in bed all day." She's getting more comfortable with me by the day. I love that she's showing what she's feeling.

"Tomorrow," I reply. "We'll spend the whole day in bed."

"Promise?"

I laugh. "Promise. You won't have to leave the bed for anything." Ryan's been like a breath of fresh air in my life. Her mood's infectious when she's happy. "But you got to get up."

She pushes the covers down to her waist with a loud sigh and looks over at me, smiling. "Morning."

"Good morning, baby."

Ryan crawls toward me and presses her lips to mine. I wonder if her shyness will come out again. She's so carefree with me lately that I'm almost sure I've knocked down the walls.

"How'd you sleep?"

Ryan stretches. "Good. Really good, actually. You?"

"I sleep better when you're here," I reply truthfully. The comment makes her blush.

Ryan gets up. "Can I use your bathroom?"

"You don't have to ask."

"Can you come with me?" she asks. "I don't want one of your roommates walking in."

I get up from the bed and head to the bathroom, letting her walk in first before closing the door behind me and locking it. Ryan gets herself together and I brush my teeth and wash my face. It's cute, watching her get ready. I'm starting to think a lot of the things Ryan does are cute.

"All done," Ryan says as she wipes the last bit of soap from her face. "What time do you leave for your game?"

"Nine-thirty." I open the door for her to head back to my room.

She doesn't ask me to leave while she gets dressed, so I get back into bed and watch TV. When I turn my attention back to her, she's dressed in a blue long-sleeve shirt and some light blue overall shorts, looking in the mirror and pulling at her clothes uncomfortably.

"This is as good as it's getting today," she whispers to herself. She tucks some hair behind her ear and catches me staring. "Everything okay?"

I nod. "You're beautiful."

She turns around. Her bare face shows off a light pattern of freckles above her nose. "And you're sweet."

Ryan walks toward me, and I reach out my hand to take hers, pulling her back in. "Stay with me until I go to the field for my game."

"I'd love to, but as you know, money doesn't grow on trees." She laughs. "You think you'll win today?"

"That's the plan," I reply. "We'll see, though."

"You'll do great. You always did before." I know for a fact Ryan has never been to any of my games, but I say nothing. I cuddle her, running my fingers through her hair, enjoying the last few seconds we have together.

My teammates fill the hallways, running around getting ready for the game. A few of them do double takes, surprised to see a girl around the morning of a game. I entwine my hand with Ryan's to let them know not to mess with her or talk to me as we walk downstairs.

We wait for her Uber in the lobby, Ryan's arms are wrapped around my waist, as Avery walks in. We make eye contact immediately, but Ryan doesn't notice.

"As always," she says, "You've been a great host."

I turn my attention back to her, ignoring his stare. "Any time." A silver Toyota Camry pulls up seconds later. "That's your ride."

"Alright," Ryan says with an elongated sigh. I lean in and kiss her, moving my hands to her ass, very aware of people's looks. I want everyone to know we're together. "Whoa . . ." Ryan laughs, leaning back. I keep my arms around her but loosen my grip. "That's a hell of a good-bye kiss."

"I'll see you after my game?"

"Yeah." She's smiling as she lets me go, but I pull her back for one more kiss. I really don't want her to leave.

"Call or text if you need anything," I tell her, but I know she won't.

"I'll see you later!" She giggles, kissing me again and then backing away toward the door. "Bye!" she says with the prettiest, most genuine smile I've ever seen on her face.

"Bye, baby." I smile and watch as she gets in the Uber. I turn around to head back but see Avery, Justin, and Davis looking at me.

"When did y'all get together?" Justin asks, but I'm sure he's doing it for Avery.

I shrug. "You know how it is, bro. We've been off and on since high school, and then made it official once we got here."

They all nod, believing the lie. If I make things look more serious between Ryan and me, Avery will back off. He has a habit of hooking up with some of our teammates' girls, but he won't try that with me. I turn my attention to him. "How do you know her?"

He must feel the pressure on him because his shoulders slump and he rubs the back of his neck. "We just hung out on the courtyard one day." He shrugs. "She never mentioned dating one of my teammates, though."

"She wasn't at the time," I reply, walking away so I don't have to finish this conversation. Something about Ryan makes me feel like she's end game. Now that I have her, I won't let anyone mess up this good thing.

***

RYAN

New relationship bliss makes the morning speed by, so I feel fresh and excited to leave work for the second half of Devyn's game.

I'm surprised to see so many people in the stands when I get there. I convinced Nico and Troy to join me (Jay declined the offer due to a hangover), and since they're waiting, I don't have to find a seat. I maneuver myself through crowds of people fast. It's an old talent of mine from growing up invisible, so it doesn't take long to find them in the third row.

"Hey!" I smile and hug them before taking my seat next to Nico. The fourth quarter just started, and we're actually winning!

"We were starting to think you wouldn't make it," Nico says. "How was work?"

I shrug. "Cool . . . not too bad." I spot Devyn on the field, then turn to Nico. "How'd things go last night?"

"Not good." She sighs. "We're going to talk again, though."

I nod.

"Devyn's playing well." Nico changes the subject, which is fine with me.

"Really?" I smile. "He's been playing a lot?"

Troy nods. "I think he's only been out for a couple of minutes." Good. From the looks of last night, he's certainly the most focused member on the team.

We spend the next hour yelling and cheering with other Truth fans. Truth ends up winning sixty-seven to forty-six, and I'm so happy for Devyn. It's cute seeing him celebrate with his teammates and Coach K after their win.

"Alright, we're out," Troy announces. "Nico's dressing me for my date tonight."

I get up and hug them. "Thanks for coming, guys."

Nico laughs. "This was my first football game, and I have to say, it's not too bad. Let me know when you want us to come again."

"You'll definitely be at more games! I'll see you guys back at home."

I text Devyn to let him know I'm waiting in the bleachers, ignoring another call from my dad in the process. I can't let him ruin my day.

"So you *have* been ignoring me." The familiar, raspy voice instantly makes my stomach churn.

***

DEVYN

The boys are wilding when we get back to the locker room after our win. Coach finished his victory speech fifteen minutes ago and niggas have already brought out the speaker, congratulating each other and dancing to our victory. Win or lose, these guys *are* my brothers—moments like this make it all worth it.

I get in and out the shower, ready to lie down for a couple of hours. The night presents great possibilities—a celebratory party for the team or some quality time with Ryan. I pull on my sweats and take my phone out of my locker to see a couple texts from my dad and a missed call and text from her.

> **Ryan:** So proud of you! In the stands when you're ready.

I can see Ryan on the bleachers from the locker room, talking to some guy, so I quicken my steps to save her from whoever's father decided to stir up a conversation. However, the closer I get to her, the more I don't like what's going on.

"Why are you here?" I hear Ryan say to him. "I told you before I left California that you'd never see me again."

"I didn't agree to that, baby girl."

I stop, hiding behind the wall so I can figure out what the fuck is going on.

"Please, Ivan, I'm tired of—"

"Stop with all that fucking crying. I don't want to see that shit," Ivan tells her. "I'm five seconds from throwing your ungrateful ass in the car and taking you back to LA. It's a long drive, but you can sit in the back and entertain the two other whores. That what you want?" I speed toward her, ignoring the ache in my tired legs. "That's what I thought. You'll give me what I want . . . it's just a weekend."

"Nah, that's not fucking happening." I walk up the stairs, catching their attention.

"The fuck are you?" He spits.

I stand behind Ryan, and she turns toward me. "Let's just go."

"Baker." Ivan's eyes are on my football bag. "Devyn Baker from G-Heights?"

"Please," Ryan begs.

"We used to bet on you when you were in high school." I look from Ryan to him. His teeth are broken and yellow, his brown skin pale, and his yellow eyes glistening and tired from drugs. His Adidas sweatsuit is dirty and two sizes too big. "What's this? You two together?"

Ryan's fear and his cockiness makes my blood boil. As much as I want to knock this nigga out, I can't do that here. And it won't help Ryan.

"We have a problem? I told you she's not going anywhere." I step past Ryan and walk forward until I'm standing over him.

He laughs. "You know who you're talking to, nigga?"

Ryan tugs on my shirt. "Devyn." She takes my hand and pulls it. Her eyes are glistening as she struggles not to cry, obeying Ivan's orders, and my heart sinks. This isn't what she needs right now. She doesn't need to be near him.

"Your dad's going to love when I tell him this!" Ivan laughs. "Little Annie went off to college and attached herself to the first nigga she could find. We thought we taught you better!" His words infuriate Ryan. "Neither of you taught me anything, you sick—" She pauses. "I got here with no help, no money, and no support. I don't need anything from you. Leave me alone, or I'm going to the police. For real this time."

Ivan smiles. "We both know you won't do that to Daddy. And don't think this big motherfucker is going to keep me away from you. You know I don't get told no."

"If I catch you here again, I swear to God, you'll regret it. You hear me?" I tell him, but I know the last thing Ryan needs is a savior. She wants to fight her own battles.

Ryan pulls me away from the bleachers. "Don't worry, you'll hear from me!" Ivan calls after us, still laughing. "I'll get you back, baby girl. And we gon' have a good ole time! No one's ever been able to keep me away from you!"

I grab Ryan and get her far, far away from his grimy ass.

***

RYAN

I'm watching him sleep.

I didn't think I'd be the kind of girlfriend that's head over heels for her man, but damn am I getting there. And it's only been a couple of days.

We've been lying in my small bed for three hours now. The first two were spent talking about the game, the team, about where Devyn wants to take his football career after college. Devyn doesn't talk about his mom, so much so that it's like she's nonexistent. They're not close, and she's not around at all. His dad could have carried him in his stomach for nine months and pushed him out himself. He's been through stuff, but he does an amazing job at keeping it together. He holds the people he loves on his back, including me. We aren't in love, but part of me does love him for the way he's taken me under his wing to protect me from my demons.

My phone beeps. I pull my phone from under Devyn's heavy body, surprised to see a text from Avery.

> **Avery:** What's up? You were never going to say anything about you and D?

I don't owe him an explanation. I was never interested in him in the first place.

"He texted you?" Devyn mumbles sleepily. I'm surprised he's up after falling asleep mid-conversation, exhausted from his game.

"No, it's just Nico." I turn my phone away from him, already feeling bad for not telling him the truth. "Why are you up?"

"I felt you get up." Devyn flips onto his stomach and grabs one of my pillows for his head. "Are you okay?"

I nod. With him here, I'm safe from my dad, Ivan, and anyone else.

"How are you?"

Devyn yawns. "Tired . . . sore . . . happy to be with you."

His sweetness makes me smile. "I'm happy you're here."

"Lay with me then." Devyn takes my hand and envelops me. "Can I ask you a question?" He brushes his fingertips down my back.

"Of course." I scoot down so our groins align, giving me the chance to rest my head in his neck.

"You seemed so calm when you were talking to Ivan. What were you thinking?"

I place my hand behind Devyn's neck to massage the spot right behind his ear. "I know how to handle Ivan," I whisper. "He doesn't like crying or screaming or fighting back. It won't make him stop. He sees what he wants to see and hears what he wants to hear."

"I could kill him for what he did to you."

"Hey." I cup his face. "I'm away from all that now."

"Still."

"If I spent my life mad at the people who've done me wrong, I'd be walking around furious," I reply. "My dad and Ivan are so drugged up they can barely tell left from right, let alone understand the harm they bring to other people. I don't want them in my life, so they won't be."

Devyn sighs against my body. "I don't know how you're able to process all of this. How you even got to that mind-set on your own. That couldn't have been easy."

"I have bad days," I admit. "But I've been rewarded with so much good lately. That's what helps me cope." He holds me tight, comforting me without words.

I mean what I say. The little things hold me together—heart-to-hearts with Nico, movie nights with Troy and Jay, the greenery of the East Coast. Or the fact I've gotten here despite every effort my father used to try to tear me down. I was strong before, but these new additions make me feel like no one can touch me. I fought my enemies until I could barely hang on, but now I have someone so big and bad on my team that he tears down my enemies before they can reach me.

I don't know how long Devyn will be in my life, so I want to appreciate every moment as best I can. "Thank you for being here," I tell him.

"Of course." His hands travel to the orange workout shorts I'm wearing. "You hungry? Let me take you to dinner."

"You don't have to do that."

"I want to."

I look at my phone. It's a little after seven. "Is this a date?"

"Do you want it to be?"

We've never been on an actual date. "Only if you do."

A smile creeps onto his face. I love that, somehow, I'm always able to make him smile without trying.

"Yeah, it's a date. But keep it casual; I'm not changing again." I hop out of the bed to put on better clothes as Devyn stretches to make himself more at home.

I keep it simple, choosing thermal leggings with a black long-sleeve shirt.

"Hey, sleepyhead." I shake Devyn, waking him. His eyes flutter open and then shut again. "Devyn," I whisper.

"I'm up. I'm up." He groans as he gets out of bed. Devyn rubs his eyes, cracks his back, and turns around to fix my bed. He doesn't have to do that, but I love that he does. I never leave my room without making my bed, so maybe he noticed.

"Ready?"

I nod, slipping on my denim jacket. "Where are we going?"

"I'm sure you're tired of Mexican food."

"Just a tad."

"I know just the place," he says. "Do you mind walking? It's probably cold."

"That's fine."

The walk to dinner is silent, but the soft blow of the wind and my hand tightly in Devyn's is soothing. Fifteen minutes later, we stop in front of a restaurant called Oohs and Aahs, a soul food restaurant I've never seen.

"This good?" Devyn squeezes my hand, pulling me into the small restaurant that looks more like a cottage. The place is packed with people, but we're seated immediately in a small booth near the kitchen. "Come and Talk to Me" by Jodeci plays loudly through the walls of the restaurant, allowing people to sing and dance along in their seats or on the small dance floor in the center of the room. The place is full of good vibes and happy black people.

"Have you been here before?" I ask Devyn as we settle into our booth.

He nods. "Yeah, but it wasn't like this. It's usually quieter."

"I like it!" I yell over the music.

We spend the next few minutes looking at the menu, and then our waiter comes to take our order. Devyn and I get the same thing—fried chicken, mac and cheese, and yams.

"When's your birthday?" I ask Devyn as the waiter walks away.

He laughs at my question. "January 11," he tells me. "When's yours?"

The waiter comes back with a lemonade for Devyn and a Diet Coke for me. I take a sip.

"December 22."

My last birthday was spent at Diana's house for a movie night and pizza with her and Hope. It wasn't much, but it meant so much that they made an effort to make it special. But the day got ruined when I got home to find my dad passed out on the porch, high as a kite, and Ivan in my bed, waiting for me.

I shake my head from the thought, reminding myself the past is the past. I promised myself to be present and focus on the future. I turn my attention back to Devyn to live up to that promise.

"Where'd you go?" he asks me.

I laugh, searching for an excuse to avoid what I'm actually thinking about. I can't ruin this date with my past trauma. "That you're too far away." His smirk makes me blush, embarrassed. "I'm sorry. I don't mean to sound clingy."

"You're not." He chuckles. "It's cute."

"Come sit next to me." I scoot over to make some room for him. Devyn gets up and comes around to sit beside me. "This is so much better!" I lean into him, pointing over to the people dancing. "You can see the dance floor from here too."

"You want to dance?" Devyn asks me as the song switches from a "Superstar" remix by Usher to "If This World Were Mine" by Luther Vandross.

I almost fall out of the booth in excitement. "Really?"

He nods.

"I'd love to."

Devyn gets up, taking my hand to pull me to the dance floor. We're among older couples, adults who have to be over forty, but it feels like we're exactly where we need to be.

"I've never danced with a guy before," I confess, but he probably knows that. I hadn't gone to any school dances back in the day.

"First time for everything." Devyn pulls me closer to him. A girl dancing beside us places her arms around her date's neck, so I do the same. "See, you're a pro," he whispers.

I close my eyes and hold him close, losing myself in his arms. He's everything I didn't even know I wanted in a man. He manages to be so big and strong and intimidating while treating me so passionately. Was it possible to fall for someone so fast? I'm willing to give him my heart, something I've never given anyone before. He's worth the risk, but can I trust him not to hurt me? How can I make sure he's never added to the list of people who've done me wrong?

The song switches to "Heaven Sent" by Keyshia Cole, and I just know the DJ made this playlist personally for me. I move my head to look at Devyn as we dance. "Thanks for bringing me here."

We look eyes, momentarily, before he responds. "You're gorgeous," he says, kissing me.

"I don't think a first date can get better than this." Devyn presses his lips to my forehead, pulling me back into him.

We dance until the waiter puts our food on the table. Devyn sits next to me in the booth without my asking this time, which makes me happy. I'm lucky to be with him, not because I'm the girl on his arm, but because he's managed to be just what I need. It's nice to have someone in both chaos and happiness.

Our food comas combined with the cold make us catch an Uber back to the dorms. We spend the short five-minute drive wrapped in each other's arms. I can't get enough.

CHAPTER 11

DEVYN

The weekend flies by, and I'm sad to see it go. We spend Sunday as Devyn promised, lying in bed. Devyn showered me with kisses and cuddles, naps, takeout, and then a little tutoring at the end. I love how his place has no interruptions. His roommates are rarely home, and the place is usually quiet. We got the day of rest we both needed.

I've slept at Devyn's place almost every night since our first kiss, and I'm not sure how healthy it is to spend so much time together. Still, my doubts can't stop the smile on my face as I enter Intro to Psych late Monday morning.

I'm so happy I can't even focus on my professor's lecture about nurture versus nature. Devyn's seeping into my thoughts. I constantly wonder how he is, what he's doing, who he's with. One weekend with him and I'm feeling happier, well-rested, and excited to see where my life will head with Devyn by my side. Life's a lot brighter when you don't feel alone. Now I have a partner, and the possibilities seem endless.

Nico and I agree to meet for lunch after class. I find her on the benches outside, dressed in some blue tribal-printed palazzo pants and a white crop top with sandals. The weather's too hot for late September, but it gives me the chance to wear all the clothes I bought in California for school. Sooner or later, I'll have to spend money on winter clothes.

"Look at you!" Nico says as she sees me approaching. Her words make me blush as I hug her. "I don't know how Devyn even let you out of his place this morning with that on." I look down at the tight blush dress that accentuates all my curves. It's revealing and shorter than I'd expected, which is why I had Devyn's jean jacket over it. "And those burgundy boots! I'm stealing them."

"Thank you." I laugh. "But I haven't seen him all day." He rushed out of his room in a hurry this morning, waking me up with a kiss before speeding to practice.

We walk into the cafeteria to get food, keeping it simple with subs and french fries. I'm eager to know about Nico's weekend and if she got to talk to Sasha, but I don't want to rush the subject in case things went left.

"What have Troy and Jay been up to?" I ask, keeping the conversation light. "I've spent so much time with Devyn, I feel like I don't know what's going on with anyone."

"They're good. Jay wasn't home all weekend, so it was just me and Troy."

"What'd you guys do?" I look around to see if it's possible that Devyn's here too, but tell myself to get over it. We're supposed to be having quality sister time.

"After the game, we went shopping, and then Sasha came over. Yesterday we smoked all day, laid in bed, and ordered food." She shrugs. "It's nice to have a girlfriend *and* a boyfriend to occupy my time."

I laugh. "You and Troy are a match made in heaven."

"If only I liked dick." Nico sighs dramatically.

"So, you know I'm waiting to hear how things went between you and Sasha . . ."

Nico can't even stop herself from smiling at the mention of Sasha's name, and I'm relieved. "Oh, she was pretty understanding about everything. We agreed to spend the whole weekend together. She was going to come tonight and hang out, but Jordan's planning our first family dinner."

"When was I supposed to hear about this?"

Nico chuckles. "He hasn't told anyone. Troy made fun of him for it last night and called him a shitty RA, so I think he got offended. He told me to spread the news before I came here, so Troy's telling Jay and I'm telling you. Six o'clock sharp."

I nod. "Cool. I'm excited! We don't know anything about Jordan."

"He's not that great." Nico rolls her eyes. "I'd make a better RA."

"You've got a point there."

Nico smiles. "Enough about me. I'm already happy and in love and all that shit. What's going on with you and Devyn?"

My smile spreads to reflect hers. "We made things official."

"Really?" Nico squeals. "That's adorable! I told you everything would work out. How was the sex?"

I laugh. "I'm still a virgin." That's an easier story than *I've never willingly had sex with anyone, but I was continuously raped for years before I came to Truth.* "We're just going to take things slow . . . see how it goes."

Nico nods. "You know, I had a feeling. You, like, never talk about sex."

"You guessed right," I shrug. "But I like him a lot. From what he says, he feels the same way. You'll have to see us together and tell me what you think."

"Bring him over." I got you," she says between bites of food. "I'm basically fluent in nigga."

We sit there talking and joking around until it's time to head to class. The more I hang out with Nico, the more I love her. She's the coolest friend I've ever had, so fun, and best of all, she doesn't reek of the essence of my past.

I notice a group of football players near the library on my walk across the courtyard and instantly find Devyn talking to another lineman. The two of them look like giants standing next to each other, everyone around them significantly smaller.

"D!" someone screams nearby, and I'm genuinely relieved it's not me. These days, my body has more control over my brain when it comes to how I act toward Devyn. But a girl in tight black spandex and a Truth Cheer shirt runs toward *my* boyfriend. I watch as she jumps into his arms, the two of them laughing and hugging too closely for my liking.

Who the fuck is this girl? She wasn't far from me when she'd called for him, and somehow, he doesn't see me. He's been out of my sight for a few hours, and I'm back to being invisible.

When it comes down to it, it makes sense for Devyn to be with someone in his own social circle—someone to literally cheer him on in all moments, someone to fuck when he wants, someone that doesn't have so much baggage and need so much protection.

I watch as Devyn puts her down, their conversation never losing its bubbliness. I can't stand here looking stupid any longer. I'm less than five feet away, and he hasn't seen me or cared to look. I leave for class, excruciatingly angry and sad. My happy mood is officially ruined, and my new relationship is already over.

***

Devyn: Miss you.

I've been looking at this text for an hour, going back and forth between telling Devyn to fuck off and just not responding. I don't want to see him after watching him and that girl, and as the day goes by, I'm only getting more upset and confused. Sitting in my room makes me overthink the situation more. I even tried to go into work, but Tony forbid me from working on my off day.

What am I going to do? If I'm overreacting, then I need to get over it, but the feeling just won't shake. Devyn's popular, he's handsome, and he's hardworking and incredibly sweet. Any girl would want that. He's supposed to be mine now, and he said he wasn't interested in anyone else. Why can't I trust that? The situation repeats over and over in my mind.

I don't like how I feel, or the fact that he didn't see me when I was two or three feet behind that girl. If I'm his girlfriend, I'm not supposed to still be invisible to him, even when a crowd of people is around.

Devyn texts me again right when I finish most of my homework for the week. At this point, I'm trying to do anything to distract myself.

Devyn: Are you okay? Haven't heard from you all day. Just seeing if you're good.

I send him the thumbs-up emoji so he knows I'm alive and that Ivan hasn't kidnapped me or something. My phone rings seconds later. I go back and forth on whether or not to answer but end up giving in.

"Hey?" he says like a question.

I get up from the table and climb into bed, hoping a nap will ease my overthinking. "What's up?"

"What's wrong?"

"Nothing."

"Where are you?"

He has some nerve questioning me on my whereabouts. He probably just left ole girl. "Where are *you*?" I retort back. My attitude takes him back. "I just got back from lifting. I was about to hop in the shower and come see you." He's his usual calm, soft-spoken self, which only annoys me. Can he not tell I'm upset?

"I can't hang out."

"You can't?" Finally, some emotion colors his voice.

"No, Devyn, I can't." I can't even stop myself from being a bitch. "I'm going to this dinner."

"Oh . . . what for?"

"Do I ask what you're doing all day?"

"You can if you want to. I definitely wouldn't give you as hard of a time as you're giving me." The irritation is thick in his voice, but I can tell he's trying to stay cool.

"I don't know, Devyn. Maybe you should find a girlfriend who's a little more obedient and happier to comply . . . like a cheerleader or something. That'd be the perfect fit."

"What?" he retorts. "Ryan, what's wrong with you?"

This is a waste of my time. "I have to go. I'll talk to you later."

"Ryan!" Devyn yells through the phone right as I pull it from my face to hit *end*.

I bring the phone back to my ear just as Nico enters the room. "What?" I yell. The look on her face tells me she's shocked by how I'm treating the person on the phone.

Devyn lets out a long sigh. "Tell me what's wrong ... please." Nico comes over and sits next to me. I know she won't leave till I tell her what's up.

"I can't talk. People are in my room."

"I don't give a fuck who's in your room. Kick them out."

"Bye, Devyn."

He pauses. "Call me after dinner," he tells me. "Whatever it is, we can talk about it. I just want to make things right."

I hang up, irritated with both myself and him.

"Weren't you just telling me a couple hours ago how much you liked Devyn?" Nico gets under the covers and lays down next to me. "What happened?"

I sigh. "I just . . ." I look at her. "I saw this girl all over him in the courtyard, and I've been going crazy ever since. I don't like feeling jealous, but it's not okay for some girl to just be all over him."

"It seemed like something was going on?"

I nod. "I read people well. I'll always be able to tell if a girl's interested in him. I don't want to feel like I can't trust him."

"Ry, he hasn't given you a reason not to. Give him the benefit of the doubt. Maybe you read it wrong. I mean, he's pushing to work things out . . ."

"What makes you say that?"

Nico laughs. "He asked you to call him later to talk. Most guys would be like, 'This bitch is crazy,' and let you get over it. No offense, but you do sound nuts."

"How do I stop this feeling? Like, I just feel so . . . possessive." Possessiveness. Something I'd never be able to take from Devyn. And now here I am. "Girls are always going to be in his face. Girls are always in these athletes' faces. What if he goes to the NFL? It'll be ten times worse."

"Trust him." She doesn't understand how hard that is for me. In fact, I'm not sure I even fully know how.

***

Jordan's girlfriend, Savannah, could win a medal for being the worst cook in the entire world. I couldn't have been more unhappy sitting on his couch eating overcooked spaghetti with sauce that has to have half a bottle of salt in it.

We're all sitting in silence in the living room. This dinner is pointless and a waste of time, especially since Jordan hasn't shown up. It's proof he doesn't give a shit about us, and the feeling's mutual. Nico could have set something up, used a hot plate to cook the food, and the night would've been a thousand times better.

"This is good," Jay lies, putting another forkful of pasta in his mouth. He flinches with every bite. Nico bursts into laughter, and I nudge her to shut up.

"I'm starving," she whispers to me.

I nod. "We're getting food after this."

Troy refused to eat after the first bite and just sits on the floor sulking.

I take another bite, forcing the nastiness down my throat. How Savannah finished a whole bowl and is working on her second one is beyond me. Hungry and irritated, I make an excuse about homework to leave, and everyone follows behind me.

"Thanks for dinner." I give Savannah a quick hug as everyone stops on their way to exit. "This was so sweet, and dinner was great."

"Of course!" This has to be the first time anyone's told her this, because Savannah grins from ear to ear. "Are you guys sure you don't want to stay and wait for Jordan?"

"Hell no," Troy blurts, and Nico nudges him, trying to hide her laugh. "I mean . . . no need to force these things if no one's into them."

"Thank you, though!" Nico adds, and we all hustle out of the room before the conversation gets any worse.

"Ryan, you're such a liar! That entire thing was terrible!" Nico laughs, closing the door behind her.

"I think I have gout now," Troy says.

"Be nice!" I exclaim, pushing him. "Is it rude if we go to the dining hall?"

"It's freezing. Let's order in," Troy says. We all jump at the idea and agree to get our things for a study session while we wait for the food to come.

I go to the bathroom to throw away the to-go plate I made to be polite. When I get to my room, the door is closed, which is weird because I'm positive I left it open when I went to dinner. One hundred percent sure who's in the room, I find Devyn sitting at the table doing homework when I walk in. He looks tired and adorable in a full navy sweatsuit. For a moment, I forget how mad I am.

He looks up as I enter. "I texted this time."

"I left my phone in here."

"I know," he says and nods at my phone sitting at the center of the table. *It was on my bed before...*

Devyn pushes his homework aside and pulls out the chair next to him. "Sit with me?" I don't have the heart to say no to him when we're face-to-face.

"Why are you here?"

"If you'd read my text, you would've known," he responds. "First, my tutoring sheet's due tomorrow and you haven't signed for all the sessions. Second, I need to know what's going on with you. I'm so confused."

"I saw you. Earlier."

He blinks at me. "And what'd I do? Because I can guarantee most of my day was spent thinking about you."

I shake my head. "That's a straight-up lie."

"It's not." Devyn turns his body toward me. "Ryan, I had such a good time with you this weekend that you've been in my head all day. I was feeling good until I got out of practice and hadn't heard from you. Can you tell me what happened? When'd you see me? If you had that dress on, there's no way in hell I would've missed you."

I took off his jacket—well, ripped it off and threw it somewhere in the closet in an angry rampage—when I got home, so my outfit's more revealing. I know he's telling the truth, and I need to do the same.

"On the yard, and some girl was all over you," I confess. "That's not cool with me, and I don't like the way it made me feel."

Devyn nods.

"It's silly of me to think that other girls aren't interested in you or that you haven't been with other girls since you got here." I'm trying my absolute hardest to keep eye contact. "It just upset me. And you did miss me. I was right behind her. I don't want to be invisible to you."

"What did she look like?"

I sigh. *That* would be the question he asks. "Long red hair. Hershey's bar skin. Huge boobs . . ."

He pauses. "You think something happened with Freedom?"

"Who?"

"That's the girl . . . Freedom."

"I don't care who she is, Devyn."

Devyn reaches over, taking my hand in his. "Ryan, I told you I'm not interested in anyone else. That includes Freedom. I'm sorry I didn't see you, but if you felt bad, baby, the only thing you had to do was come over, and I swear everybody would've known I'm yours. I can't get enough of you . . ."

I don't know how to respond, so I say nothing.

"You have to talk to me when something's bothering you. You asked me not to ignore you when I'm upset, and that's exactly what you did."

"I really was at dinner."

"But I called to work things out before that. I called you and I tried to see you." He scoots his chair a little closer to me, his knee brushing mine. "Plus, dinners don't last all night."

He's saying all the right things and sounding reasonable. I can't be mad at him for having friends, but that Freedom girl was too affectionate. I have to find a way to control my jealousy, but he also needs to be aware of it.

"I'm sorry for icing you out. I just don't know how to deal with . . ." I can't use the word possessive without sounding insane. We've only been together for a few days. "These new feelings. But there's no way in hell I'm just going to walk up to you if some girl's in your arms."

"She wasn't *in my arms*." Devyn laughs. "It was a hug."

"You can't tell me that was a normal hug!"

"Baby, I hear you. I'll handle it." Devyn laughs, squeezing my hand tightly. "But the only girl I like in my arms is the one I'm looking at right now. You don't pay attention to the kind of affection I show you." He pulls me out of the chair and into his lap. My hands wrap around his neck and I'm hugging him before I can even think about it. It's a natural reaction at this point. "See, there's no way in hell I was hugging her like this." He squeezes me tightly. His hands rest on my lower back.

"You're pushing it," I mumble in his neck. "I missed you."

"I missed you too," he says. "The next time you deprive me of this, we're really going to get in our first fight."

I giggle and move my head to kiss him. I melt into his embrace and lips.

"Can we be friends again?"

"More than that," I say, making him smile, and kiss him again.

"Good," he says, our lips still touching. "But I do need your help with this paper. It's due tomorrow."

I lean back, putting my hands up in surrender. "Okay, I'll be good. Let's get to it."

I get up, but Devyn pulls me back down. "Tell me about your day."

I sigh. "When I wasn't mad at you, I was thinking about yesterday . . ."

"What about yesterday?"

"How much I loved it."

Devyn's face erupts in a cheeky grin. "We'll have plenty more."

Entranced, I touch my lips to his. He's just too damn cute. "How was dinner?"

I laugh. "Disgusting."

"For real? What'd you eat?"

"My RA's girlfriend made spaghetti. It had so much salt, it soaked up your saliva with every bite."

Devyn laughs.

"We're about to order food now."

"I brought you some," Devyn tells me.

"You did?"

He nods. "I thought you were lying to me about dinner, so when I got food, I just got you something too." It's funny how Devyn's always trying to feed me. I'm not malnourished, and I sure don't look like it.

"What'd you get?"

"Wings." He then adds, "They're good . . . definitely better than salty spaghetti."

"Thank you. I'm so hungry, I could eat you right now." I laugh. "How was your day?"

Devyn sighs. "Long, tiring."

I rest my lips on his chin. His freshly cut beard's in the way, but I don't complain.

"Can I spend the night?" he asks.

"Of course, but do you think it's healthy to spend every night together?"

"Why wouldn't it be?"

I chuckle. "You're going to get sick of me."

Devyn snorts. "I doubt that." He kisses my forehead. "I love spending time with you."

I cup his face, really about to get lost in his lips when the door opens. Devyn leans over to see who it is, but I'm feeling bold and kiss him anyway. Whoever it is can wait. Nico's in the doorway, laughing.

"Looks like the lovebirds made up," she teases.

I cuddle into Devyn, giggling. "Devyn, this is Nico. Nico, this is Devyn."

"I'd get up to hug you, but it doesn't look like she plans on getting up any time soon." Devyn sticks his hand out, and Nico walks over to shake it.

"You're good." She smiles. "I wouldn't either if my girl was here."

"Where is she?" I ask.

"Library working on a group project."

I nod.

"I was coming to see if you still want food."

"No, I'm good."

Devyn's hand glides up and down my back.

"I had a feeling you were." Nico smirks. "I'll leave you two alone. I can't leave Jay and Troy in my room by themselves for too long before they get rowdy or try to smoke my weed." She looks at Devyn. "It was nice meeting you."

"You too."

"Love you!" I call as she exits the room.

"Love you too!" she calls back as the door closes.

Devyn and I look at each other. "That's your best friend, right?"

I nod. "Yeah, here, she is." I wonder if Devyn knows my friends back in LA. In high school, he balanced himself between athletes and Manny, his best friend since preschool. Manny played basketball, so he and Devyn hung out in similar circles. Manny lived right next door to me. "You ready to start homework?"

Devyn groans, and I get up to grab my laptop. I'm feeling more relieved now that we've talked things out. We're back on the same page, and all my stress of this not working out starts to evaporate.

He works diligently for the next hour while I sign his forms and play around on social media. I wonder if it's weird to start putting pictures of Devyn on Facebook or Instagram. We've followed each other and have been friends for years, but he's never posted a girl he's dated. It's not that big of a deal, but I don't want to be his secret.

"Devyn?" I feel bad for interrupting him, but not bad enough to stop me from doing it.

"Ryan," he says, his eyes and fingers never leaving the computer.

"I'm allowed to tell people about us, right?"

He stops typing and lifts his head to look at me. "Of course." He leans back into the chair. "Why do you ask?"

I shrug. "I was thinking we don't have any evidence we're a couple."

"Evidence?" He peers at my computer and sees I'm on Facebook. "You mean like we don't have pictures together?" I'm being serious, but somehow he's amused.

"Yeah. Why is that?"

"Maybe because we've been together for less than a week, and most of our time is spent in bed or tutoring." Devyn chuckles.

He's right. I'm being silly and overthinking again. This is my first relationship, and I don't know how anything's supposed to go. "I know. I'm just saying."

"Come here," Devyn pushes his chair back and pulls me into his lap. "You don't need any more reasons to get yourself worked up tonight." He reaches over me and goes to his computer, pulling up the Photo Booth app.

"We don't have to do this now. I look crazy." I chuckle.

"No, no . . . you asked for this." Devyn laughs. "And you look good. Stop all that."

"Maybe we should go out this weekend and take one," I suggest.

"You want to hide your face?"

I laugh. "What?"

Devyn clicks the button to start the time, and then pulls me into him, pressing his lips to mine passionately. I get distracted by his kiss and the way his tongue plays against mine. I wrap my arms around his neck, allowing him to deepen the kiss. His erection pressing against my leg makes me stop. I don't want to start anything I can't finish.

"I'm sorry." He presses his forehead against mine. "Between the giggling, you, and this dress, I can't handle it."

"It's not your fault." I blush.

"Let's look at these pictures." Devyn turns me around in his lap so I'm facing his computer, my back toward him. You can barely see our faces, but we look like two fools in love, completely wrapped up in each other. It's kind of cute. Devyn takes the picture and uploads it to his Instagram; a simple red heart is the caption. "Happy?"

"Yeah," I respond and kiss him one more time for being so sweet. "Very. I'm always happy when you're around."

***

DEVYN

"What's your favorite holiday?"

"Thanksgiving."

"What's your biggest fear?"

"Death."

Ryan turns to look at me. "Really?" She's been playing this random question game with me for the last forty minutes. "Why's that?"

I shrug. "I don't want to die a nobody."

"That's impossible," she replies. "You're hard to forget."

She lays her head back down on my chest and continues her game. "Um . . . if you were stuck on a deserted island, and you could only bring one thing with you, what would it be?"

"You."

Ryan laughs. "You're cute, but you're lying."

"I'm not!" This girl keeps a smile on my face. "I wouldn't want to be alone on the island, and if I brought anyone else, I'd just wonder what you're doing—" She interrupts me with a kiss. "My turn to ask questions," I say.

"Ask away."

I somehow have to incorporate that I went through Ryan's phone and saw how Avery had texted her multiple times this week. She didn't reply, but if she had, this conversation would've started much earlier. After our little fight, I'm not trying to have another one.

"Who's your favorite person in the world?" I smile, mainly because I already know her answer.

"Hmm . . . either you or Nico. It just depends on the day."

I ignore that part. "Favorite song?"

"Depends on my mood." She pauses. "Right now, it's "Lay You Down" by K-Young."

We don't have the same taste in music, but R&B's our common point.

"What's your dream job?" It's weird I don't know this.

"I want to write TV shows—some kind of black soap opera for young adults. Probably in high school or college," she says. "Nothing too stereotypical, though. It has to make people think."

"Have you started writing any?"

She nods. "I have, but it's been a while. I've got about two seasons finished."

"Can I read it?"

"Of course. I'd love to hear what you think." We go on like this for a while, discussing turn-ons and turn-offs, favorite movies, and so much more. I love getting to know Ryan. Things with her are easy, despite the obvious complications of her father and Ivan.

Even with Ryan's trust issues and trauma, I know how hard she's trying to make things work. The small fight we had was based on her insecurities, not my actions. She doesn't need to worry about me with other girls. She's my girlfriend, and I'm not going to hide that, which is different from my past relationships, where I kept things very private. But I'll take her feelings into consideration and use a more hands-off approach with female friends.

"I wonder if anyone saw your picture." Ryan checks her phone. "Whoa, look at all these comments . . ."

"From who?"

Mostly people from high school comment with the looking-eyes emoji, with "Congrats," or with "Who's the girl?"

You can't really tell it's Ryan in the photo, so I'm not surprised by the confusion. None of my college friends really care enough to comment on if I'm in a relationship or not. "You gon' tell them who you are? Or is this a guessing game?" I let her decide, since she's the one who brought all this up.

She takes her phone back, pausing in thought before matching my caption and comments with a red heart. She puts her phone down, and I pull her into me, wrapping my arms around her. "Any more questions?" she asks.

Now's the best chance to get my questions about Avery answered. "When's the last time Avery hit you up?"

Her eyes lock with mine. "You went through my phone, huh?"

"Answer the question."

"Yesterday. I was going to say something, but I didn't respond."

"I'll talk to him." I'm getting defensive, but he doesn't need to be talking to her.

"That's unnecessary," she replies. "He just wants a reaction, Devyn. Don't give him one. I'm not interested in him."

"What's he been saying?"

"I thought you read them."

I did, but I want to hear it from her. "I just saw he texted you."

She sighs. "Well, at first, he just asked why I didn't tell him we're together, and then he was like, 'Does your boyfriend not allow you to have friends?'"

I laugh. I'm going to kick his ass.

"I think it's about the chase, you know? You always want what you can't have."

"And he definitely can't have you," I say. "Ever."

Ryan scoots closer to me, pressing her lips to mine. "You're the only guy I want, Devyn."

I pull her in and kiss her again.

"You have nothing to worry about," she says against my lips.

I know Avery's no threat to our relationship, but he still needs to be put in his place.

"It's not about being worried. That shit's just not cool," I tell her. "He's my teammate."

"He'll get the hint eventually."

"He'll get it even faster when I say something."

"Devyn..."

"Ryan." I don't want to stir up any more fights, but she'll only be more upset if I did it without telling her. "I'm not letting this nigga hit up my girl and think I don't know. That's only going to give him more of a reason to think he's got a chance."

"He doesn't."

"I know." She doesn't need to reassure me. "I'm handling it."

CHAPTER 12

RYAN

I'd taken sleeping with Devyn for granted because a few days later, I endured the worst sleep of my life—suffering bad dream after bad dream, tossing and turning. Thoughts of Ivan consumed me. I could feel the way his hands once touched me, the things he'd done and said, like they were haunting me.

Thursday morning, I jump awake from my sleep, startled before realizing I'm thirty minutes late to my 8:00 a.m. class. I can already tell it's not going to be my day.

Last night I worked overtime. It seems like the restaurant only gets busier as the weeks go by. We'd had a huge impromptu party, so there was tons of cleaning once they left. I clocked out at 1:30 a.m., missing another scheduled tutoring session with Devyn. Our conflicting schedules kept forcing us not to see each other, and the distance must have more of an effect on me than I thought. I never have bad dreams on nights I sleep with Devyn.

I jump out of bed, throw on some jeans and a sweatshirt, and sprint to class, making it in six minutes. As hard as it is to stay awake, I manage to get through with good notes for the quiz we have next week. When it's over, I run to the cafeteria for some breakfast and much-needed coffee. I'd miss my next class, but today I couldn't care less.

"Morning, sunshine," someone says while I'm pouring as much cereal into a bowl as I can. I'm happy to find Troy standing next to me. "You're never here at this time."

"I'm thinking about taking a personal day," I tell him. "I'm exhausted. I slept terribly last night." I'm highly considering calling out of work too. "I figured food might wake me up."

"Good idea," Troy replies. "You look awful."

I laugh. "You're *so* sweet, Troy."

"Just being honest." Troy laughs. "Nico's here. She's not doing good."

"What's going on?"

"Sasha asked for a break . . . she cried all night."

I turn around to see what Troy's talking about. Nico is resting her head in her arms at a booth near the window.

"I'll go talk to her." I grab my food and rush over. "Hey." I slip in beside her. She looks at me with red, puffy eyes as I pull her into my embrace. "What happened?"

Tears fall down her face, and I regret asking. "She said it's too hard to balance work, school, and a relationship. She's a DJ. That doesn't make sense!" Nico cries. "I came here for her, and she breaks up with me less than a month into school."

I squeeze her tightly. "She's going to realize she fucked up. You can get any girl you want. It's her loss."

"You don't mean that."

"I do!" I chuckle, trying to cheer her up. "Have you seen yourself? You're one of the coolest and hottest girls in our class." I'm gassing her up, but that's what friends are for. "You can do whatever you want, now. Date other people—"

"I don't want that," she cries.

"Then just work on you—do hair, DJ a little bit, focus on school and friends."

Nico nods, wiping tears away.

"I'm here for you—any time of day."

"I love you." Nico hugs me. "Thank you."

I squeeze her tighter. "I love you too. I promise it'll be okay."

"Can I get a hug?" Troy sits across from us and pushes a plate of waffles, grits, and fruit in front of Nico. "It's okay to be sad, but you're not getting depressed on me . . . we just smoked three blunts, so we're not leaving until you clean that plate."

"You let her smoke?" I scold Troy. "When she's this upset?"

Troy shrugs. "She was a mess. You were gone, and I didn't know what to do."

Nico nods, putting a spoonful of grits in her mouth. "I'm a lot calmer."

I couldn't even be mad.

"You should smoke with us."

"Not happening," I laugh. "But getting high isn't a way to cope with sadness."

"It is today." Nico takes another bite of food.

We talk for about an hour, but Nico doesn't cheer up. Between that and my exhaustion, this isn't our happiest meal. Poor Troy tries his best to keep smiles on our faces. I take his advice and agree to skip my next classes. When they rush off, I stay behind to clean our dishes. I'm about to take the best nap of the year, and nothing and no one can stop me . . . well, maybe except for the nightmares.

While I exit the building, I'm surprised to see my boy-friend standing in front of the door with a crowd of football players and cheerleaders by his side. Is he ever alone?

Freedom is pressed next to him.

I take a minute to get myself together, breathing slowly. I can't get myself worked up. Devyn said they're nothing, and I'm going to believe him.

It also doesn't help that I look absolutely crazy. I hoped the next time I ran into Devyn and his friends, I'd be feeling myself and more dressed up. Today's not that day. Devyn told me to just walk up to him when I see him on campus, but he has to know me well enough to understand that's not happening.

However, staring at him, I feel a little lucky. Even just in his sweats and T-shirt, he's sexy.

And all mine.

I stare a second too long, because his eyes lock with mine, and the smile on his face widens. He leaves the group mid-conversation and heads toward me.

How mad would he be if I full on sprinted in the other direction?

"I knew I'd run into you today," he says, strutting toward me with strides so prideful and confident, it makes me more insecure. I'm not in a state to be seen with him, and we've officially caught the attention of his friends.

"R-really?" Did I just stutter in front of all these people? "How?"

Devyn smiles. "Fate, or I was going to make it happen." He bends down and kisses me, his lips lingering against mine.

I hold him to me. I've missed this so much the last few days. I take a moment to appreciate it. Again, he's managed to be just what I need. For a moment, I forget everyone's watching. "I missed you," I say into his neck.

"Missed you." Devyn holds me, one hand around my waist, the other on my butt. He's claiming his girl, something he'd done the last time we were in front of his teammates, but I act like I don't notice. "You've been busy."

"Sorry. Everything's been so stressful."

Devyn takes a seat on the bench behind him and pulls me in between his legs. "You haven't been sleeping."

How'd he know?

He cups my face; the pads of his fingers gently rub underneath my eye. "It's all in your face, baby."

I sigh. "I have so much to do, and my mind's been racing . . ." I don't want to mention my bad dream. It'll only worry him. "I just need sleep."

"How many more classes do you have?"

I shake my head. "I'm skipping. I'm too tired."

"Call off work too."

I chuckle. "Are you going to pay me for today's hours?"

"If I have to," Devyn takes my hands, bringing them to his lips. "You don't have off days?"

"A couple."

"Take one." I know he's right. I'm exhausted. "Text Tony and see what he says. Go if they need you, but you should rest."

"I'll think about it," I tell him as he pulls me closer. "You're causing a scene." I glance at a couple girls staring at us. Freedom included.

"Fuck them," Devyn says. "I've barely seen you all week. I'm not gonna hold back 'cause people are around." He kisses my chin and then my lips. "I like your outfit."

"D, we're going in. Are you coming?" some girl asks, interrupting us.

Devyn pulls me into his lap before responding. "I'll meet y'all in there." She looks at me and then at him and then walks away. Devyn's lips press against the back of my head. "Should I have introduced you?"

I shake my head. "On a day where I look better."

"You look beautiful . . . always."

I pull my phone out to text Tony, telling him I'm swamped with homework. He replies immediately:

> School comes first. Take the day off. My treat!

"That was easy," Devyn says, kissing my shoulder.

I get up. "I should get going." I yawn. "Go eat. I'm sure you're hungry. Plus, your friends are waiting."

"I don't mind eating alone." Devyn shrugs.

"Go. I want to go lie down anyway, and it's cold," I say, making him laugh.

Devyn grabs my sweatshirt, pulling me back. "Let me help." He wraps me up in him once again. "You're going back to your dorm?"

I nod. "Where else is there to go?"

"I don't know. I can give you my keys if you want to go to my place."

"It's okay, I want to change . . . and then sleep. All. Day. Long."

"I'll call you after practice," Devyn replies.

"Looking forward to it." We kiss again before going our separate ways.

***

DEVYN

I thought Coach K was going easy on us after our win, but tonight's practice changes all that. I'm still winded as I walk back to the dorms. Guess this is his way of making sure we don't get cocky anymore.

Sneaking into Ryan's dorm is easy. I walk in, flash my ID to the half-asleep guard, and take the slow-ass elevator up to the dingy fourth floor she calls home. Her door's always open, so I walk in. She's out, sprawled across the bed in nothing but the black T-shirt I gave her the first time she spent the night at my place, her underwear, and some purple ankle socks.

I'm worried about how tired she looked earlier, and I'm happy she decided to take the day off. She needs to cut back her work hours, but I know she'll never agree to it. That's a battle I don't know how to win.

I set my things on the little couch thing she made out of the other bed and get into bed with her, startling her awake.

"It's just me," I whisper, picking her up and getting under the covers in one swift motion.

Her sigh of relief is loud, and she closes her eyes. "I was hoping you'd come," she mumbles.

I make myself comfortable as Ryan clings to me in her way—face between my neck and shoulder and her arms around my waist.

The room's cold from the open window, and her hands are colder. "Are you spending the night?"

"Do you want me to?"

"Every day." I know she doesn't mean to say it out loud. She just mentioned it might be a bad thing the other day.

"Then I'll stay."

"I don't think the nightmares will come if you're here," Ryan slurs.

"Nightmares?"

"Ivan and his friends come get me. I can never find you."

She must be tired, because she'd never tell me this on a regular day. At least not this easily.

"That'll never happen." I rub her back to soothe her back to sleep. "Get some rest, baby. I'll be here when you wake up." Ryan stirring in my arms wakes me from my own sleep. The lamp in the corner dimly lights the room. The setting in here is dark and depressing, but somehow, I can't be happier.

"When'd you get here?" Ryan cups my face and pecks my lips. Does she not remember that whole little moment we had?

I look at the clock. It's a little after nine. "A couple hours ago," I reply, my voice quiet. "How are you feeling?"

"Sleepy." She yawns. "I can't get enough sleep these days."

"You sleep okay?"

Ryan smiles. "I did . . . waking up next to you is a good surprise. I'm glad you came."

"I missed you." I kiss her again. "I'm worried about you."

"Why?"

I sigh. "You're pushing yourself so hard." Ryan plants a kiss on my jaw before nuzzling into my neck. "You need to get more rest."

"I could say the same thing to you." Football's a few hours a day, while Ryan runs around all day working, studying, tutoring me. Her stress takes a toll on her physically as much as it does emotionally.

"Baby, it's different. I see when you're stressed or too tired. You can't hide it from me."

Tears fall instantly down her face. I don't know why.

"I think that's why you're having nightmares—everything with school and work and Ivan and your dad." I face her and wipe the tears away. "You don't have to take all this by yourself anymore. I'm here, and I want to help you any way I can."

"I don't know what you can do." She scrubs her face, taking a minute to get herself together. "I've been feeling overwhelmed since we saw Ivan. What if he didn't leave?"

"You think he'd stay?" There're ways to figure that out without getting anyone into trouble. At the very least, I can call Manny.

Ryan shrugs. "I don't know, but I'm scared."

"You said you can't live your life scared of him and your dad," I remind her. "You just got to hope he's not here, baby, but be watchful."

"It didn't matter until I started having these awful nightmares." She sighs. "They freak me out. Last night I woke up crying, twice. And when I have them, they don't shake. I was up all night just thinking about it." Ryan rubs her arms, soothing herself. She sits up to talk to me.

I wish she had called me about the nightmares. If sleeping with me makes things better, then I'll make sure we sleep together more often, but it would be hard on weekends I have games. We just need to find a way around this.

"Remember they're just dreams." I take her hand in mine. "If you have a bad dream tonight, I'll be here to help you out."

Ryan nods.

"But you're going to be fine. And you have me. Believe me when I say no one can touch you without getting through me first."

Ryan chuckles, and then lets out a long, deep sigh. "You're a good boyfriend."

"It's not fair, all you go through."

Ryan sighs. "I just need some time, but I'll be okay." We sit in silence for a minute before Ryan decides to change the subject. "I'm hungry."

"What do you want?"

"Let's go to the café," she says. "I've never had their late-night menu."

I laugh. "It's the same shit that's always in there." I get off the bed to put on my shoes while Ryan goes to put on leggings. I watch her get dressed and put her hair into two long braids. She ignores my mesmerized stare. I really am a lucky man.

"I'm ready," she tells me, looking at herself in the mirror. Ryan glances at me. "Do I look okay?"

I nod. "If only you could hear the things going through my head." Ryan fails to hide her smile while pulling on a pair of black Ugg boots.

I'm surprised to see so many people in the café this late at night. We go our separate ways to grab food. I head to the pasta line for spaghetti.

"D." I look up from scrolling through Twitter to see Royal, one of my roommates, coming toward me. Freedom, who seems to be around him often these days, walks behind.

"Wassup?" I slap his hand and give Freedom a quick hug. I look around for Ryan, who's busy conversing with the chef preparing her food. I step away from Freedom to avoid her getting any more ideas. I don't want Ryan getting jealous.

"What are you doing here? I thought you went to hang out with ol' girl?"

"She's right there." They both look over to eye Ryan. "We got hungry. What're y'all doin here?"

"I haven't eaten *all* day," Freedom chimes into the conversation. "I was at your place, so I dragged Royal along." I move in the line and take the plate of spaghetti from the counter.

In the corner of my eye, I see Ryan coming toward me and know she'll try to avoid me with Royal and Freedom nearby. She gets shy around my friends, so I head toward her.

"What'd you get?"

"Chicken nuggets." She shakes the Styrofoam container her food is in. "Are we eating here?"

"Yeah. You want something to drink?"

"I'll go with you," she replies and takes the lead to the vending machines.

I press my body to her back as she pours our drinks. I'm being showy with our relationship, and I know she loves it. Ryan's not used to affection in any form, but I know PDA is something she enjoys. I set my plate down and wrap my arms around her.

"You're bothering me." She giggles as I kiss her neck.

"No, I'm not," I flirt, making us both laugh. "You look too good; can't have other niggas thinking they can come talk to you."

Ryan grabs another cup and puts ice in it. "There's like fifteen people in here."

"Can we sit with you guys?"

Freedom and Royal stand behind us. I don't want to be bothered with them; I enjoy being alone with Ryan.

"Yeah, sure," she says right as I open my mouth to tell them no.

I look at Royal and he shrugs.

"Sit wherever, and we'll meet you?"

"Sounds good!" Freedom chirps, pulling Royal over to the tables.

Ryan hands me a drink. "You didn't have to say yes," I tell her. "I don't want to have dinner with them."

"Be nice," Ryan scolds, giggling.

"You're too nice," I whisper. "I'm with them all the time. I want to be alone with you. What's wrong with that?"

"Nothing's wrong with that," she replies, "but it's rude to say no. They're your friends, Devyn. I don't want them to think I'm taking you away from them."

"Baby, I'm with them all day—"

"And a little longer won't hurt." She smiles as she picks up my plate and hands it to me. "Come on; it'll be less than an hour. If anyone'll be uncomfortable, it's me. These are your people we're about to hang out with." Ryan lifts onto her tiptoes to kiss my lips. "We can be alone in bed later." I sigh as she kisses me again.

I know Freedom has staged this as some kind of test. I hooked up with a couple of her friends over the summer and got with Ryan right as she started to make her move. I'd never tell Ryan that, because it's nothing. I'm not interested in Freedom, but she's a good friend who'd hook a guy up. I can tell that my settling down upset her, but I couldn't care less. I meant it when I told Ryan these people in my life are new. They shouldn't feel any ties to me. Royal won't say anything out of line—he's one of my closer friends here and knows how important Ryan is. But girls like Freedom kept me from having a girlfriend in the past.

Ryan and I sit across from them in a long booth in the center of the dining room. I can tell Ryan's nervous, which only furthers my reasons why we don't need to be having dinner with them.

We sit in silence for a while, until Freedom speaks. "So, are you two ready for the game this weekend? Everyone says Savannah State'll be an easy win."

Royal shrugs between bites of alfredo. "If we play like we did last week, we'll be good. Offense gets cocky; we never have problems with the D line."

"They're working on it," I say, pulling Ryan closer. "Coach K almost beat Avery's ass at practice today."

Royal laughs. "That nigga's a bitch; he's the reason we lost the first game." That's not a hundred percent true, but Avery's cockiness does often get in the way of his playing.

"The reason you lost the first game was because majority of the team was hungover." Freedom laughs. "Especially Avery—he was in bed with not one but two of my girls that night."

"You sound proud." Royal snorts, and Freedom playfully shoves him. I turn my attention back to Ryan, who's silently eating and texting Nico. She notices me looking and turns the phone so I can't read the messages. Her back's slightly toward me. I wrap my arms around her while Freedom and Royal discuss our game.

I take her hand and kiss it, watching her relax before my eyes. Our eyes lock, and her face turns up in a smile. She scoots closer, rubbing her hand up and down my leg. There's my girl. We're both learning how to tear down each other's walls, even when we try to put them back up. I know hearing about the stuff that happens at the hotel bothers her, but she doesn't need to worry. I was with her that night.

"So, Riley, have you been to any of the games?"

"Ryan," I correct defensively. Ryan squeezes my knee.

"Yeah, I went to the last game."

Freedom nods. "Do you have a favorite team?"

Ryan laughs. "I've never really been into sports until I started dating Devyn. What's yours?"

"The Ravens." Freedom's from Maryland, so that doesn't surprise me. "But it's crazy that you've never, like, been into sports. You never played as a kid?"

Ryan shakes her head. "No. I was more into academics. But it's cool. I don't know a lot about what happens on the field, but I like watching Devyn."

"Aw, how cute. But I'm surprised you're not used to it . . . since you've been watching him play for so long."

"Because we went to high school together?"

"Yeah," Freedom replies. "You guys have been together for a minute, right?"

She must know what I told Avery about us dating since high school. Did they put her up to this?

A couple good characteristics about Ryan is that she catches things easily and reads situations well.

"Yeah, but I didn't go to a lot of his games in high school. My dad's kind of"—she looks at me—"strict." I nod, and she turns back to Freedom. "I'll attend more when my work schedule allows it."

"Where do you work?"

Ryan swallows her food. "This Mexican restaurant down the street."

"Is it any good?"

"Yeah," Ryan replies. "About as close as it gets to California."

"Really?" Freedom laughs. "I'll have to try it! Do friends get, like, discounts?"

"Cheap!" Royal teases.

Freedom rolls her eyes. "I'm just asking."

"Honestly, I don't know," she responds. "No one really visits me at work."

"I do," I butt in before Freedom can say something.

Ryan laughs. "Yeah, but you come after closing."

"And never brings food home for his roommate, knowing damn well I'm hungry!" Royal jokes.

"Nigga, I don't think about you when I'm with my girl," I retort. "I told you that before."

Royal looks at Ryan. "See how he does me?"

"I didn't know." Ryan laughs. "One of these days, I'll send him home with a to-go plate for you."

"I knew I'd like you," Royal says, making Ryan smile. She wants acceptance from my friends, but I don't care about that. I already know who she is.

We finish our food and go our separate ways. Ryan and I are back in her room by twelve-thirty. The vibes in her room are so different from mine. I feel a personal touch in here you only see in a girl's room, but my place has a lot more space, which is nice. I can sleep here occasionally, but it's hard being in her twin XL.

I watch as Ryan goes to her closet to take off her shoes and grabs her laptop before getting in bed. "Did you finish your essay for the week?"

I nod. "Yeah, last night. I sent it to you."

"Great." She smiles at me. "You make my job easy."

"I try," I say, taking my homework out of my backpack. It's not due till next Wednesday, but I want to be productive while Ryan edits my paper.

I snuggle up to her as she reads, and she kisses me. "I love having you here."

She's always finding cute ways to compliment me.

Fuck homework. We've barely gotten any time together this week, and I miss her. I take the laptop and move it before pulling her into me. "Let's edit this later," I say as I taste her lips.

Her giggle instantly makes me hard. I can't even think about sex with her, though. I know she's not ready and that she'll say no. I promised myself I'd wait until she told me otherwise.

Ryan leans back on the bed, pulling me on top of her, which only excites me more. I try to relax and enjoy the kissing. I want Ryan bad, in more than just a physical sense. I want to be closer to her than any man ever has, wash away the damage Ivan and her dad caused, and make her forget any other nigga who tried to get at her. But it's harder than I thought. I desire an emotional connection to Ryan. At first, I just wanted to get to know her, be there when she needed me, and make her see she has someone to protect her. But as time goes on, I'm starting to get more attached in ways I never thought I would be. I'm scared, but it's cool knowing I'm talking to someone so dope, they can completely change my view on women.

"Hey." Ryan cups my face. "Are you okay?" Her eyes are dilated like she's holding something back. Does she feel the way I do? I doubt it.

I nod, going back to kiss her shoulder and neck before flipping over so she's on top. "I'm done with homework tonight."

Ryan sits up, straddling me, her smile big.

"You haven't even started." She crosses her arms over her chest. "I told you, I can't lose this job if we're together. I need to . . ."

"I know," I reply. "But I finished everything that's due tomorrow, and the essay's due tomorrow around midnight, so we have time to edit it."

Ryan sighs.

"I know how important working is to you. I've been doing my part, right?"

"You're right, but I have some work I should do . . ."

I nod. I'm not getting in the way of that. "Then let's get back to work."

CHAPTER 13

——

RYAN

The last time I saw Devyn's friend Freedom was that weird dinner we all had together in the dining hall, so I'm surprised to see her and half of the varsity cheerleading team walk into my job during a busy Friday evening a couple weeks later. They all enter as I drop off two plates of beef enchiladas to a cute old gay couple that comes to the restaurant regularly. My initial response is to be self-conscious. I feel a little insecure that I'll be looked at as "help" to these girls instead of the friend I hope to be. I'm not that into girl groups, but I want Devyn's friends to like me.

"¡Hola!" Maria greets them. She and Tony get excited when big parties come in since it brings so much money into the restaurant. I decide to be happy they're here, at least because of that. "How many?"

"Fourteen. You got this?" Tony says from behind me as Maria leads them to their table. "A lot of them have on Truth sweatshirts. They your friends?"

I turn around to look at him. "Not really, but they know Devyn."

Tony nods.

"I have to serve them all?"

"You'll get a good tip." Tony shrugs and heads back toward the kitchen. Despite my urge to hide in the bathroom for the remainder of their time here, I toughen up and head to the dining room.

"Look who it is!" says a girl sitting next to Freedom. She wears the worst curly wig I've ever seen, but her makeup is so nicely done, it makes up for it. Freedom looks up from her menu and smiles at me.

"Hi, ladies. Welcome to Mi Mexicana Cocina," I say with a bright smile on my face. I need to make these girls think they don't intimidate me. "I'm Ryan, your server for tonight. Can I get you guys started with some drinks?"

"How about some margaritas?" Freedom says, and all the girls jump with excitement. "Let's do green apple for all of us." She closes the drink menu and hands it to me.

I know damn well Freedom's a freshman, just like me, so it only makes me question how many of these girls are under twenty-one. I already know Maria's somewhere keeping an eye on this party of girls. She's nosey like that.

"Okay," I play along. "I just have to see some IDs first." All of the girls look around at each other.

Freedom turns to me. "About that . . . none of us here have fakes yet, but I told them you wouldn't mind." She pauses. "Since you and I are friends and all."

I nod, a little afraid to get on her bad side. "I'll see what I can do."

I write on my notepad, APPLE MARGARITAS X14 VIRGIN.

"I'll give you girls time to decide on what you want."

Freedom's face lights up like a kid in a candy store. "I knew you'd help! Thanks, babe."

I put on my fake smile and head to the kitchen.

"You make sure those girls behave," Maria says to me, coming into the kitchen. "They look suspicious."

I nod. "I'm on it."

Twenty minutes later, I'm back with three other waitresses to pass out the drinks. They all jump for joy as we place a large glass in front of each of them.

"Ryan, come here for a second." Freedom motions toward me, and I walk over. "I've had a margarita before, and this definitely doesn't have alcohol in it . . . do you think we're stupid?"

"She's not a fool," the girl next to her says.

"Yeah . . . my boss wanted to come in and double-check IDs, so I told her this was an AA group at Truth and all the margaritas were virgin." The lie's stupid, but they believe me. "They're obligated to call the police if they found out, and I know you guys don't want that before the big game in DC."

Freedom chuckles. "Good looking out. Luckily, I brought back-up." She reaches in her bag and pulls out a small bottle of Everclear, pouring some into her glass before I can speak. "We're getting lit tonight, bitches!"

Fuck, they're trying to get me fired.

"Please be careful not to get caught. I . . ."

"I'd never think of it." Freedom chuckles. "We're friends, Ryan. You make sure we don't get caught, and I won't tell your boss you're the one who gave us the bottle."

What am I going to do? She's manipulating me. I want to call Devyn for help, but I know he's on his way to DC for his game tomorrow and don't want to bother him. So instead, I walk away, praying that they don't get caught. Arguing with Freedom is pointless; she'll have a whole team of girls to defend her if things go bad. So instead, I say a little prayer and begin taking orders. The fact they put in advanced dessert orders make up for their secret bartending. So at least I'll be getting a decent tip. College students are cheap, but hopefully they'll be lenient since we're all "friends" now.

"So, how do you know this girl?" one of the girls asks as I'm about to walk into the dining room to give them more water.

There's a pause before Freedom responds, "That's Devyn's girlfriend. The one who's suddenly made him stop his fuckboy tendencies." I know Devyn used to get around, but I never guessed he was a whole fuckboy. At least they know he's changed.

"Shut up!" one of them gasps. "I'd never guess he likes fat chicks. All the girls he hooked up with over the summer were so skinny." They all laugh.

"You would know, wouldn't you?" says another, causing more laughter.

"Turns out they've been together this whole time. She either doesn't know or doesn't care he fucked around." Freedom tells them. The alcohol in her system makes her loud, so it's easy for me to hear what they're saying. "Anyone that wants him still has a chance. When she's out of sight, she's out of mind."

"Great!" another girl says. "'Cause I'm all over that when we get to DC tonight. That was the best dick I've ever had!" More laughter.

Tired of this conversation, I walk into the room, and all the girls go mute. Their words begin to play at my jealousy, anxiety, and definitely my trust issues. I shove my rage deep down. They can't know they got to me.

"Can I ask you a question?" the girl next to Freedom says as I place a glass of water in front of her. The room falls silent.

What the fuck did these bitches want to know now? "Sure."

"You're Devyn's girlfriend?"

I nod.

"How long have y'all been together?"

I'm not sure why Devyn lied to them about how long we've been together, but I agreed to go along with his on-again-off-again story. "Officially about a month. Maybe a little longer."

"You guys weren't together in high school?"

I chuckle. "You're so full of questions."

"We're wondering! He never mentioned you over the summer, so finding out he has a girl is surprising." She pauses before adding, "He didn't act like it, either."

"I'm sure." I laugh, trying to play cool. "It took Devyn a while to realize what he wanted." I rush away to hold myself together. I'm not sure how I'll get through this night.

"Ryan! Food's ready!" Maria calls, so I run back into the kitchen to serve the girls. I'll be happy when they're well fed and out of my sight.

An hour later, the entire cheerleading team is tipsy and stuffed from all the food and drinks consumed. I don't know how they manage to stay in shape when they eat like pigs. I'm ready to go home and go to bed. These girls' constant demands and requests are exhausting. Trying to hide the fact that they're drunk doesn't help, either.

I'm hiding in the kitchen, tired and parched from all the running around when a coworker comes in looking anything but happy.

"I can't do this anymore," she whines. "I'm about to clock out early."

I take a sip of the tall glass of water I just poured. "Don't. It'll just make my night so much harder!"

Kiana chuckles and crosses to the cupboard to get a glass.

"How did you manage to cover that whole table by your-self?" she asks. "Those girls are absolutely crazy."

I sigh. "It doesn't help that they've been spiking their drinks since they arrived." She goes wide-eyed. "One of the girls is pretty good friends with my boyfriend, and she's such a bitch."

"You should've told Maria!"

"I know, but they threatened to tell her I gave them the alcohol. There's like twenty of them; who's going to believe me?"

"Maria knows you."

"You know how serious she is about this place, and I didn't want to—" A loud scream from the dining room cuts me off.

"What the fuck is that?" Kiana says. We run to the dining area.

Maria's blocking the door from Freedom and her friends and yelling in Spanish. I can't make out what she's saying, but I'm am a hundred percent sure it's about money.

Half of the girls have already left, but the rest are huddled up in a pack, hovering over Maria, causing a bigger scene than the one she's already caused.

"Listen, I already told you . . . we're not paying for this," Freedom slurs. "We were told we could get free drinks and food on Friday nights."

"That's not true! You need to pay!" Maria yells.

"I'm ready to go," another cheerleader says.

"I'm going to call the police!"

"Call them." Freedom laughs.

"Tony!"

"Bitch, I said move!" Freedom grabs Maria and throws her to the ground and out of their way, completely shocking everyone in the room. Kiana and I rush to her side. "Thanks for a great night!"

The girls run out of the restaurant, laughing.

"I'll help, Maria," Kiana says.

"Find Tony," I say, bolting out the door. Freedom's getting into the cheerleading van when I get to them.

"Hey!" I yell.

"Hey, girl!" Freedom smiles. "Thanks for a great night! We had fun!"

"What the fuck are you doing?" I'm furious. "Do you know how much money you're stealing from these people?"

Freedom giggles. "I really don't care, but you got this one, right? Employee discounts and all?"

I'm so pissed I don't know what to say. Freedom gets in the front seat and leans out the window. "Look, I owe you one! If I ever decide to be a busboy, I got you."

"You—"

"I did you a favor, Ryan. This job's lame, so not only did I give everyone a show, you get to tell your friends something exciting happened to you today. Your life seems pretty dull." Freedom laughs. "I'll see you later, okay?" The car starts and they drive off.

I don't know what to do except face the consequences of being an idiot.

"Oh, Ryan!" Freedom calls out the window. "Don't worry, we'll take good care of D tonight! I'll make sure to tell him you said hey!"

They zoom down the street, leaving echoes of laughter behind them.

Those bitches took advantage of me. I know they spent over three hundred dollars and I can't afford to cover their bill. Tony and some other coworkers are consoling Maria when I walk back in.

"I'm so sorry," I tell her but am immediately startled when she snaps on me.

"Those were your friends!" she yells in my face. "You let them sneak alcohol and steal from us! After all we've done for you!"

How did she know about the alcohol? "Please, Maria, let me explain. I didn't know they were coming. I had—"

"You're fired!"

**

DEVYN

Ryan can't catch a break. Something or someone is always against her, and in this case, it definitely has something to do with me. Those girls didn't know Ryan existed before we started dating. I'm livid. They won't get away with this.

It takes almost two hours to talk Ryan down after Maria fired her. And to think I thought this was going to be a boring night.

Most of my teammates went to one of the seniors' rooms to smoke and drink to end the night, but Royal and I stayed behind. Coach K already told me he plans on checking rooms, and I won't be in that crossfire. The clock just hit midnight, and I know I should be resting, but I don't want to hang up on Ryan. When she first FaceTimed me, she sounded like someone died. I know how much she needs this job, so this is hard for her. As strong as Ryan is, she suffers from her fly-on-the-wall tendencies. She's not going to stand up to

Freedom or her friends because she sees them as popular and that scares her.

Watching her lying in bed, I desperately want to be back in New York, comforting her. I hate being so far away when she's upset. Royal heard me trying to calm her down, so he sits in bed quietly watching *The Fresh Prince of Bel Air.* "What time do you have to be up?" Ryan asks. She's been silent for the last half hour. "I don't want to keep you up." "Nah, it's still early, and I don't have to be up till, like, nine. It's not like I'm doing anything strenuous."

She nods. "No parties or anything?"

I shake my head. "You getting sick of me?"

Ryan cradles her pillow. "Never." I can tell she's tired. "I miss you."

"I miss you too, baby." I wish she wasn't so sad. "We'll figure things out when I get back."

She doesn't respond for a minute. "I don't know how to fix this," she whispers. "I can't afford to pay them back, but I did let them sneak alcohol in there. Maria and Tony could have lost their liquor license if they were caught."

"How would they get caught, Ry? Tony seems pretty understanding. Have you tried talking to him?" Tears cascade down Ryan's face. I'm not helping. "Look, I'm sorry. I don't want to upset you more than you already are."

"It's not your fault," she cries. "Can we talk tomorrow? Just call me before your game. I don't know how to deal with this right now, and I don't want to ruin your night."

"You're not," I soothe. "Just try to relax. We don't have to talk; close your eyes and get some sleep." Ryan turns off her lamp before pulling the covers over her body. She's still crying, and hanging up the phone will only make things worse. I don't like her trying to hide her pain from me. But

I'm surprised she called so quickly to let me know what's going on. It means we've taken another step forward. Ryan is knocked out in twenty minutes, but I don't hang up. Instead, I mute my phone not to wake her.

"Sorry about this, bro," I tell Royal, taking off my headphones.

He shrugs. "You good. Your girl alright?"

"Freedom and her friends went to her job, messed with her, and got her fired."

"What?"

I wipe my hands over my face, still in disbelief myself. "She really needs that money. What they did was some high school shit. I didn't know girls still played those kinds of games in college."

"Want me to talk to Freedom?"

I shake my head. "Nah. This shit's just weird."

"You really like her, huh?"

I laugh. "What's not to like?"

Royal laughs.

"I know a lot of annoying females in the world, but Ryan's not one of them. Shit, she and my little sister are 'bout the only ones I can stand being around . . . I just don't want Freedom or anyone else thinking they can just mess with my girl. Why did they do that shit?"

"Freedom's bored. No one wants to cuff her, so she messes with people to look cool. Plus, you fucked her best friend, so she's mad about you having a girlfriend."

"I didn't then. Ryan and I were both very aware we weren't together before now."

"Nigga, you didn't mention her," Royal says. "And we had a whole conversation about back-home girls."

"She wasn't even fucking with me," I half lie. I look at my phone, watching Ryan sleep as I try to figure out the right words to say. "I fucked around a lot before, and she was done with me for a minute. Not answering my calls or nothing, so I wasn't going to tell y'all I had a girl who was not only going here but wasn't even fucking with me."

"How'd you get her back?"

"I don't even know. I ended up moving her in on move-in day . . . she wasn't fucking with me at all."

Royal laughs.

"But she's changing. She was so secretive about everything in high school. I didn't get the chance to know her. Now she's happy and opening up—the more I find out about her, the more I like."

"Damn, nigga, you whipped."

I laugh. Royal's a good friend, but he doesn't take much seriously. "I don't know about all that, but that's my girl, and it's gonna be like that for a while, okay?"

"Don't worry, boy, we'll keep this between me and you." Royal laughs. "Go to bed. We gotta be up soon."

CHAPTER 14

RYAN

Nico and I spend the next evening moping in bed. She's still heartbroken about her breakup and I'm still upset about my job. I should have spent the day searching for another one, but today I can't find the strength. A weekend of grieving will give me the will to go out and find something better, even though I really loved my job and everyone there.

I haven't heard from Devyn since I woke up to him brushing his teeth on FaceTime. It's cute that he'd stayed on the phone with me through the night. I feel special knowing how much he cares for me.

Ready for him to get back, I send him a quick text.

Me: Where are you?

"What should we watch next?" Nico asks as she takes a bite of the licorice in her hand. Troy dropped off snacks earlier for us to pig out on.

"You choose."

Nico scrolls through Netflix, then selects *Love Jones*.

"Good choice."

She laughs. "A little corny, but a straight romance movie won't bring me to tears. I don't envy heterosexual couples at all."

I shake my head, laughing as my phone buzzes with Devyn's reply.

Devyn: OMW.

Before I can text back, the door flies open, and in comes my giant, handsome boyfriend. Unconsciously, I jump out of bed and fly toward him. I've missed him so much, and we've only been separated a little over twenty-four hours.

"Hi to you too." I hear his smile. I wrap my arms around his neck, holding back unreasonable tears. "Hey, Nico," Devyn says.

"Hey," she says kindly. "I was just filling in while you were gone. How was the game?"

"We won . . . but it was close." I squeeze him a little tighter to congratulate him without words. "Thanks for taking care of my girl."

Nico laughs, getting out of the bed. "She did most of the comforting. I'm going to bother Troy." I peek behind Devyn's shoulder to look at her, and she blows me a kiss. "Have fun, lovebirds."

"Night!" I call out as the door closes.

Devyn puts me on the ground. "Pack a bag. We're going to my place."

"No celebratory party for your win?"

"Yeah, but we'll lock the doors like last time." Devyn shrugs. "I just want to be in a bigger bed."

I've yet to go to a college party, and the one in Devyn's dorm intrigues me. "You don't want to go?"

He looks at me suspiciously. "Do you?"

I'm embarrassed to admit it. "I've never been to a party before . . ."

Devyn smiles. "I know. And you want to go to this one?"

I nod.

"Freedom and her friends will be there."

My good mood evaporates.

"Word gets around fast. I'll tell them not to come if you want."

Maybe those bitches need to see firsthand that I'm not going anywhere and that they can't mess with me or my relationship. "It's okay, just don't leave me alone with them."

Devyn shakes his head. "I tend to be a little overprotective when it comes to you—I won't leave your side."

I rush to the closet to throw some things in an overnight bag. "What should I wear?"

"Wear what you have on, for real."

I frown at my baggy sweats and oversized T-shirt.

"That's cute. I'm the only one that should be looking at you, anyway."

I walk over to him and kiss him. "Thanks . . . but we both know I can't wear this shit. You want your friends to have even more to say about me?"

"You know I don't give a fuck what they think about you," he responds. "Their opinions can't change mine."

I kiss him again before going back to the main topic. "So, what should I wear *for you*?"

Devyn pauses. "The dress you wore a couple weeks ago— the short one with the little straps." I walk to the closet to pull out a different tight dress—this one strapless. I'm sure the party will be hot, but I'll bring a jean jacket just in case, matching it with white sneakers.

Devyn offers to invite my friends when we're back in his room. The idea's comforting, but I want to be alone with Devyn in his environment. He changes and then leaves me alone to get dressed.

I have to look my absolute best. Usually around Devyn's friends, I look tired from work and school. But tonight gives me the opportunity to switch things up. I keep my hair straight, give myself a full contour that highlights my bone structure, and add pink eye shadow. Luckily, after many lessons from Nico, I'm close to mastering a natural, glowing look.

The party gets loud right as I finish. "Caroline" by Aminé booms through a speaker in the living room. My hair and makeup look flawless and my outfit has come together perfectly, hugging my curves and making my boobs perk up. I can't deny I look hot.

Devyn disappeared into the party and hasn't come back, so I throw away the idea that he'll come get me, shake off any nerves, and walk out of Devyn's bedroom into a crowd of about forty or fifty people in the living room and kitchen. The only familiar faces are some of the cheerleaders from last night. A couple of them give me dirty looks before turning back to their conversations, only emphasizing how much I need to find Devyn. Sadly, Avery finds me instead.

"Goddamn!" he exclaims. He doesn't tower over me the way Devyn does. Instead, we're eye to eye. "I didn't know you clean up this good."

I fake a laugh, trying to be polite. "Thanks, I guess."

"Where've you been lately?" Before I can respond, Devyn's massive body presses against my back, stopping me. *Thank God!* I lean back and let him wrap his arms around my chest. "What's going on?"

I know he's trying to make a statement. Even I'm aware of Avery's intentions with me. "Nothing. Avery's just saying hello."

"I see."

Avery drinks out of a red Solo cup he grabs out of nowhere. "Actually, I was just letting your girl know how good she looks tonight."

Devyn's laugh is forceful. He moves me from his front to his side, bringing his hand to the curve of my back. I look at him. He's looking at me, a certain sparkle in his eye. "I'll agree with him on that one. You do look sexy, baby."

Smiling, I get on my tiptoes to kiss him, but one kiss isn't enough for either of us. Our bodies yield together, colliding as we deepen our first real kiss of the day. I love how I can get as much PDA as I want, whenever I want. I love that my affection is always reciprocated.

Devyn laughs against my lips, interrupting our moment. He turns his attention back to Avery, who stands watching us. "We'll see you later, Ave."

Devyn's blasé order to go surprises him.

"Y-yeah," he stutters. "I'll see you guys around." Devyn shakes against me, still laughing as his teammate walks away.

"You're mean." I playfully push him away, and he bounces back closer.

"He was too close." Devyn leans in, pressing a gentle kiss to my lips. "I told you, I don't play when it comes to you."

I feel the same way about Devyn talking to other girls, however, Devyn's more in tune and assertive with his jealousy than I am.

I pull him closer and wrap my arms around his neck. "You have nothing to worry about."

He presses his forehead to mine. "I missed you today."

"I missed you," I tell him. "Do you like my outfit?"

"Hell yeah." Devyn steps back and spins me around to get a better look. "You know you look good in everything, though, right?"

"You're full of compliments tonight."

"Just being honest," he says. "So . . . do you want a drink or something?" He seems nervous to ask, but I want the complete party experience. I know I'm safest with Devyn by my side.

I nod. "Yeah, sounds good." Devyn takes my hand and pulls me to the kitchen, where a guy mixes a large punch bowl. The two of them slap hands as we walk past him.

"Baby, this is my other roommate, Kenny." Kenny's shorter than Devyn and Royal, but I can instantly see he's another lineman by his size. He reminds me of Kyle Massey from *That's So Raven* with his circular physique, short haircut, wide smile, and chestnut skin.

"Ryan!" He smiles and gives me a tight bear hug. "It's nice to finally meet."

"Right," I say. "You're, like, never around here." He releases me from his embrace and Devyn pulls me back.

"Kenny's girl goes to NYU, so he's there a lot."

I nod. "Is she here?"

"Nah." Kenny shakes his head. "She's an actress, and she has a show tonight. You'll see her around here soon, though."

It pleases me to know at least one of Devyn's friends is also in a committed relationship. "Looking forward to it!" Devyn disappears to the refrigerator and pulls out a bottle of green apple Amsterdam. He walks over to the counter, and I follow to see what he's up to.

"I can't drink what Kenny's making?"

Devyn grabs a shot glass from the cabinet. "There's codeine in it," he says, pouring the clear liquid in the glass. "You should take it slow. It's your first time."

I've never told him about my freshman week excursion with my floormates.

"Try this." He hands me the shot and I throw it back. The alcohol burns the back of my throat.

"Not a fan?"

I shake my head, making Devyn laugh.

"Okay, let's mix it."

Devyn goes back to the refrigerator to grab a bottle of orange-mango juice and then a can of pineapple juice. The front door opens, and my attention turns to Freedom as she and a couple other girls walk in. They enter as if they own the place, and all their eyes instantly lock on me.

"For you." Devyn hands me the drink with a kiss on the lips, not noticing. "Better?"

I take a sip, barely tasting the alcohol this time. "Much better! Are you drinking?"

"Nah, that's all you, but I'll smoke if that's cool?"

"Go ahead." I want him to have a good time too.

Devyn opens a drawer and pulls out a pre-rolled blunt and a lighter. A year ago, I would've judged a couple for doing what I'm doing right now, but I can't find much fault in it. I want us to enjoy this new memory, despite the fact I don't know or like most of the people here.

I watch Devyn light his blunt and take a long pull before offering it to me. Part of me feels like I should decline, but my curiosity gets in the way. I take a long hit and choke immediately. My lungs burn with smoke, and I instantly question *how* and *why* people do this for fun. I give it back to Devyn. I chug the rest of my drink to ease my burning chest.

"Damn, baby, you don't mess around." Devyn laughs. "You want another drink?"

I nod, and he gets to mixing.

An hour later I'm on the couch with Devyn, a couple of his teammates, and some other girls, watching them play an intense game of Uno. The three drinks Devyn made me have hit, making me looser, bolder, and more talkative than before. Meeting people isn't so hard, and Devyn's the perfect wingman. I'm enjoying myself!

"Uno out!" Devyn yells, slamming his purple card on the table.

"You're fuckin' cheating, man." Kenny leans back in his seat, rubbing his face.

Devyn falls into me, and I grin at him. "Uno is a talent . . . and you don't have it." His hand glides down my leg, and he turns to me. "You good, baby?"

"Yeah." I laugh. "Why?"

"Just checking," he replies before kissing my cheek and turning back to his friends. The urge to tell him I love him smacks me, and I hold my lips together tightly to conceal the drunken thoughts from escaping my mouth. It's too soon. Maybe I am too drunk.

I do want to be intimate with him tonight. He's been a perfect gentleman, friend, and partner tonight, and my heart and body ache to be closer to him. I touch him to get his attention, and of course he gives it instantly to me. "I need to talk to you."

He puts his arm around me, bringing his face close to mine to whisper, "What's wrong?" Even in a room full of people, my needs are most important to him.

Royal calls Devyn from the kitchen, and I'm interrupted. Devyn tells him to give him a minute and turns his attention back toward me.

"Go," I tell him. "It's not important."

Devyn gets up from the couch and sticks his hand out for me to take. "Come with me?" He pulls me to the kitchen and motions me toward the fridge. "You need water," he says, going over to Royal by the stove. I watch as the two of them have what seems like an important conversation until I feel someone's hand on my shoulder.

"Ryan?"

I turn my head to see Freedom and one of her friends.

"Wow, I couldn't tell that was you!" She laughs. "You actually look pretty."

As much as it irritates me, I ignore her backhanded compliment. I can't let them rile me up any more than they already have.

"What are you doing here, girl?"

I get a water bottle off the shelf in the refrigerator. "My boyfriend lives here."

Freedom and her friend look at each other.

"You've never been to a party before—" Royal steps forward and whispers something in Freedom's ear just as Devyn comes over to me. "What? We're just talking," Freedom argues.

I look at Devyn. "What's going on?"

"You good?" he says to me.

"Ryan, you can't fight your own battles?" Freedom yells. I turn back to her. "Excuse me?"

Her smile grows big and mischievous. "You weak *bitch.* Of course you'd have Devyn and Royal bodyguard for you." Freedom takes a step toward me and presses her chest against mine. "You feel safe? You're fucking pathetic. Any smart person would've known what we were up to from the moment we walked into that nasty-ass restaurant." Royal grabs her arm, and she shoves him away.

"Back up, Freedom," Devyn says from behind me.

She looks at him. "You better shut up before I tell your girlfriend who you really are."

My blood boils with every drop of spit that hits my face as she talks.

"So, tell me." She gets closer, our noses inches apart. "Do WE HAVE A PROBLEM?"

My fist hits her face before I can even think about it, and Freedom falls to the ground. I see red. I lost my job because of this crazy bitch. She's talked about me numerous times and hurt Maria when we did nothing to her. I'm not a fighter, but I'll defend myself and anyone I care about. Especially when it comes to bullies who just fuck with people for no reason.

Her friend pushes me, but I attack, hitting Freedom in the face again. "Do not fucking mess with me!"

"Ryan!" Devyn scoops me up. I'm so mad that I try to fight him off, but he's too strong.

"Don't touch me!" I yell at him. "She keeps fucking with me!" I fling my fists at her again, but Devyn tightens his grip and rushes back to his bedroom.

If people didn't think I was crazy before, they do now. The last thing I see before Devyn closes the door behind us are all eyes on me and Freedom's girls crowding around her.

"I can't believe you!" I push Devyn away as soon as he places me on the ground. "You're my boyfriend, not my dad! I already told you, I don't need a fucking bodyguard!" Devyn reaches toward me, and I push him away, banging my fist against his rock-hard chest.

"Stop!" he yells back, grabbing my hands so I can't move them. I go mute, shocked by the roar of his yell, and he loosens his grip instantly. "Please relax, Ry. You're drunk... you're just upset."

"I will not spend college with your friends thinking they can push me around! Not after—"

"Shh." Despite my effort to fight him off, Devyn still manages to wrap his arms around me. "I know. Just try to calm down so we can talk. If you want to fight Freedom after, I won't stop you." Hot, angry tears rush down my face as I try to control my rapid breathing.

"I'm so sorry," I sob. "I didn't mean to embarrass you."

Devyn laughs. "That's the last thing you did, Ryan." I let him pull me closer. "Relax..." He carries me to the bed and sets me down in his lap. I wrap my arms in their usual place around his neck as he hugs my waist. "On the bright side, I know you can defend yourself now," Devyn says, making me laugh. "One punch knocked Freedom out."

"I don't know what got into me," I say into his neck. "Your friends probably hate me now."

"You're fine," Devyn tells me. "You're more important. They should be trying to impress you."

His words mean so much. "Really?"

"I don't know why you need them to like you." Devyn leans back to look at me. "They can't change how I feel about you. I know you better than they ever will, plus our relationship is about us."

I love him. I'm sure of it now. He always knows what to say and what to do to make me feel like the only woman in the world. "I still want to fight her."

He tightens his grip around me, shaking with laughter. "No, you don't. You're not a fighter, Ry." I look at this perfect man. My man . . . the perfect image of an ideal boyfriend. As hard as it is for me to admit to others, I know I've fallen for him completely. "What did you want to talk to me about?"

"Huh?"

"Earlier, you said you needed to talk," he explains.

"Oh . . . that." The desire to be close and intimate hasn't wavered, even with all the fighting. But I'm too nervous to tell him what I want, so instead I lean in and kiss him. "Nothing. Just thank you for always being so understanding."

Devyn smiles. "You make it easy." I kiss him more, pushing my tongue into his mouth as he falls back on the bed. My dress rises up above my thighs as I straddle him, and I don't fix it. I'm ready to be intimate. To have sex and take our relationship to the next level.

Devyn scoots back, allowing both of us to tumble fully on the bed, and I roll to my back, drawing him closer to me. "Ryan," he murmurs against my lips. I feel his erection against my thigh, and he tries to pull away, but I scoot closer. He's not going to deny me.

"I want you," I murmur against his lips. Devyn stops and stares at me, but I don't want to get anxious, so I kiss him again.

"What do you want to do?" he asks and I pause. "Say it."

"Really?" I scoff.

My irritation surprises him. "You're drunk, baby." He gives me a kiss and flips onto his back. "Before you get upset, just hear me out." I look at him to find him already looking at me. "I want to have sex. I want to do more than just have sex, but not like this. You've been drinking and aren't fully capable of making that decision." Devyn pauses. "I just can't do something that'll make you resent me in the morning."

"I won't resent you."

Devyn sighs. "Honestly, neither of us know how you're going to feel after. For real, babe, there's no rush. We can wait. I'm not going anywhere."

"I won't be a hundred percent sure until we try," I admit. I know how important sex is. I crave intimacy with Devyn in all ways, but sex has never been that dreamy fairytale you see in movies or hear about from your friends. I've never enjoyed it, and I don't know if that'll change.

"We have time, Ryan." He yawns, his demeanor extremely relaxed from all the weed he's smoked tonight.

I don't know what to say. I know that as much as Devyn likes me, I'm not tending to his physical needs the way he's always tending to my emotional ones. It's not fair to him. But I'm scared that the one who robbed my virginity permanently damaged my attitude toward sex. Even thousands of miles away, Ivan's still manipulating my life and my relationship.

The low hum of Devyn's snoring silences my negative thoughts. I get up and change into one of Devyn's practice shirts. His aromatic scent is on it . . . it's him . . . my home . . . my new home, at least.

Somehow, I manage to take off Devyn's shirt without waking him. He kicks off his shoes and climbs under the covers, falling back asleep instantly. I turn off the lights and lock the door. The party is still loud, so I connect to the speaker and let the soft sounds of Syd's "Drown in It" fill the room.

The bed feels heavenly against my heavy, drunk limbs, making them tingle as I lie across the soft sheets. Devyn turns toward me in his sleep, and I cuddle into him. I hug him and leave a soft kiss on his chest. "I love you," I whisper. It scares me, but I do.

I know I'm too deep into this. He's saying he won't go anywhere, but what if my rushed feelings push him away? I close my eyes, hoping the thought of him loving me will somehow pop into his dreams. Definitely too drunk and in my feelings, I hold on to him a little tighter and fall into a deep sleep.

CHAPTER 15

DEVYN

I'm surprised to find Ryan isn't next to me in the bed when I wake up. The silence and brightness of my room is calming among the fuzzy drowsiness I'm feeling. Something about Sunday makes you appreciate everything—God, good friends and family, and a great girl to cuddle at night and wake up to in the morning.

Well, most mornings, anyway.

The door opens, and Ryan comes in. She looks exhausted, her hair tied in a low ponytail, glasses on. One of my T-shirts hangs sexily on her body, ending on the top of her thighs. Did any of my roommates see her half-dressed like this?

"Where'd you go?"

"I needed Advil," she whispers, crawling toward me on the bed. She sits astride my hips, pulling a water bottle out of nowhere and taking a sip. "I have a little headache."

"Hungover?" I ask, sitting up. Ryan presses her forehead against mine, kissing me, and wraps her arms around me for a hug. I rub her back and rest my face in the crook of her neck. She smells like the sweet, addicting scent I can never describe and can never get enough of. "Good morning."

I hear the smile on her face. "Morning." Her voice is low as she squeezes me tight before leaning back. "What are we doing today?"

I cup her face. "First . . . we're going to get your job back."

"That's impossible."

Ryan's bosses seem like they can be won over easily with a little begging, especially Tony. "You haven't even tried." Fighting for her job would be easier than getting a new one. Especially one that's so flexible with tutoring and school. Her silence tells me she knows I'm right.

"What are we doing after that?"

"I'll take you to lunch, and then we should probably do some homework."

Ryan sighs. "It's sad you have to remind me to do homework when I'm your tutor."

"Can I ask you something?" She's been acting so cool. I wonder if she forgot about last night. "Do you really think you're ready to have sex?" Her body immediately tenses in my arms, but she keeps her eyes on mine.

"I don't know," she says. "Last night I felt really bold I guess . . . and fearless. I didn't expect for you to reject me."

"I didn't reject you . . ."

"I should be relieved you didn't want to have sex while we were both intoxicated, but now I just feel . . . unworthy."

I don't understand how she can feel that way, especially after telling her how much I wanted to have sex. However, I push my feelings aside, nodding to seem more understanding.

"I don't want to trigger"—I pause, trying to find the right words—"feelings you may have had with Ivan. I want to be with you too, baby, but I need you to be sure."

"I told you before, that can't happen if we never try," she retaliates. I know she's still partially mad about last night. "Devyn, I know I'm not giving you everything you need."

"You told me you didn't think you could give me sex less than two weeks ago, and I'm trying to honor that." I must've said the wrong thing, because she hops up and goes to grab her bag. "Where are you going?" I ask her.

"To get dressed!" she shouts.

"What did I say? I'm trying to talk things out."

"You being all understanding isn't you being truthful. All guys need sex, Devyn. Do you really expect me to believe you're fine with just making out all the time?"

"Yes!"

"Well, I don't! I'm annoyed I'm so fucked up that I can't even hook up with my own boyfriend!" Tears fall from her glistening eyes. "So when I try to have sex, I'd appreciate if you just let me."

"We both know this conversation would be ten times worse if we had sex last night." She's being completely irrational. "I'm not going to take advantage of you the way Ivan did!" I regret my words the moment I say them.

Her chest moves up and down rapidly as we stare at each other in silence. "I'm going to take a shower, and then I'll go talk to Maria and Tony *alone*." She walks out of the room, slamming the door behind her.

Fuck. What a great way to start the day.

I'm not wrong. I would've been more upset with myself for giving in to sex than I would for doing the right thing. Ryan's mad only because she's embarrassed. But I'm not going to punish myself. Sex isn't going to just be some risky, hit-or-miss thing that could potentially end our relationship.

I pull on a pair of black sweatpants and a matching shirt and hoodie. It's rainy, foggy, and probably freezing outside. I sit at the foot of the bed and wait for Ryan to come out. I won't let her irrationality ruin our day.

Almost thirty minutes later, Ryan walks into the room in black leggings and a dark gray T-shirt emblazoned with BLACK GIRLS ROCK in sparkly black letters. Her glasses are off and her hair's down. I can't tell if her eyes are red from the shower or if she's been crying.

"Can we talk?" I ask. She stares at me with her arms crossed over her chest. "Please?" I don't know how long she's going to be silent, so I start talking. "You're right when you say sex is a big deal, but it's not everything, and I'm not going to risk your mental health for it." I keep my eyes on hers, but she breaks eye contact, looking down at the ground to wipe her eyes. "I don't want to feel incompetent, baby. I want you . . . I told you that last night, but I mean it when I say there's no rush."

Ryan sits next to me on the bed. She doesn't look at me, but she rests her head on my shoulder, letting me know we're not fighting anymore.

"I can't believe you're this perfect," she whispers. "That you can hold out for this long without temptation. I know girls must throw themselves at you. I know you're wanted."

I sigh. She obviously doesn't listen to me. "You're worth waiting for. As long as I get to see you and touch you and be with you . . . that'll hold me." I take a moment to see if I can come to a happy medium for both of us. "Why don't we try walking before we run?" Ryan looks at me, so I turn my body toward her. "We're not going to have sex right now, but we can do other things." Ryan's hands don't go near my dick when we're making out, so I don't believe we should jump straight to sex. She has it so wrong.

Nodding, she seems to relax. "Alright. That's a good idea." I take her hand and draw her into my lap for a hug. "Thank you. You won't regret it."

"I don't doubt I will." I'm scared of how she'll react to certain things. I wonder if I can talk to someone about how to date the sexually assaulted.

Ryan lets me go and walks over to the closet to grab one of my hoodies. It looks like a dress on her, falling right above the knees, but it still looks good. "Maybe if we match every day, then girls will think you're whipped and will stay away."

I laugh. If only she knew how whipped I already am. "I'll tell you what I wear every day if it means we don't have a repeat of last night's throwdown." I'm still baffled by how easily Ryan beat Freedom's ass.

Ryan laughs. "She deserved it."

In the end, Maria and Tony don't take a lot of convincing to give Ryan her job back. Maria even admits to overreacting. They won't make her pay them back, but they cut her days to four instead of her usual five. She's not happy about it, but I'm glad she'll have more time to rest and relax. I pull her out of the restaurant as soon as they're done. She doesn't need to be there on her day off.

***

RYAN

I love you.

Why can't I say it?

I know it's only been a couple weeks, but I feel like a coward. I should be able to voice how I feel when I feel it unapologetically. But instead, I'm staring at this big, strong, gorgeous man, able to say anything but the words I want to. Is it too soon? The thought's been driving me mad since I admitted it to myself. I'm overemotional all because I can't be honest with him. And to top things off, I'm almost certain Devyn agrees I'm acting crazy. I can't control these feelings. Liking someone is different than loving them—the pull's a lot less overwhelming.

We're back in Devyn's room after spending the afternoon in an Italian restaurant in the city. One thing I'm learning about Devyn is his excellent taste in food and his love for trying out new restaurants. My drowsiness has kicked in from all the delicious carb loading. I'll have to add exercising to my list of things to do since Devyn's always feeding me. Who knew relationship weight was really a thing you had to work to avoid?

I lie on Devyn's bed as he sprawls on his back at the other end, reading *Native Son*. He looks relaxed, and I can tell he's enjoying the book from all the annotating he's been doing. To think it upset him when I made him start taking notes, and now he seems to enjoy it.

What if I just say it? Would he really leave me because of it? I'm clearly already obsessed.

"I . . ." I open my mouth but can't get the last two words out. Devyn looks at me. "You what?"

Fuck, I need to get it together.

"I'm exhausted. I can't get any work done like this." Luckily, I don't think he notices how hard I'm trying to conceal my emotions. "How's the book going?"

"It's pretty good, for real."

"Yeah?" I smile, genuinely enjoying his new love for reading. "Do you want to take a break?" He's been working hard for almost two hours, so it won't hurt.

Devyn rests his book on his chest. "Sure. Want some water or something?"

I nod, and he lurches up, disappearing from the room. I sit in silence, contemplating again on whether or not I should let him know my true feelings. I want him to know, but I'm afraid he won't feel the same way.

"I love you," I say out loud. I practice a couple more times, and it's not hard. However, I'm back to speechless when Devyn walks in.

"I brought you this in case you need some caffeine." He hands me a Diet Coke. I take it as he sets a water bottle on the bed next to me. "What are you working on?" Devyn plops next to me on the bed. Luckily, I started the paper already, so it doesn't look like I've done nothing. He presses his lips against my shoulder, eyeing my laptop. "What class is this for?"

"Psychology." I sigh. "It's due on Thursday, but I figured I'd start it." I put my computer aside and climb on top of him. I cup his face, admiring his smooth skin, beard, and high cheekbones.

"Admiring the view?"

I smile, lean in, and plant a kiss on his full lips. "Always." Devyn envelops me in his arms, pressing my body to his, making the kiss more intense.

He rolls us over, tucking me underneath him. He adds tongue to the kiss before pulling away. "You have to let me know if I'm doing something you don't like."

What's he talking about?

"If you get weird thoughts or feel bad, say stop. If we're going to be more physical, I think we should be a hundred percent honest with each other from now on."

What are we about to do? All these questions run through my mind. "I promise." I nod. "I'll tell you to stop if I need you to." I look him in his eyes, so he knows I'm being genuine. "How—" He pauses. "How far did Ivan go with you? Foreplay wise?"

I shook my head. "Just sex."

"I'm your first," he whispers, trying hard to conceal the smile on his face. The conversation's getting weirder and weirder, but I just nod. "Okay, well," he says, "Let me try something, and we'll go from there."

"Kiss me," I blurt before I start getting nervous. I pull his body on top of mine. Our mouths collide as Devyn's hands travel under my shirt, cupping my breast over my sports bra. His lips move from my lips to my neck, and he sucks on it. Butterflies enter my stomach as my body heats up from his touch.

"Can I take this off?" he asks. I nod, and he yanks my shirt over my head. I think he's going to take off my bra, but instead he leans back, looking at me with an expression I can't read.

"What?" Instantly, I cover my stomach, but he grabs my hands and entwines them with his.

Devyn shakes his head. I notice him smiling but am too nervous to ask why. "Don't hide yourself from me," he says, taking off his shirt so we're mirroring each other. He leans in to kiss me again. I don't know what's going on, but I try my hardest not to let my thoughts ruin this moment.

He kisses my neck, and his hands are on my butt, pulling me closer. The feeling of his erection pressing against my leg excites me rather than evoking anxiety for the first time. I like the feeling of his bare skin against mine; the warmth and vulnerability is different, but it makes me get into things more.

I pull him closer, kissing him. I'm in this just as much as he is, maybe more. A moan escapes the back of his throat, and it makes me giggle.

"What?" he says in between kisses.

"I love you." The words fall from my lips. Devyn stops and looks at me, and I instantly regret it. Fuck! I release my arms from him and sit up on my elbows. "I mean . . . I think I am . . . I don't know . . . I'm sorry."

"Don't apologize." My confession has flabbergasted him, and I've completely ruined our amazing moment.

"You don't have to say it back, I just . . ."

"I love you too, Ry." I don't know what to do. I pull him into me, and he hesitates before hugging me back. "I've never told anyone that before," he tells me.

"Neither have I." I hug him a little tighter. "I was so nervous to tell you."

"You can always be honest with me, Ry. It doesn't matter what it's about." I know that's true, but it's easier said than done. "I'm nervous too."

"Why?" I ask, but Devyn's lips are back on mine before I know it. His hands move to the waistband of my leggings, and I'm thankful he doesn't ask if I'm okay again. I lean back and lay down on the bed, both nervous and excited for whatever's about to happen. The energy in the room gets hot and heavy as Devyn's eyes burn holes into my skin. It's just me and the person I'm most comfortable with. I couldn't ask for more.

"It's okay," I whisper, closing my eyes. He's about to turn all the bad memories into good ones, and I'm ready. The feeling of Devyn planting a kiss on my hip bone sends shivers down my body.

"Look at me." I open my eyes and they immediately lock with his. "Trust me." It sounds like a statement more than a question, but I nod anyway. He pulls down my leggings slowly. He's just as nervous as I am, and that makes me love him even more.

Devyn slides down my underwear and tosses them off the bed before trailing French kisses up my thighs. The anticipation kills me, and loud gasps escape my lips as his warm, wet tongue hits my opening. The sensation is something I've never experienced but absolutely love.

"*Fuck.*" The word escapes my mouth in a whisper. Devyn's hands travel from my waist to my boobs as he pushes up my bra and pinches my already hardened nipples. I can no longer keep my eyes open as my back arches from the constant combination of pleasure and excited nerves traveling through my body. "Devyn," I moan, only making him suck harder and stroke deeper with his tongue.

He's completely taken me by surprise, only adding to the long list of what makes this man so great. The room spins and stars form in my eyes as I reach my first orgasm. My body shakes under his hold and I feel elated. Devyn backs away, wiping his mouth with the T-shirt he dropped on the floor earlier, and then he gets next to me in bed.

"Good?" he asks, making me laugh. I'm in nothing but my bra, which is pushed up over my breasts, and couldn't care less. I roll into his body and kiss him. Devyn rubs his nose against mine. "I really do love you," he says, making me smile. "Part of me feels like I always have."

His words make tears instantly fall from my eyes. I kiss him again and don't stop for the rest of the night.

CHAPTER 16

RYAN

Weeks go by like days, and with time, I get accustomed to living in New York, being in love for the first time, and balancing school, football games, friends, and seeing Devyn as often as possible. Before I know it, it's the beginning of October and I'm caught up loving every part of my hectic new life. For the first time, I wake up happy and go to bed even happier. I feel like my life's headed in the right direction; however, I know so much more is coming.

Devyn and I are still holding off on sex. While the foreplay is amazing every time, after thinking about it, I realized we really do have time. We're allowing for the moment to happen naturally and we're having fun pushing the limits. For me, every new thing we do is exciting. It makes us closer, makes us both feel good, and even creates a bond that both of us are experiencing for the first time. We take things step-by-step, Devyn always cautious, but at this point, we both know the time's bound to happen sooner than later. I'm excited for whenever the day comes, but sometimes I get nervous. Sex is the only step Devyn and I haven't taken, and the one thing I've done with Ivan. I'm not sure how I'll react.

I call an Uber from work to the dorms. The temperature has dropped from the high seventies to the low forties in a matter of weeks, and I'm having a hard time adjusting. The East Coast winters have a sharp pain that hits your skin the moment you go outside. My LA ass could've never prepared for it.

Eager to get to my tutoring session with Devyn and under the cloud-like fabric of his comforter, I practically prance out of the restaurant. After a brief overview of what he's working on and what he has due this week, I plan to knock out. In a short amount of time, Devyn's managed to keep up in most of his classes and barely needs my help. I think the reason he makes sure we keep them is to guarantee we get ample alone time.

I cage my desire to jump out of the car without as much as a thank-you to the driver. I'm so glad the day's over, and even happier to spend the night at Devyn's, which has become more common on nights we have tutoring. Both of his roommates are sitting in the living room playing some 2K game when I enter. Royal smiles at me as I set a takeout bag on the counter.

"Please be for me!" he exclaims.

I nod. "It is."

"You're amazing," he jumps off the couch, skipping over to me. The quick side hug I get as a thank-you makes me laugh.

"I know," I respond, taking out the container with Devyn's food from the bag. "Kenny, there's one for you too." I leave them to their burritos and head to find Devyn.

The room's set in its usual dim hue when I enter, but I'm surprised to find Devyn putting clothes in a bag rather than his usual sleeping, doing homework, or watching TV. "Hey." I smile, happy to see him. He's wearing black Adidas sweatpants, and a white long-sleeve shirt clings to his body, showing off bulging muscles, gut, and a muscular physique. He looks too good to be sitting in the house, even in sweats. "I brought you something." I put the food on his desk. He looks over at it and resumes folding his clothes. "Thanks."

"No problem," I say, walking toward him. "Can I have a kiss? I haven't seen you all day."

He pauses, taking his time to stop from what he's doing before leaning down and kissing me briefly. Ignoring his curtness, I take a seat on the bed.

"Did you finish homework already?"

"Haven't started."

I laugh. "I had a feeling. What do you have due?"

"I'm not doing that shit tonight, Ryan," he snaps at me.

Why is he angry?

"Are you mad at me?"

Devyn sighs, shaking his head.

"Why haven't you looked at me since I got here?"

He looks at me, revealing bloodshot, glistening eyes. "I am looking at you, baby."

"What'd you do?" I say without thinking. My question angers him, but he's hiding so much emotion. He has to be guilty of something.

"Manny was shot in the back of the neck," Devyn strains, holding back tears. We keep our eyes on each other for a couple seconds before he turns around, grabs some shoes, and throws them in the bag.

I feel terrible. This isn't the time to ask questions about what happened or be upset about his distance. I push his duffel bag aside and crawl into him, wrapping my arms around his neck.

"Don't assume the worst in me," he says. "I haven't done anything wrong. You know that."

I nod. "I'm so sorry."

Devyn wraps his arms around my waist, holding me tightly.

"Is Manny . . ." I don't want to finish my sentence.

"He's in surgery right now. The earliest flight I could get was for tomorrow." The thought of him leaving already starts to make me physically ache, but I understand he has to go check on his best friend. "We've got to be out of here by 10:00 a.m."

I lean back, looking at him. "What?"

"I'm not leaving you here."

Has he lost his mind? "Devyn, I'm not going. I have work . . . and class."

"You can take some time off, Ryan."

I need to be honest. "Devyn, I told you a long time ago I'm never going back there."

"You're really doing this right now?" he asks me. "You know I wouldn't ever put you in harm's way. No one is going to touch you; you'd be with me 24-7."

"I'm not going."

"I already bought your ticket."

"I didn't ask you to do that, but I'll pay you back. How much was it?"

"I don't want your money, Ryan!" he yells, making me jump. Tears instantly fall from his eyes. "This isn't about you." Devyn steps away from me and uses his shirt to wipe away his tears.

"Maybe you should wait until after your game? We can talk about it more and you'll feel better . . ."

"Ryan," he begs. "My best friend is dying. What part of that don't you understand? Nothing else matters right now. I don't care about football or your job or class or Ivan or whatever other problems we got going on. I'm going home, and I want you to come with me because I love you and I . . . I fucking need you by my side." More tears fall as he struggles to keep it together. "I'm going with or without you."

I spend the rest of the night silently watching Devyn. He packs, gets in the shower, and then climbs in the bed, falling asleep while browsing through his phone. I don't know if he needs alone time, but I want to be there for him. I know he's scared and upset . . .

And worst of all, angry with me.

I take my time in the shower while Devyn sleeps, but I'm surprised to see him awake and on his phone when I come back. Too afraid to open my mouth and ask for pajamas, I go over to what's now "my drawer" to grab an old T-shirt and a pair of underwear I'd left here.

I lie in bed, feeling bad. I don't want to fight with Devyn, and I don't want him to go to California with a bad taste of me in his mouth. We lie in bed for what feels like forever as I figure out what to say to fix things between us.

"I love you." I turn toward him. His eyes are closed, but he's facing me, so I know he's listening. "Can we talk?"

He moves his head, nodding slightly.

"I don't want you to be mad at me."

"Then come with me," he responds.

"Devyn, you know I can't go back to California." My voice cracks, and I push my emotions deep inside. It's not my time to cry. "It's not safe for me. You know how much power Ivan has back home."

"Nothing would happen to you," he says. "We'd be together the entire time. We'd stay at my dad's . . . I have everything planned, and you won't even try? You said he won't touch you if you're with me." I lie there in silence, not knowing what to say. "I know it's going to be hard, and that this is scary for you . . . I just want you by my side. But if you don't come . . . well, I'll be upset, but it's not going to change anything between us."

"Are you scared?"

He doesn't answer my question.

"Let me hold you." Devyn pulls me into him. My chest crushes against his as we hold each other tight. "I love you too." He cries in my neck. "I get why you can't come. I respect your decision."

I hold on to him for what feels like hours that night, listening as Devyn cries himself to sleep. His pillow is stained with a puddle of his own tears when he knocks out.

It's my turn to be strong for both of us.

***

I wake up the next morning still wrapped in Devyn's arms, the annoying beeping from my alarm waking me up for class. I need to make sure Devyn's good before he leaves for the airport, but I don't want to wake him. This will be our last morning together for I don't know how long, and I'm already missing him dreadfully.

Fuck class. I have more important things to worry about today. I grab my phone and turn it off.

"What time is it?" Devyn groans sleepily.

"Seven. You don't have practice?"

Devyn scratches his head, turning to wrap his arms around my body. "I'm excused from practice and the game."

I stop questioning him and instead snuggle closer.

"I'll miss you," he whispers as his hand rubs up and down my hip.

Thinking of how long we'll be apart makes me panic, but I try to keep it together. "I already miss you," I say into his chest. "But we'll talk every day and FaceTime and stuff."

Devyn snorts. "FaceTime?"

I look at him. "Yeah, what's wrong with that?"

"It's just not this."

"Manny's going to be okay," I say, changing the subject. "I know you're scared, but—"

"We don't know that," Devyn interrupts. "I mean, getting shot in the back of the neck isn't really an easy thing to recover from."

I'm an idiot for thinking that talking about Manny would make him feel better. I don't want him to start crying again, so I just nod and keep quiet. Devyn kisses my forehead, letting out a heavy sigh.

"Is there anything I can do?"

"You're doing it, Ry," he whispers. I press my lips to his. Saying I love you in this situation just isn't enough. "Well . . . maybe we can make out before I have to get ready to go? That would definitely make me feel a little better."

I smile, pulling Devyn on top of me. "Anything for you."

"I love you so much." He smiles against my lips.

My anxiety is trying to crawl out of my skin as Devyn and I enter the airport. I'm not prepared to say good-bye to him, but I won't break down or cry. Devyn must sense my nervousness, but his corny jokes and quiet affection on the way here can't ease my worries.

I watch as he checks his bag, and then I walk down to the security check with him. Since he's not a child, I doubt they'll allow me to follow him to his boarding gate. I'm too afraid to ask, anyway.

"You sure you don't want to come?" he says as we approach the long line of people. I open my mouth to speak, but he continues talking. "I know, I know . . . I'll stop asking." Tears instantly fall from my eyes, and before I know it, Devyn's holding me tight. "I'm sorry; I shouldn't have done that."

"It's not you." I step away from him, wiping my eyes. "I just don't want to say good-bye."

"I'm coming back. It'll only be a couple of weeks."

I nod. "I know. It'll just be weird . . . being here by myself again . . . not having you around."

Devyn reaches over and brushes the tears off with his thumb. "You're not by yourself, baby."

"You'll text me before you get on the plane? And when you land?"

"Of course," he responds. "Ryan," Devyn says as more tears fall. I pull him down to hug me, and he scoops me into his arms.

"I'm trying to be strong for you."

"You don't have to do that." He rubs my back to soothe me.

"I love you so much," I cry. "I'm here whenever you need me . . . no matter what or when."

"I know," Devyn whispers. "I love you too. Kiss me." I move my head to plant a long, lingering kiss on his lips.

Devyn puts me back on my feet. "Okay, I'm good." I laugh. "Maybe you should go before I completely fall apart."

Devyn nods. "Okay." He leans down and kisses me again. "I love you."

"I love you." I kiss him back. "Be safe."

"Always."

***

"Ryan, there's no way in hell I'm letting you mope in bed until Devyn gets back," Nico says, busting into my room later that evening. I texted her frantically the entire Uber ride home. She was in class but spent my hour drive back trying to console me over text.

Instead of going to school, I went to work earlier, so I'm already home by five. Devyn has a layover in Atlanta and is still on his way back to California, but I'm already antsy and missing him. With no desire to be productive today, I came home and got straight in bed.

"I get that you're sad, but you're being ridiculous, babe. You have a great boyfriend you'll talk to every day, and that's just as sad, if not more, as you are. We have to find other things to occupy the little bit of free time you used to hang out with him."

"I just miss him," I pout. Nico comes over and gets under the covers beside me. "I'm scared of him being back home."

"Why?" No one knows about my past except for Devyn, but I know I can trust Nico with a little information about where I grew up.

"It's just not safe. California's got a lot of gorgeous places, but G-Heights isn't one of them." That's the easiest way to explain things without giving any more info.

"You really think Devyn's hanging out with, like, criminals or people that'll get him in trouble? He doesn't seem like that kind of guy."

"He's not, but what if Manny is?"

"You don't know that," Nico tells me. "It's fine to worry, Ry, but Devyn will be fine. Be worried about his mental and emotional state. He might lose his best friend. He's going through a lot right now."

I know I'm bringing my own homebound insecurities into what's going on with Devyn. I just have to trust that he'll be safe and take care of himself. He made a way before me and he'll make a way now. All I can do is be there for him as best I can.

"I just need today," I tell Nico. "Let me mope about Devyn leaving, and tomorrow I'll go to work and class and bother you . . . which'll be my new way of occupying what little time I have."

"I'd love that! You can help me find a new girl." Nico's slowly getting over Sasha, but she still has times when she gets really sad. This mostly happens at night, but Troy's always the one to help her when she needs it. They've been spending a lot of time together, cuddling in one of their beds, watching movies, eating in the cafeteria, and smoking tons of weed. If I didn't know Nico was "very gay"—her words, not mine—I would think they had little crushes on each other.

"Getting back out there?"

"Kind of." She sighs. "I'm thinking of being in a polyamorous relationship."

I laugh, putting my feet in her lap. "What the hell is that?"

"I don't want just one girlfriend anymore. It's college, and I've already decided I like girls, so this is my new experiment. I want two girlfriends."

"For real?"

"Yeah, like we *all* hang out and go on dates . . . we *all* have sex . . . and we *all* are there for each other emotionally," Nico says. "That way, if someone's busy, there will be another girl to do things with, meaning you won't get lonely. Less heart-break in the end."

I don't know if that'll work, but I keep my mouth shut. "I've never heard of anything like that."

Nico chuckles. "Well now you have! I need something new, you know?"

"I think it's a cool idea." I don't have the heart to barrage her with all my questions. What if two people like each other more than the third person? Regardless, she's set her mind to this idea, and I can't change it.

"Really?" Nico smiles, excited. "I thought you'd think it's weird."

"I mean, I'd never do it." I laugh. "But I'm all for taking chances these days. Do you have anyone in mind?"

"No one you know," Nico says. "I'll keep you updated if anything gets serious."

I nod, taking note again of how special a friend Nico is. "But speaking of new experiences, have you and Devyn—"

"Nope!"

"Why?" Nico bellows. "What's stopping you?"

I shrug. "I mean . . . I love him so much."

Nico laughs at my words.

"And I want to, but we just decided to wait until the time's right. No planning, no specific dates . . . when we can't take waiting anymore, we'll do it."

"That'll cause some serious energy," she responds. "I have to tell you something, though. I sit next to this girl, Freedom, in my—"

"Ugh . . . fuck her."

"You know her?"

"Sadly. I think she hooks up with one of Devyn's room-mates," I tell her. "She's the one that got me fired."

"*That's* her?" Nico says. "She's always talking about Devyn, and she makes him sound so unlike the person you talk about or even the guy I've seen. He's always so caring and attentive toward you."

"Devyn wasn't the best guy when he first got here," I tell her. "I mean, I didn't know him that well in high school, but he seemed like your typical athlete. He was kind of a dick, got away with a lot, but for some reason, girls still wanted to fuck with him. I guess Freedom hooked him up with a couple of her friends, but he's always saying I'm the only girl he's ever felt this way about. Maybe that's why he's so different." I don't even want to know what Freedom had to say about Devyn, and honestly, I don't care. I know who he is, and nothing anyone can say or do will change that.

"Good, 'cause they make him sound like an asshole, and I'm not trying to fuck up your boyfriend anytime soon," Nico says, making me laugh.

"I wouldn't want that, either." I figure a healthy distraction will be better than moping around until Devyn calls. "How about a movie? Your pick."

Nico smiles. "I'd love to! They just put every season of *Game of Thrones* on HBO Go, and I've been dying to get into it."

"*Game of Thrones?*"

"How do you want to be a film writer, and you don't know about the most popular fantasy show out right now?"

I shrug. "I didn't have cable in LA."

"We'll start from season one. You'll be addicted, and there're eight seasons . . . that's plenty of time to distract you till Devyn comes back." Nico takes my computer to find the show. I hope she's right about the distraction. I have a feeling I'll be worrying about Devyn a lot over the next few days.

CHAPTER 17

DEVYN

Even with the welcoming feeling of smoggy air and the familiarity of the LAX airport, I'm not happy to be home. The only joy comes from getting off that long-ass plane ride.

"Surprise!" a high-pitched female voice says, and I'm ecstatic to see none other than my seven-year-old baby sister standing next to my dad outside on the Tarmac.

"Cara!" I drop my bag and pick her up as she collides into me. She's exactly the same as I left her, with her hair in curls just below her shoulders, a round face, chubby cheeks, and a gap between her two front teeth. Cara's bigger than her twin brother, Cory, with the genes from my dad's side. Cory has the lanky, skinny figure of our mom's side.

"I missed you," she says as I envelop her small, round body in my arms.

"I missed you more." I put her on the ground as my dad walks up. "Hey, Pop," I say, giving him a hug. Being so close to my family after this long makes me a little nostalgic, but I keep a brave face.

"Son!" My dad holds on to me tightly. He'd called me about Manny in tears. Manny's been my best friend my whole life and is like a third son to him. "How are you?"

"I'm okay," I say.

"Ryan didn't come?" he asks, releasing me.

I shake my head. "Nah, it's just me." I'm sure he's got his own conclusions on why Ryan didn't come, so I don't need to explain. He knows enough.

"Who's Ryan?" Cara says, wrapping her arms around my waist.

I look down at her. "You still nosey? I thought you'd outgrow that trait while I was gone."

She shrugs. "I tried, and I can't."

I laugh, picking her up as my dad grabs my bag so we can leave.

We walk back to the car, Cara going on about the new basketball team she's on and how she's the best because she's the biggest. I'm happy she's still at that age where she doesn't care about her weight yet but instead takes pride in it.

My dad's mostly silent until we get on the freeway. As much as I want to go see Manny, it's after nine, and visiting hours are closed.

"Have you seen him?" I ask my dad. Cara's watching a movie on the old car's TV in the back seat, her headphones loud so she can't hear us. I remember how excited my dad was when he got this truck right before the first day of my second grade. We spent hours driving around, and I sat in the back seat watching *Spider-Man*. I like to focus on those times—when we felt like an actual family and things were good. However, when thinking of home, the bad memories of my mom always overshadow the good.

"Yeah, we saw him before we came to the airport," Dad tells me. "Cory cried the whole way home, so we dropped him off at the house with Sashanie."

Sashanie, or Shae, as we call her, is Manny's older sister. She's twenty and has a two-year-old son, Jodeci, who she named after her favorite R&B group (we begged her not to do it, but she never listens). From the time Jodeci was born, Cory had an instant attachment to him. For a while, Cory refused to let anyone else hold him and would even cry when Shae took him away to breastfeed or change his diaper. My dad and I would get so mad at him for acting like that, but Shae thought it was cute for a five-year-old boy to have such an attachment to a newborn.

Shae went through a bad time around the end of my sophomore year and started hanging around Ryan's dad, Javon, for a brief period of time. A couple months later, she got pregnant and told us she had no clue who the father was. You'd think a situation like that would make you hate men and maybe even regret the life inside you, but one night a few weeks after Jodeci was born, she, Manny, and I were hanging out, and she confessed that Cory made her want to keep her son.

"I hated Jodeci when they first put him in my arms after the delivery," she said in the living room as she smoked a blunt Manny had rolled for us. "But I saw the way Cory looked at him with so much love, and I wanted that. I learned to love my own son through a little kid, and that's crazy . . . but I know now I would do anything for my son and for my family. I had to stop being selfish for him."

"Thank God," Manny joked as Shae passed the blunt to him. "Me and Mom thought we was gonna have to raise the kid. I love my nephew, but a little boy don't look good when you're

trying to get a girl." We'd all laughed too hard at his joke in
our cloudy states.

That's Manny, though. Forever fucking clowning, even
during the serious moments. He always finds a way to keep
a smile on our faces.

God, let him be okay. Please don't take my brother away
from me.

"He's stable," my dad says after minutes of silence. "In a
coma and on an oxygen tube, but he's alive and the bullets
have been removed from his neck and back. We just gotta
take it day by day."

"How's his mom?"

"Awful," he says. "But we're all going to make it. We got to
hold it together for Manny and his family. He was the glue
that held them together—"

"And he'd do it for us."

My dad nods. "He'd do it for us . . . without even thinking
about it."

Ten minutes later, we pull up to the row of palm trees
that tell us we're near Garden Heights. Dirty sidewalks with
patches of weeds coming out, buildings with chipped paint
and broken ceilings, homeless men and women fooling
around on the streets, a liquor store on every corner. I'm
already missing school with Ryan.

I send her a quick text since I forgot when I landed. I'm
hoping she's asleep, but I know she won't until she's heard
from me. She worries too much.

Just got to the house. I'll call in ten.

I grab my bag as Cara bounces out of the car. "I've been sleeping in your bed since you left," she tells me as we walk through the garage door.

"Well, you're not sleeping with me," I laugh. "You need to go to your room."

"It's so dirty." She yawns.

"Better start cleaning," I say, letting her dart past me into the living room.

My house is one of the better-looking homes in this shitty neighborhood, but that's not saying much. Every house in the area is over forty years old, and most of the neighbors inherited the land from family members who've passed. Even my dad got this house from his great-grandfather. My dad was pretty young when my mom got pregnant, and his grandfather had given him the house as a going-away present. He died a few months later from lung cancer no one had known about.

Cory and Jodeci are asleep on the couch as I walk in, and Shae's watching TV, braiding her hair. "Hey!" she says when she sees me, quiet enough not to wake the boys. She gets up slowly to hug me. "It's so good to see you! How was your flight?"

"Long." Shae's the older sister I never had. We hadn't gotten close until Jodeci was born, but she's always had an energy about her that brightens the mood. She's bubbly and all smiles, even when she's been through hell. "How's everything with you?"

She shrugs. "I'm keeping it together. That's all I can do right now." I know exactly how she feels. We'll get a chance to really talk once everyone goes to bed. "But I'm excited to hear all about you and college. Manny said you love New York, and your dad said your new girl came with you."

"She ended up not coming," I tell her. "She's actually from here."

"D!" She laughs. "The point of going to college was to get away from the G-Heights ratchets!"

I laugh. "It just happened. She's different, though."

"Who is she?"

"Ryan McKnight."

Her entire facial expression changes. "Javon's daughter?" she whispers. "Isn't she like . . . sixteen?"

I shake my head. Does Ryan look that young? "No, she's my age. In my class and everything."

Shae seems to want to say something she can't in front of my dad and the kids. She pauses a moment, thinking hard. "She's pretty." She nods. "I've never heard her talk or anything, though."

"She's shy." I laugh. Ryan and I have come so far in the couple months we've been together. "I don't know how I got her to start talking to me."

"You're charming as fuck, Devyn." She chuckles. "I doubt it was that hard."

"Sashanie," my dad interrupts, coming into the room. "Are you staying here tonight? I'll put the boys in Cory's room, and Cara can sleep with me, so you can take her room. I just cleaned it up."

"Yeah, that'd be great." A shy smile creeps to the corner of her lips. I figure her mom's still at the hospital with Manny and she doesn't want to be alone.

"I'll help you," I tell my dad. I turn my attention to Shae. "I'ma hop in the shower, but give me like thirty minutes. We'll talk?" She nods and I go to grab Jodeci from the couch. The kid's so cute with his dark chocolate skin and freshly done cornrows. He feels a little too light in my arms.

"Thank you," Shae says, her eyes glistening with tears. My dad smiles at her before heading back to the bedrooms. "We're family," I whisper to her. Jodeci wraps his small arms around my neck, murmuring something under his breath about Batman. "We got you; we'll get through this together." I kiss her forehead as tears stream down her face. She pulls me into a hug. "It means so much that you came back—to me and my mom. You have no idea how much we need you."

"You know it's no problem." Shae lets me go, and I hurry to Cory's room to put Jodeci down. I still need to shower, call Ryan, and comfort Shae before I can even think about sleep.

Unlike Cara, Cory's weirdly clean. Everything in his room has to be a certain way, and if you knock it down, he'll immediately let you know he doesn't want you in there. He'll follow you closely to make sure you don't mess with his things. Meanwhile, Cara's room usually looks like a family of eight lives in there.

I carefully lay Jodeci next to Cory and pull the covers over the two of them. My dad turns off the lights. "Going to bed?" I ask him.

"Yeah, it's way past my bedtime." He jokes and pulls me into another hug. My dad was always affectionate, but never as much as he's been tonight. "Good night, son."

"Night." I hug him back. "Love you."

"Love you too." He plants a kiss on my forehead. He's taking it too far now, but I keep quiet to not ruin his moment. "I'm happy you're back."

I go to my old bedroom, closing the door to FaceTime Ryan.

"Hi, handsome." Her face pops up on my screen, showing off a warm smile. She's in bed, glasses on and with a bonnet on her head. As much as I hate the thing, it always makes me laugh when she remembers to wear it.

"Hi, Ry."

"How's it going?"

I sigh. "Everyone's just trying to keep it together from what I can tell." I close the door behind me and plop onto the bed. "How was your day?"

"Have you heard of *Game of Thrones?*"

I laugh. "I have . . . I didn't know you watch it."

"I didn't, but Nico and I watched like half the first season, and it's so good! Who knew those little fantasy characters could be so"—she pauses, blushing—"sexy and interesting."

"I've never seen it."

"Really?" Ryan replies. "I'll have to show you; you'll love it," she says. "That's basically all I did today. Other than miss you, of course."

"I miss you."

"You've been on my mind all day." Ryan tends to be a little bolder over the phone than in person, but the last couple of weeks, she's become flirtier.

"What about me?"

I know she's smiling without even looking. "Like I said, I just miss you," she tells me. "Just being around you . . . holding you, kissing you, and stuff."

I laugh. "And *stuff*, huh?" She's giggling, which only drives me crazy. My attraction to Ryan grows more intense with every day.

"How's it being home?"

"Weird," I confess. "The same unresolved issues."

"What do you mean?" Ryan doesn't know a lot about my family other than the fact that my mom's not around and that I don't talk about her. I'm not sure if she even knows who Manny is, besides knowing he's my best friend.

I wonder how much she knows Shae . . .

"It's just the same ole shit. Everyone's still broke, the neighborhood's still ugly, but now, Manny's not around to hang out with or distract me." I sigh. Being home does suck once I think about it. I don't blame Ryan for not coming.

"Have you seen him?"

"No, visiting hours were over by the time my flight landed. I'm going first thing in the morning. His sister's here, though. She's gonna sleep in Cara's room."

"Manny has a sister?"

I get up to change clothes. "He does. Sashanie. You might know her."

She contemplates. "I don't know . . . the name sounds familiar." I don't want to push, afraid it'd open up a sore wound from her past. I look at the screen to see her eyes closed. She's starting to relax.

"You want me to let you go, babe?" I ask her. "I know you're tired and you have class early."

Ryan yawns. "I want to talk to you." I change into basketball shorts and a T-shirt and get back in bed. "I wish you were here."

"I wish you were here too." I hope my words don't restart the argument from last night. Ryan keeps quiet, and I know she's avoiding the same thing. "What are your plans for this weekend?"

She sighs. "Nico said I'm not allowed to mope around, waiting until you come back . . ."

"I completely agree."

"I'm sure you do." She rolls her eyes. I need to talk to Shae, but Ryan wants me to stay on the phone. Hopefully she's asleep soon. "But I don't know. Maybe I'll hang out with her or with Jay and Troy."

"Who?"

Ryan giggles. "My floormates."

I didn't even know Ryan had male friends, so it's weird that, with all the time I've spent in Ryan's room, I haven't met them.

"I've told you about them before!" she replies, that infectious smile on her face. "This just goes to show how much you listen to me."

"I do listen to you, baby." To be honest, I probably wasn't in that moment. Those are two names I wouldn't forget. "I just forgot. Who are these guys?"

"Like I said, they're my floormates. Pretty much the only friends I have besides you." True. "I tried to introduce you once, but you weren't in the mood to meet them."

"When?"

"After practice—" A knock on the door takes me away from listening to Ryan.

"Come in!"

Ryan asks, "Who's knocking on your door?"

Shae walks in with bloodshot eyes.

"Hey." I smile at her. "I was just about to find you."

"I wasn't sure if you fell asleep."

No way in hell Ryan'll let me just say good night to her with no explanation. She gets jealous so easily.

"No, I'm just talking to Ryan. But I was about to go look for some food if you're hungry."

"Your dad has stuff for grilled cheese. I could make it for you, if you want." I'm about to decline her offer when she adds, "I'm getting hungry too."

"Thanks. Give me five minutes."

Shae nods and exits my room without a word, closing the door behind her.

"You have to go?" Ryan asks when my face appears back on the screen.

"I don't want to hang up, but I know Shae needs to talk . . ."

As always, Ryan's facial expression tells me how disappointed she is. "I'm sorry, baby."

She gives me that fake smile I haven't seen since we first met. "It's fine! I'm tired anyway . . . I'll talk to you tomorrow."

"I'll call you when I'm done. Don't wait up, though. Just go to bed, and if you hear the phone, answer it."

"You sure?"

"Yeah, give me an hour."

"Okay. I'll take a little nap until you call."

This way we end the conversation on a good note, which hopefully means sweet dreams and no overthinking. "I love you."

"I love you too. Good night."

"Good—"

She hangs up before I finish, telling me she's definitely mad.

I text her, ignoring how immature she's being.

> Don't be mad. I'll call you back. You know I have a lot going on. I love you.

I go to the kitchen to find Shae cooking. She smiles at me as I enter.

"I'll be done in a second," she says, flipping the sandwich in the sizzling pan. I wait until she sets my food on the table, unsure of how to start this conversation. However, she breaks the ice.

"So, you really like Javon's daughter, huh?" she says, going back to the stove to fry her own sandwich.

I nod. "Yeah, I do. Did you know about all the stuff that goes on in that house?"

She takes her time responding. "Um, I don't know . . . what'd she tell you?"

"Just about her dad—how awful he is . . . all the women, the drugs . . . Ivan." I was scared to bring up Ivan but wanted to see her reaction at the mention of his name.

She laughs. "You do know how Jodeci was brought into the world, right?"

"Dumb question . . . my fault."

"She shouldn't have told you that," Shae tells me. "The stuff that goes on in Javon's house"—she pauses—"I never wanted you or Manny to know about."

"It's a huge part of her life. She can't even come back here."

"Really?" Shae looks at me, surprised. If she knows what goes on in that house, why is she so shocked? "Javon and Ivan only talk about her behind closed doors, and I only saw her maybe a handful of times when I used to run with them. She was *so* quiet, but they'd say the nastiest things to her. I mean, she wouldn't get to her room without them saying something. I always thought she and Ivan had something going on, though. He's obsessed with her. I was surprised when they said she'd left for school."

"What makes you think they had something going on?" We aren't talking about what needs to be discussed, but Ryan's past has so many pieces I can't put together. I've always been confused about Ivan's possessive obsession with her.

"He has this nickname for her . . . it's weird." She puts her grilled cheese on the plate, turns off the stove, and comes to the table. "It was *Eternity.* Maybe it was a code name between the two of them. He has it tattooed in big letters on his chest too. She'd go to her room, and we'd be hanging out, partying or whatever, and he'd just go back there. Javon would do nothing. I mean, Ivan's the boss, but Ryan's his daughter . . . he couldn't just . . ." She stops talking, deep in thought.

I can't tell her what Ivan did to Ryan. It's not my story to tell, plus I don't want to make the night more depressing than it already is. "I don't know everything," I lie. "I just know that some fucked-up stuff went on in that house. She can't even talk about it."

"As she shouldn't," Shae says. "Javon and Ivan are really big on discretion."

"Do you still talk to them?"

Her response is instant. "Nope." She shakes her head. "They kicked me to the curb the moment I decided to keep my baby."

"That's fucked up."

She nods. Part of me feels like she still has some loyalty to them; she seems to be picking her words. "A baby doesn't fit into that life. I'm happy I got out when I did. Jodeci doesn't need to be around that."

"And you had Manny . . . he's better than any other guy around here."

"Definitely." Shae laughs, tears falling down her face instantly at the mention of her brother. "What am I going to do if he doesn't make it?" she whispers, wiping her tears. "What are *we* going to do?"

"You can't talk like that. What have the doctors said?"

"The coma was induced to help the swelling in his brain go down. He lost a lot of blood, though, so we just have to take it day by day for now." We can do nothing to help him. "I just hate seeing him like that . . . tubes down his throat and shit. I know he hates it." She's right. If Manny has any awareness, he's not happy being so weak.

"I miss him." I don't have the words to make her feel better or ease her thoughts. I'm going through all the same emotions. Manny has always been my confidant, my brother, my protector. I've always been bigger, and when our other friends got caught up in gangs or selling drugs, he'd been the one to influence me to take the football route. "Do we have any idea who did this to him?"

She shakes her head. "The police said he was just walking home. They tried so hard to put the blame on him, asked us if he was involved in a public shooting." Shae's breath shakes as she continues to cry. "Once you left for college, he started hanging out with some of y'all's high school friends that worked for Ivan. He promised he wasn't involved with selling the girls. Just weed . . . nothing bad."

"You let him do that?" Ivan and Javon have their shit wrapped up in too many of my people's lives.

"How could I stop him?" Shae yells. "He made up his mind, and he had *no one* after you left, especially good influences. We needed money, and all of a sudden, Manny started coming home with some. Not a lot, but enough to make things easier. He told me he wasn't into the serious shit, and I didn't question him after that."

I try my hardest to suppress my anger. I can do nothing now, except make sure our families are safe. "Are Javon and Ivan behind this?"

"I don't know. I don't think so. The police are investigating, but we haven't heard anything yet." She places her hand on top of mine, tears falling down her face. "I already feel bad.

I should've stopped him . . . your dad and my mom know everything now."

I pull her in for a hug. "It's not your fault," I say, trying to make her feel better. "You didn't shoot him."

CHAPTER 18

DEVYN

My dad takes his sweet time getting to the hospital, which does nothing to ease my nervousness about seeing Manny. My mind's racing with thoughts. How will he look with tubes down his throat and a bullet wound in his neck? I need to get this over with—the sooner the better.

After I spent the morning FaceTiming Ryan, my dad had the bright idea to go out for a family breakfast, only prolonging the time. After we wait for everyone to get ready, including Manny's sister and mom, it's damn near three o'clock by the time we pull into the parking lot. Everyone's demeanor changes the closer we get to him, and the absence of smiling and joking puts me on edge. If I wasn't ready to see Manny before, I'm definitely not ready now.

We take the elevator up to the seventh floor. The ICU looks more like an insane asylum with its white walls and white floors. Hospitals are not places of comfort. It's all cold and unwelcoming, as if the building itself was trying to push everyone out . . .

Is that why Manny's here?

"Do you want to go first? Only two people can go in at a time," Manny's mom asks me as we walk into the lobby.

"I can go with you," Cory says. I know Shae wants to come with me, but I don't have the heart to tell my little brother no. We haven't talked much since I got back.

"Let's go." I put Cara in the chair next to my dad so that she can go back to sleep. Shae sadly slumps in the chair on the other side of him, but I ignore her. I don't have the strength to focus on her right now.

Cory takes my hand. "He's in here." He points to the slightly open door with 703 on the front. As we walk in, an old man sits consoling two adult children as a woman sleeps silently in a hospital bed. I keep my eyes down at my little brother, not wanting to interrupt their moment.

Manny's on the side closest to the window, which makes his area of the three-person room a little less cold. He lies on his back, a large blue oxygen tube down his throat. He's grown out his Afro since I last saw him, which is huge and touches his shoulders. He looks sick, his light brown skin pale and his face skinny. He hasn't been in the hospital for a week yet, and he's already fading before my eyes.

"It's okay if you have to cry," Cory whispers, squeezing my hand. "I did."

I need to be strong.

How can someone go from so healthy and happy and alive to so dead in days?

I take the chair from the corner of the room and set it next to Manny's bed before pulling Cory into my lap. "You think he can hear us?"

His little shoulders rise in a shrug. "Dad said he might be able to." He reaches over and grabs Manny's hand. "I miss you, Manny. We usually play basketball on Friday nights, and I'm going to miss that tonight."

I smile, surprised by the fact that Manny keeps his and my tradition from high school going with Cory. "Even though you always win and pick on me the whole ride home . . . I wouldn't be mad if you picked on me today."

Tears fall down my face, and I brush them off. *Be strong.*

Cory looks at me. "Your turn."

"I came all the way here just for you to be laid up in bed." I chuckle.

Cory nudges me, telling me to be serious. He's still holding Manny's hand, despite the fact he can't hold it back.

"Nah, but for real, I miss you. I'm sad not having you around . . . maybe that's how you felt when I left for school. You never told me if it was." I pause for a moment to pull myself together. Cory's not looking at me, but he's listening. "Come back to us, Man. Your family needs you . . . Shae's going to lose it soon. We always said we were going to get the fuck out of here, and that can't happen if you're not here. I'm holding onto my end of the deal . . . you have to do your part too."

Cory turns to look at me. "He heard that."

I laugh as a couple more tears fall from my eyes. "Yeah?" I wipe my face. "What makes you say that?"

"You just have to believe it." Cory lays Manny's hand back on the bed before giving me a hug. "I know I'm not big like you and Manny yet, but I'm here for you. He was my brother too."

I used to get on Cory for being so emotional, and Manny used to get on me for calling him soft. He always said there'd come a day when I'd need him more than he needs me, and that softness would come in handy.

Who would've thought he'd be right?

***

RYAN

I forgot how much fun it is to get dressed up and go out with your friends.

Not that I went out much in high school, but getting cute, taking pictures, and going out is just so exciting. It's different from dressing up to go out with your boyfriend.

We decided to go for dinner and drinks at this Mediterranean restaurant that doesn't card. Nico told us about the place, and we're meeting in her room at eleven o'clock sharp. However, the clock just hit 10:40 p.m., and I've just finished getting dressed. I look in the mirror, taking in my tight black jeans and low-cut bodysuit, feeling good. I rush to the closet to pull on hot pink, heeled boots I've been saving for a day like this and then grab my phone to show Devyn my outfit. However, I see he texted me over an hour ago.

> **Devyn:** Are you home? Need to talk but don't want to stop your fun.

I call him, happy when he answers the phone immediately.

"What's wrong?" I ask before his face appears on the screen. However, when it does, I see puffy red eyes and a deep frown. He's been crying.

"Where are you?" he snaps.

"Home. I didn't hear my phone earlier." I go over to the table and sit down. "Are you okay? How's Manny?"

"He's in a coma. Tubes down his throat. He can't move. On the outside, he looks pretty dead to me." It hurts me to hear his words, so I know they hurt to say. "Don't talk like that, baby. He could be healing for all you know." "He's stronger than me," Devyn says. "He took care of everyone. I can't do that. It's too hard to be strong for everyone. I almost lost it in that hospital room earlier. Everyone's dependent on me to find a way to suddenly heal him, or worse, heal them from their pain, but I can do nothing to make things better. I can't take this shit." Devyn stops talking and lets out a loud sob. He covers his face with his hands, hiding tears. I've never seen him like this. Not even when he first found out about Manny. "I can't be there for everyone while trying to keep it together myself. He's my brother too. No one sees that."

I know only one thing I can do to make things better. Despite my fear of going home, I'll do it for Devyn. I love him way too much to watch him suffer. He's always so strong, but the weight of this is too much.

"Let me be strong for you," I tell him as calmly as I can. I don't know if he heard me through all the sobs, but he doesn't need to worry about my anxiousness too. "I'm coming to LA."

CHAPTER 19

DEVYN

I know I'm an awful person for letting Ryan come back to LA, but I need her here more than I care to admit.

Seeing Manny so helpless in the hospital was hard for me, and being back in this fucked-up neighborhood makes things harder. This place can't do anyone any good. I could easily ignore all G-Height's problems when I wasn't here. But the burdens don't usually fall entirely on my shoulders.

Before, I could get out of situations with words and the credibility I got from football. People saw my talent and knew I could get out of here. They knew I'd take care of my family and Manny's. But until the time comes, Manny's supposed to hold down the fort. I'll make the money and he'll be in charge of our family's protection. When I make it to the league, he'll be my right hand and make sure my family's covered.

Acting as another older brother for my siblings and a son to my dad while taking care of his own family, he's exceeded my expectations. My dad works a lot, and Manny took on what I could no longer do while at school. He's there for Cory, understanding him in a way I can't. He plays an important role in both our families, and I'm not the person to take on his tasks. How am I going to keep it all together?

Ryan's presence here will give me the smallest outlet to vent in a way I can't with family. She's an even bigger confidant than Manny. You can't be vulnerable with your niggas the way you can your girl. Last night, she caught a seat on the last red-eye to LA, so her flight lands at 7:05 a.m. I'm in baggage claim, waiting for her to land.

> **Ryan (6:37 a.m.):** In LA! Hope you're awake. Should I meet you at your house?

> **Me (6:37 a.m.):** I'm here. Did you check a bag?

> **Ryan:** Nope.

I wait at the bottom of the escalator with the other friends and family members. After fifteen minutes, people come down in pairs, only increasing my anticipation to see my girl. When she appears, a weight lifts from my shoulders. She smiles when she sees me, practically pushing people out of the way as she runs down the steps toward me.

"Hi!" she exclaims, jumping into my arms. I squeeze her, so happy she's here and she's made it safely.

"You okay?"

She leans back and attaches her lips to mine. "I'm good. I missed you."

I hold onto her, not saying anything. It feels too great to have her back in my arms. She'll never understand how much her being here means to me.

The ride back to my house takes less than twenty minutes, and I instantly kick myself for not taking a longer way to ease Ryan into being back home to her personal hell. Her demeanor changes before my eyes as she slouches down in the seat so no one can see her and her words shorten. She's crawling back into the shell I pulled her out of two months ago.

I park my old black Nissan Xterra in the garage, waiting to speak until the door's all the way shut. Everyone's home, so I'll take my time going inside. I need to make sure Ryan's good.

I unbuckle my seat belt and kiss her, knowing affection will melt some of her worries. Her response isn't immediate, but she kisses me back. "Talk to me." I press my forehead against hers. "Tell me how you're feeling."

"I don't want to be another burden for you."

I kiss her again. "You're not a burden, Ryan."

"I hate it here," she whispers. I look for tears but don't find any. "Everything about this place is filled with a bad memory, and it's scary. You know they're eventually going to figure out I'm back."

She's right, but they can't touch her around me, or in this house. I wouldn't have asked her to come if I thought she'd be in danger. "I hate it here too."

A sigh of relief flies from her body. "You do?"

I nod. "I *promise* you. We won't be here for longer than a week, and one day, we won't ever come back. I'm going to make sure this place is just a memory for both of us." I reach over to unbuckle her seat belt and tug her toward me, so she's straddling my waist. Her short, curvy body fits perfectly in my lap, as usual.

"You're amazing." Ryan looks at me through glistening, dilated eyes, and then leans in to kiss me. "I'm here to help you in any way I can."

"You already are." The accumulated sexual tension from days of separation sparks. Ryan only gets sexier the more confident she becomes. I lean in, pressing my head against hers. "I want to be alone with you, but we have to get past my family." She giggles, and I give her another kiss. "Nervous?"

She nods.

"It's not like it's your first time meeting them."

"The circumstances are a little different this time."

I shake my head. "They'll see what I see—you're perfect."

We kiss some more before Ryan climbs back to the passenger seat and gets out of the car. I follow her lead and get her suitcase, surprised when she doesn't fight me for it. She takes my hand and we enter the house, where I can instantly hear everyone in the kitchen.

"Dad!" I call. "We're home!"

"Kitchen!" he calls back. My dad smiles when he sees us. "Hey!" he says as he sets a plate of sausage in between Cara, Cory, and Jodeci, who are all devouring bowls of Captain Crunch.

"Hi!" Ryan smiles at him. My dad comes over to give her a welcoming hug.

"I'm so happy you decided to come," he says once he lets her go. He's never been so friendly to my other friends, so he must like her. I think he grew a soft spot for her after taking her to the airport.

"Thank you for letting me stay here." She smiles. It's her shy smile, but it's genuine. "I'm sure you know how much it means to me."

"It's no problem. Welcome home."

I squeeze her hand, knowing I'm right—there's nothing for her to worry about. My family is overly welcoming to whoever enters our gates.

"You guys hungry?"

"I'm okay. I ate on the plane." The pitch of her voice changes, and I know she's lying.

I pull her into me, wrapping my arm around her shoulder. "We're going to lunch sometime before or after we see Manny, so I'll wait too."

"Well, we have more than enough if y'all change your mind." The oven beeps, and Dad excuses himself to turn it off before pulling out a tray of biscuits from the rack. Damn, he's going all out.

My siblings are being shy, so I pull Ryan over to the kitchen table to introduce them. "Cara and Cory, have you guys met Ryan?"

They shake their heads. "Are you Devy's girlfriend?" Cara asks Ryan. I grab the sausage off her plate, and she hits my hand. "There's a whole plate right there!" she yells, then uses her chubby fingers to grab three more.

"It tastes better off your plate." I laugh. "Yes, Ryan's my girlfriend, and she'll be staying with us for a few days. She came to help me take care of Manny."

Cory puts some sausage on Jodeci's plate, saying, "Sit next to me." Ryan visibly relaxes and lets go of my hand to do as she's told. "I like your name, Ryan. I only know boys named Ryan."

"It's different, huh?" She chuckles. "But I'm glad you like it. You must be Cory."

"Yep!" He smiles big, showing off a missing front tooth. "And that's my sister Cara, and this is Jodeci. He's my nephew."

I laugh. "Say hi, Jodi. Don't be rude."

"Hi!" Jodeci screams with a mouthful of cereal.

"Hey!" Ryan smiles. "Cara, that's a very pretty dress you've got on."

She's wearing an orange dress with a white long-sleeve shirt underneath.

"Thank you!" she says. "My dad got it for me."

"Yeah? Your dad's got an eye for fashion."

"I think so too." She giggles. "I love dresses."

Ryan leans against the table, intrigued by her conversation with my little sister. "Well, you look great in them." She smiles. "I love dresses, too, but it's a little too cold in New York for me to wear many."

"We can match one day! I've never done that before."

"I'd love that," Ryan gasps. "I'll be here all week, so just give me a day, and we'll work something out."

"Cool." Cara smiles. I go over to the stove to grab a couple of biscuits, figuring I don't need to listen to this conversation. I make Ryan a plate, assuming she's hungry despite her words.

"Can I have my girl back now?" I ask as they laugh over something Jodeci says.

"How rude, Devy," Cara says. "We're having a conversation."

"Ryan's your brother's guest," my dad intervenes. "You'll have more time to talk to her later."

"Of course you will." Ryan smiles, getting up from the table.

"We can eat in my room," I suggest. Ryan nods. "This way."

"It's so different from your room at school," she says once we've opened the door. I set our plates on my bed. Ryan looks around at pictures and football trophies. "Less grown but still very *you*."

I smile. "Well, it is me." A lot of memories were made in this room I know she doesn't want to know about. I pull her into me for a hug. "Thank you," I whisper. "I'm so happy you're here."

Ryan wraps her arms around my neck. "I'm happy to be back in your arms again." I back up and sit on the bed, pulling her into my lap. "Is it bad we feel this way after only a couple of days?"

I laugh. "A couple days too long."

"Right." She giggles. "I feel the same way."

"I hope my family wasn't too much for you."

"Of course not; they're great. It'll be nice to get to know them." She pauses before adding, "If that's okay."

That's my girl. Always second-guessing herself, even at the most irrelevant times.

"Why wouldn't it be okay?"

She shrugs. "It's your family; I don't want to overstep my boundaries."

"You're family too," I say, making her smile. How doesn't she know I want to spend the rest of my life with her? To me, it's obvious. "Don't overthink it, Ry. Spend as much time with them as you want." I grab one of the plates and hand it to her. "Eat up."

"But—"

"Eat," I say again. "I know damn well no food is offered on an economy flight from New York to LA." She doesn't argue but instead takes a bite of the biscuit on her plate.

"I was hungry," she admits, making me laugh.

"I don't know why you said you weren't," I tell her. "There's enough for the million people in this house, trust me."

My dad rushed to the store when I told him Ryan was coming. He'd grown up in one of those houses that always had snacks and people coming in and out at all times. I think he wants our home to be like that, too, but sometimes things are hard.

"Are you missing football?"

I shake my head. "Just games. It's nice to have a little break from practice, but I still have to keep up with workouts."

"You do them here?"

"Running and lifting. I know all the plays."

Ryan finishes her biscuit and hands me another one.

"We have a bench press in the garage, so that'll be easy. And I can run anywhere."

"Be careful, okay? I don't know what I'd do if something happened to you."

I nod. "Always." I laugh. "I don't know why you don't believe me when I say you're going to be stuck with me for a long time."

"I'm holding you to that." She leans in and presses a kiss to the corner of my mouth.

***

RYAN

Devyn is *home*, no matter where it is, and being back in his arms is perfection. We finish breakfast, spend the morning lying in bed, and take our time getting ready to see Manny.

I make sure to keep my head low as we pull out of the garage and turn toward the hospital. I know that either my dad or Ivan are bound to figure out I'm here soon, and I need to prepare for what's coming.

We drive in silence, the DVSN album the only noise between us. I pray Devyn won't have another breakdown. I'm more nervous for him to see Manny than I am for myself.

I only ever saw him in passing at school or messing around outside his house with Devyn or Jodeci. From what Devyn says, he seems like a great guy—friend- and family-oriented, caring, and a brother to Devyn. He cared for Devyn's family while he was in New York, and I'm sad this happened to such a good person.

I take Devyn's hand as we walk into the doors of the hospital and to the ICU. A small Mexican woman walks out as we get to the door. Devyn lets go of my hand to give her a hug. "Baby, this is Manny's mom," he tells me after they exchange words. "This is Ryan."

"Nice to meet you." She gives me a smile that doesn't reach her sad, glistening eyes. "I'm sorry it's under these circumstances."

"Me too." I shake her hand. "Is he getting better?" I'm afraid I asked the wrong question but can't tell by Devyn's face.

"The doctor says he's healing better since the blood transfusion, so that's a start." She looks at Devyn. "We just have to be patient."

"A little better is something, right?" I say to encourage them. Instantly, I can tell it's the wrong thing. I need to shut up; I'm no help.

"You're right," Manny's mother says with a forced smile. "I'll see you guys later." She touches Devyn's shoulder on her way down the hall.

"Come on. Let's go say hello." Devyn motions for us to go inside.

I take a seat next to him beside Manny and listen as he talks to him about school. He apologizes for not calling once a week like he originally promised, explaining he got caught up with football or school or tutoring (which I think means me). He gets lost talking about the season and how much he loves college, saying he wished Manny would've come. Who would've known Manny also got a scholarship to Truth? I'm hypnotized watching Devyn get so wrapped up in talking to his best friend. I know he misses him and blames himself for not keeping better tabs on him.

I think Devyn even forgets I'm there, because the clock strikes three by the time he finishes. "I hope you wake up soon," he says, letting me know he's done. Devyn turns to look at me. "I'm sorry if that took too long."

"It's fine." I smile. "I'm sure it means a lot to him that you came all this way to make sure he's good." I reach over and place my hand on his leg. "I love you."

I get the first genuine smile from him since we found out about Manny. "I love you too." He leans in and kisses me. "Hungry?"

"Starving."

"That's what I like to hear." Devyn gets up from his seat. "Let's get out of here." He takes my hand and gently pulls me from the chair.

"I wish I could've met him under different circumstances," I admit.

"Me too." Devyn sighs. "But he'll be okay . . . we just need to stay positive." Devyn cups my face and slowly kisses my lips. "It's good he can't see us right now, though," he whispers. "He'd definitely have something to say about how I can't stop touching you."

I laugh as Devyn showers me with kisses. "We're being rude." I step away from him and grab my purse from the chair. I place my hand on top of Manny's and give it a little squeeze. I really do hope to meet him soon. "See you tomorrow, Manny."

***

Despite all our drama, Devyn and I manage to have a good day. We go to Melrose for lunch and spend the day walking around, filling each other up with affection. For the first time, I'm enjoying being back in my hometown. California's nice without the heavy weight that sat on my back before. While it took us thirty minutes to get there from the hospital, it took triple the time to get back to his house. We're both exhausted when we arrive at Devyn's and immediately fall into bed. An hour later, I'm in the arms of the man I love, a *Snapped* marathon playing behind us as we devour each other. I'm tucked underneath him, our lips and tongues colliding and hips perfectly aligned as we grind against each other. We're still clothed, but I'm panting and ready for him. With every moment like this, my want for him grows.

I pull off his shirt, figuring he's waiting for my signal, and quickly unbutton his shorts. Devyn sucks on my neck as his hands search for the tie that will unleash my body from my halter dress.

His eyes lock with mine. Our noses touch as we take a moment to catch our breath. This isn't our first time being nearly naked in front of each other in nothing but our underwear, but something feels different. The last bit of sun glimmers through the window, giving his room an auburn hue, making the room hot and his body glow. This is the moment I've been dreaming about for so long.

"Should we stop?" Devyn breathes. He rests a little of his weight on me but instantly pulls away as his large erection presses against my inner thigh.

"I don't want to." I wrap my arms around him and pull him back, kissing him again and adding tongue.

"Ryan." He stops me again. "I'm not trying to ruin this, but I need to know how—"

I kiss him again to shut him up. I don't need him to worry. I'm about to give myself to him completely. I'm not worried, and I need him to know I trust him with everything.

"Make love to me." That's what I need. Not just sex or fucking or hooking up. I need to have this experience with the man I love. The only man I've ever loved. He's enamored me with his friendship and love and care for me, treating me with more kindness than anyone ever has. I will always love him for that.

Devyn gets up from the bed to lock the door. I keep my eyes on him as he goes to the dresser to get a condom from the top drawer, and then steps out of his underwear before coming back to the bed.

He climbs on top of me, and I pull him close, excited about how naked he is pressed against me. "Are you sure?" he asks in between kisses. "I love you so much, Ry. I can't mess this up."

His vulnerability turns my soft heart into melted goo. Horny and riled up, he still manages to worry about me first. "I have no doubt in my mind about having sex with you right now," I say, making him laugh. "I love you and I want to be close to you. I'm never going to regret that."

Devyn pulls me into another kiss. His hands fall to my panties and he pulls them down, and then he moves to press his mouth against my vagina. He sucks harder on my clit than usual, making my arousal come fast, and then slides two fingers inside me. A soft moan falls from my lips as his fingers move in and out. He waits until he brings the stars back to my eyes to remove his mouth, keeping his fingers inside.

He lifts himself so we're eye to eye, still massaging me inside with his fingers. When he moves them, he aligns his erection to my opening and pushes against it.

"Look at me." I open my eyes and they lock with his. I gasp when he slides inside me. "I love you." His breath hitches as he pulls me closer. He kisses me before going deeper. "Fuck..."

"I love you," I pant as he rocks his hips, moving back and forth, massaging me in just the right spot. He's everywhere, his weight fully on top of me, his lips on my neck and his hands in my hair, completely covering me in his love. This moment is better than I could have ever imagined. I'm with the person I want to spend my life with, making love and enjoying it. I'm able to be intimate with Devyn in a way I didn't know was possible. He's cured my disgust of sex, and I'm so happy it brings tears to my eyes.

Of course, he instantly catches my crying. "What's wrong? Am I hurting you?" He stops, but I'm happy he doesn't pull out.

"No, keep going." He pulls me on top and sits back on the bed, somehow still inside me. The shift of motion hits me in a sensitive spot deep in my belly. Devyn grabs my hips, rocking them back and forth slowly. We both let out in-sync moans as his head falls back on the headboard.

His slanted eyes move with mine as I find my rhythm. He lets go of my hips and lets me do my thing, bringing one hand to my face to wipe away my tears. "You're still crying," he whispers.

I pull him into me, going from rocking my hips to bouncing them on his erection. I kiss him again. "I want this forever." His hips meet mine halfway, and more pleasure splurges through my body. I pull him closer, moaning. He places his lips on mine to silence me.

"I want *you* forever." He pulls my hips down and moves them backward and forward, faster. More pressure builds inside of me, and I want to scream. "You feel . . . so . . . good." His fingers move back down to my clit and he rubs it in slow circles, kissing my lips. Devyn uses his other hand to rock my hips faster, and I lose it. My body shakes and sparks seem to fly from my mouth and ears and eyes. Devyn holds my shaking body tightly, my mouth buried in his chest as I let out a loud moan. The orgasm hits like a tidal wave, and then slowly gets calmer. My blurred vision clears. Devyn and I are both breathing hard. I don't even notice him come and pull out.

I wrap my arms around his neck, burying my face in the nape. "I love you." I travel kisses from his neck to his cheek to his lips. "We did it."

Devyn laughs, wrapping his arms around me, his eyes on mine. "I mean what I said. I want you forever. I want this forever. I can't imagine there ever being another time when we aren't each other's."

"Me either." I kiss him again. "You're everything I could ever want and more. I want to be with you forever too." He flips me back onto the bed and we're at it again.

CHAPTER 20

RYAN

A loud thud comes from another room in the house. My eyes fly open and my heart stops. The room is pitch black, the only light coming from the clock on Devyn's cable box.

Screams echo from the same distant place, and I reach over to find that Devyn's not next to me. I instantly jump up, knowing he's somewhere near the noise and hoping it's not him. I pull on a pair of pajama shorts and a T-shirt and rush out of the room, stopping in the hallway to avoid being seen once I hear the familiar voice of my father.

"You're going to let me see my daughter!" he slurs angrily. He's high as a kite. How'd he find out I was here already? It hasn't even been twenty-four hours. I peek at them from behind the living room entrance.

"She doesn't want to see you," Devyn's father says. At least Devyn's not alone with him. God only knows what would happen. "Give her a break, Javon."

"My own fucking daughter comes all the way back here and doesn't tell me? All y'all got me fucked up!"

"She didn't come here for you," Devyn says, his voice stern.

My father laughs. "You think because she gives you pussy, you get to control who sees her and who doesn't? Fuck you!" The volatile words make me flinch. More commotion comes from the entrance of the house as he tries to push past the door and past Devyn and his dad into the house. "Ryan! Ryan!"

I need to shut him up. He'll wake the little kids if he continues, and this is the last thing they need to see. I step into the living room, and his screaming stops. His eyes go wide as he sees the new, college version of his daughter instead of the shy, insecure, and hidden girl he forgot to take to the airport my last day here.

Devyn comes over to me, but I keep my eyes on my dad. He's made all this ruckus about seeing me, and I want to know what he has to say. He looks older, paler, and even dirtier since I last saw him. His black hair has grayed, running past his shoulders, and his teeth are yellow. He's an exact example of how this community can destroy you, filling you with drugs and alcohol and let it consume you. Devyn touches my arm, breaking my eye contact.

"I got this," he says for only me to hear.

I look at my father, who's still stunned in silence. Devyn's dad still has an arm on him, guarding him from me. "Get out," I tell him.

"Y-you're coming with me," my dad stutters. He tries to slap Devyn's dad's hand away as he stands up straighter to assert himself. "Pack up your shit so I can take you home."

"She's not going anywhere with you," Devyn scoffs, but I touch his arm to stop him. He can never fight the battle between me and my father. I've fought this battle my whole life.

"I already told you I'm never going back to that house, and that you'd never see me again. After all the pain you've inflicted on me, the least you can do is leave me alone."

"You call taking care of your fat ass pain?" He laughs again. "The only thing I did was save your ass from living on the street."

"Just go!" I raise my voice. "Go! I'm not going anywhere with you!"

"Yes, the fuck you are!" He loses it, punching Devyn's dad in the side of the head and rushing toward me. "You think Ivan will let me—" Devyn shoves me behind him and uses his other hand to easily knock my dad to the floor. He hits the wall with a thud and then collapses.

A scream makes everyone pause, and I turn to find Cara in the hallway, watching us. She cries frantically, and I run over, rushing to get her out of the room. She clings to me immediately.

"Get Cara out of here," Devyn's dad says. Devyn is at his side. My dad lies nearly passed out on the floor, murmuring something I can't make out.

I hurry to Devyn's room, closing the door behind us so Cara's sobs don't wake Jodeci, Shae, or Cory. "Did that man hurt my dad?" she cries once she eventually calms down.

I shake my head. "No, he'll be fine." I sit on the bed, still holding her.

"I don't want him to be in the hospital like Manny." Tears continue to trickle down her face.

"He's not going to the hospital." I wipe her cheeks. "Why would you say that?"

"My dad said to stay away from that guy, because he hurt Manny."

Before I can ask her more questions, Devyn enters the room looking unfazed. "Javon's gone." He comes over and sits next to me on the bed. Cara climbs onto his lap and he envelops her in his arms. "You okay?" She nods as he wipes away her tears with his thumb.

"How's your dad?" I ask.

"He's lying down. The hit just winded him." His attention is focused on his sister. "He wants you to sleep in his room, Cara. He needs someone to keep an eye out on him."

"What if something bad happens? We should take him to the doctor," Cara replies.

"He's fine." He smiles warmly, and all I can do is wonder what's really going through his mind. He puts on such a brave face. "If you get worried, come wake me up, okay?" He kisses the top of her head. "Go get some sleep; Dad needs you." Cara hugs him and plants a kiss on his cheek before sliding off his lap.

"Good night, Ryan," she says, hugging me. I hug her back and watch as she skips out of the room, happy her father is safe and she gets to take care of him. That type of happiness can only come from caring for a father who's cared for you, and I envy her.

Devyn waits till she's in their dad's room before getting up to close the door and shed his clothes. He gets back in the bed, and I follow his lead, extracting my clothes and getting in next to him.

We lie in silence, my mind playing what just happened over and over. What gives my father the nerve to disrupt these people's lives after everything they've been through? Especially if he has something to do with what happened to Manny. And poor Cara. The last thing she needs is to be exposed to this. She's too pure and surrounded by too much love to ever have to deal with the hatefulness of this place.

"How'd you get him to leave?" I ask.

"Threw his ass right out and left him on the curb. All the police that roam the streets around here at night—they'll deal with him."

I've caused all this commotion, possibly scarring his sister for life just by being here. "I'm sorry," I tell Devyn.

"What're you apologizing for?"

"This is my fault. If I hadn't come back—"

"Stop." He turns his body toward me, resting his head in his hand. "I asked you to come." He sighs. "We knew there'd be problems."

"I didn't think my dad would barge in here in the middle of the night."

"He's a drug addict, Ryan." For some reason, it hurts me to hear what I already know. "He's unpredictable." Devyn holds my waist and pulls me close to him. "I didn't want you to know he came."

"It could've been worse if he hadn't seen me. What if he woke up the boys? Who would've known what we'd be dealing with now?" Does Devyn blame himself for this too? "I have to tell you something."

"What is it?"

I'm nervous about how he'll take this. He might really blame me after hearing what my dad could have done to Manny. "Cara told me your dad said Javon was the one who hurt Manny."

"What?" Devyn's eyes go wide. "He's never said anything about that to me."

"Why would he say something to Cara?" We're close, talking in hushed tones so no one can hear. "What if he hurt Manny because we're together?"

"That's sick." Devyn shakes his head. "But nah, that can't be it. Manny was working for your dad and Ivan. Shae said he was selling for them."

"Selling?" Maybe Manny wasn't such a great guy . . .

"Just drugs. If they did something to him, that has to be why."

"Why didn't you tell me before?"

"Because I know you, and you'd only blame yourself," he replies. "You're doing it right now. But, baby, this life you were put in will never be your fault."

I hold back the tears his healing words bring. "Devyn, being with me shouldn't bring harm to your family. Manny could die all because I fell in love. I won't do that to you."

"So, what's your plan?" His words are defensive, and I know I've upset him. "Go talk to your dad? Go back to that house?"

"Why are you mad? I just want everything to go back to normal . . . for you to be happy!"

"Because no matter what I do, who I fight, who I try to protect you from, your only solution to fixing things is to end this. To let niggas who hurt you, who *raped* you, destroy our relationship? And for what? So we can both be miserable? To make them think they have even more control over you and my family and everyone else who comes from G-Heights?"

"But what do I do to protect *you*?" I sit up. "They can't touch you, Devyn. My dad and Ivan, they know we're here, and I don't know how far they'll go to do what they want to do to me. I love you more than anyone in this world, and I think they know that." Tears fall from my eyes at the thought of harm ever coming Devyn's way. "I will lose it if they hurt you. I will lose it and I will never come back from it."

Devyn sits up and takes my hand in his. "A few hours ago, we agreed that this is forever. Don't you think that's worth fighting for?" I see the sadness in his eyes as he begs me to hold on. "I love *you*, Ryan. I'd do anything for you, and I'm not afraid of your dad, Ivan, or anyone else. No one can keep me away from you as long as you want this."

"I do want this."

"Then let's figure this out together." He squeezes my hand. "No matter what happens, you're the only one who can really hurt me. Without you, this shit isn't worth fighting for."

"It's not worth fighting without you, either," I whisper. He's right. If I end things, we'd both just be fragile.

"Fight with me." He pulls me into his lap, and rests his forehead against mine. "Combine your fighting style with mine, and they should be afraid of us."

I laugh, loving him for making me smile even in sadness. "What're we going to do?"

He cups my face and kisses me, slowly and sweetly. "We'll talk to my dad and ask him about what Cara said. I'll go to the police and see if they have any leads on what happened to Manny. He'll get better, we'll make sure everyone's good, and then we'll get the fuck out of here. Back to school and tutoring and football. Back to focusing on each other."

I'm not sure I can trust his words, but I'd do anything to make this work. To make sure his family is safe and that mine is far away from them.

***

The kitchen looks like a busy restaurant after I shower and come down for breakfast. Devyn's dad cooks like a madman as the kids run around him, playing. Pots fill the sink and what looks like a dozen different platters of food are placed on the table.

"Hey." Devyn's dad smiles at me as he sets a pitcher of orange juice on the table. "How'd you sleep?"

"Good," I tell him. "How's your head? Can I help with anything?"

"Nah, I'm almost done." Cara runs past him, carrying a doll with a matching princess dress in her hands, and he stops her. "We'll eat after Cara sets the table." She rolls her eyes but runs to the table to do as she was told.

"Your head?" I ask again.

"All good," he tells me. "Are you doing okay?" I nod as Devyn strides into the kitchen. He comes over and wraps his arms around me from behind.

"Morning." I smile as he plants a kiss on my cheek. His dad escapes to the table to assist Cara.

"Good morning." I turn my head so Devyn can kiss me. "People are outside for you."

"Who?" I ask, praying it's not my dad.

He shrugs. "Some girls."

I creep to the front door, Devyn following behind, and see my oldest and best friends, Hope and Diana.

"You *are* here!" Hope exclaims, rushing to hug me.

"Wow! Hi!" I hug her back, and then hug Diana standing next to her. "What are you guys doing here?"

"Seeing you," Diana says. "Why didn't you tell us you were coming back?"

I'm happy to see them, but with everything going on, they're the last two people on my mind. "I got back yesterday,"

I tell them. "We just came to check on Manny." I look behind me and motion Devyn to come closer. "You guys know Devyn, right?"

"Hey." He smiles at them.

"Hey," they say in unison.

"Wait . . . I thought you said you were his tutor?" I see Hope's just as blunt as she was before I left. It's been weeks since we've all talked, so they don't know we're together.

I laugh, leaning into Devyn behind me. "I'm his girlfriend too." Hope and Diana look at each other, exchanging secret glances I can't read. I'm not surprised. They believe all the things I thought about Devyn before I got to know him.

"How long are you here?" Hope asks.

"Just a few days."

"Can we take you to breakfast or something?" Diana asks next. "We need to catch up."

"Obviously," Hope adds, motioning toward me and Devyn.

I know Devyn won't mind, but we have a full day of investigating to do and little time to do it. "I can't today," I tell them. "We have to go see Manny once visitor hours open." Neither of them attempts to hide their disappointment.

"Maybe tonight?" Hope responds. "Come on, we need a little time with our girl. We haven't seen you in months."

"Tomorrow?" I suggest. "We can go to breakfast." I'll feel bad if I don't manage to schedule a little time with them before I leave . . . especially now they know I'm here.

"Perfect!" Hope says. "My mom has the late shift tomorrow, so I'll borrow her car and pick you up."

"I can drop her off on my way to see Manny," Devyn butts in. He looks down at me. "I mean, if you want."

I can tell Hope's about to refute him, but Diana quickly steps in. "Either one. As long as we get a little time with you, Ry."

I nod. "I promise . . . I really miss you guys."

Jodeci dashes through the door, a piece of bacon in his little fingers. "Time to eat!" He runs over to Devyn and hands him the bacon, making him laugh.

"I'll give you a minute," Devyn says to me. He picks up Jodeci. "It's nice to see you guys."

"You too." Diana smiles at him.

Devyn plants a kiss atop my head and goes into the house, leaving the door open. I know it scares him to leave me here alone, where my dad or Ivan could see me, but I love him for giving me this time with my friends.

"When did that happen?" Hope says, turning my attention back to them. "Last time we heard from you, you were about to quit your job 'cause he was such an asshole."

I shrug. "Things just happened. We stopped fighting, started talking, and discovered a lot more to love about each other than to hate."

"Is he, you know, faithful?" Hope retorts. "Because in high school—"

"I remember," I interrupt her. They can't tell me anything about Devyn I don't know. They know nothing about the real him. "He's different than we thought, guys."

Diana shifts on her feet uncomfortably. "We just want you to be happy. When we found out you were back, we assumed you dropped out."

"You guys know how important school is to me. That'll never happen."

"We know, but college is different . . . harder."

I'm insulted these girls who've known me forever think so little of me. Never in my life have I neglected my education. It was the one thing I always knew could get me out of here and to a better life. "I'm doing fine in school." I try my hardest to not sound as offended as I am. "How could I be a tutor if I was failing?"

"Like we said, Ry, it was just a thought." Hope laughs at me. "Don't be so sensitive."

"I'm not," I respond. I leave the conversation before I get irritated and cancel my plans with them completely. "I should go back and join them; I don't want to be rude. Devyn's dad put a lot of work into breakfast." I pull Hope into a quick hug, and then hug Diana.

"We'll call you in the morning," Diana tells me.

I smile, secretly wishing only she and I could just go to breakfast. At least Diana communicates in a way that doesn't make me feel bad. I'm not even sure why I feel bad . . .

"Sounds good." I wave at them before turning around and going inside, exhaling a sigh of relief when the door closes behind me. Everyone's around the table eating when I get to the kitchen. A vacant seat next to Devyn waits for me. A look of genuine concern is on his face as I sit beside him. He must still be worried about our talk last night, or maybe it's my conversation with Hope and Diana.

Devyn brings my chair closer to his and cuddles me into him, half listening as Cara talks about some girl in her class. He always knows just what I need, including food, because my plate's prepared before I get to the table.

He plants a kiss atop my head, and all the surrounding voices fade into the background as we slip into our bubble. "You okay?" he whispers.

I nod. "Just tired." I don't know why I'm so bothered by my conversation with Hope and Diana. We're no longer close, obviously. Their thoughts are just wrong—about me, about school, about Devyn.

"Why didn't you tell them about us?"

I instantly feel bad. That's why he's so concerned?

"I haven't talked to them since before we got together . . ." I touch my hand to his, leaning in so no one can hear us. "I didn't expect them to come; it's not like we've kept in touch. I'm sorry if that upset you."

He shakes his head. "It didn't. I was just confused. You've never kept us a secret, so it's just weird to feel like one to people you used to be close to. I thought it was because they didn't like me."

"Does that bother you?"

"Not if it doesn't bother you."

I kiss his cheek. "I don't care what anyone says about you, Devyn. They think the same untrue things I used to believe."

"I don't want you to feel that way again . . ."

We'd be taking a huge step back if I went back to thinking Devyn was just a stereotype. "That can't happen," I promise. "I know you better than they ever will." He visibly relaxes at my answer and pulls me into him again, this time kissing me.

"Ewww." Cara scrunches her face at us. "You two are gross."

"I agree," Devyn's dad says in between bites of scrambled eggs.

"My bad." Devyn chuckles. He plants one more kiss on my forehead. "It's sick how unwelcoming this family is to a little love around here."

Devyn's dad coughs up his food, surprised by his son's words. They don't know the affectionate, extremely loving man I spend most days with . . . or they're not used to him voicing it.

"Hey! We love," Cory argues.

***

The police station, and just police in general, often have a way of making any black person uncomfortable and scared. You'd think in a predominately black neighborhood like G-Heights, one might feel a sense of community because, oftentimes, police officers are people who've grown up with our parents or grandparents. Sadly, none of that's true.

Devyn and I walk toward the glass entrance, hand in hand. Just in the seconds since we've gotten out of the car, he's walking straighter, his grip on me firmer, and his demeanor extremely professional, telling me he's already on edge. We've never discussed police or altercations with the police. Mine have only been a few visits to Javon's house for noise complaints or "suspicious activity," but they never had a warrant and were just checking in. Devyn, being as big as he is and as a black man living in a neighborhood with one of the highest crime rates in LA, probably has some stories of his own.

A female officer with skin the ashy color of wheat bread and a slick low bun sits at the front desk, busily answering and hanging up the phone. The lobby of the small building is empty, so she sees us the moment we enter.

"Good afternoon," she says, putting the phone on its holder. "How can I help you?"

Devyn pulls me with him all the way to the counter. "Good afternoon. We'd like to speak to an officer about the case on Emmanuel Flores." He keeps his demeanor soft and straight. It's different than the usual relaxed charm he has with everyone else.

The woman arches one eyebrow in suspicion, looking at Devyn as if he told her the sky's purple. "Speak? Do you have any evidence in regard to his case?"

Devyn shakes his head. "No, ma'am. Emmanuel is my brother, and neither I nor anyone else in my family have been updated on the progress of his case or even whether the police are looking into it."

"Mr. . . ." She lingers on the *r*, and pauses before asking, "What's your name?"

"Devyn Baker."

"Brothers with different last names?" she questions.

"Different dad." Devyn shrugs.

The woman rolls her eyes. "You can be sure the police are doing their job. If they haven't contacted you, they're probably looking for more information."

Devyn sighs. "You can't tell me anything?"

"Nothing. That's for the detectives working on the case. As you see, I'm sitting here at the front desk."

What's with this chick?

"I understand." A look of defeat slaps across his beautiful face. "Thank you for your time." He turns around, tugging me with him.

"Wait." I stay in place in front of the desk. "Ma'am, no offense, but you didn't even look up the name of the person we've mentioned." At one time, I wouldn't have questioned her either, but Devyn and his family are hurting. They need answers. I need answers.

"And?"

"*And* do you know Emmanuel Flores by heart? I'm sure you're from here, so did you know him? Do you know what happened to him? The least you could do is act like you care before sending us away. We didn't come here for fun."

"Look, it takes hours, sometimes days, to get people processed—"

"He was not processed," I interrupt her. I don't give a fuck if this woman's in a police uniform or not. She's messing with the love of my life, refusing to help him, for what? Because she's lazy? Because she doesn't want to do her job? "He was shot in the neck."

The officer's eyes widen.

"Luckily, he's alive, but we haven't heard anything about the person who did this. Can you give us some sort of information, or even better, direct me to an officer who can?"

Devyn says nothing. The officer says nothing. But they both stare at me.

The officer takes a second to type something on the computer. "The detective in charge of this case won't be back until three." I look at the clock. It's 1:19 p.m.

"We'll be back then. Thank you." I turn around, pulling Devyn out of the office.

"You're so fuckin' tough." Devyn laughs as the door closes behind us.

I wrap my arms around his waist and let him pull me into his chest. "She's a bitch."

"You handled her. You didn't even flinch when she grabbed her taser."

"She did not!" I laugh. "She assumed we were bailing Manny out or something and was completely wrong. Isn't the whole point of becoming an officer to protect and *serve*?"

"You know how it is around here." Devyn shrugs.

I know all too well, but even if the G-Heights police are tired of pushing back against the poison in this community, they still need to recognize when it's time to help. I lean back to look at him, instantly noticing the smile still on his handsome face. He likes when I trample people for him, which is relieving, because I can't help but defend him. I look back into the lobby to see the officer looking our way. She catches us staring and immediately looks down at her computer, which makes me laugh. Never in my life have I instilled fear in someone like this! "So, what should we do now?"

He wraps his arm over my shoulder and walks us to the car. "We better figure something out. You embarrass any more police today, and we might end up on the news."

CHAPTER 21

DEVYN

I don't want to drop Ryan off with her friends the next morning. I'm ready to get out of here. Ready for Manny to wake up. Ready to get back to football and school. Ready to get away from all the drama of the past. But it seems like as days go on, my time here just gets shorter and my questions remain unanswered. The police were no help in figuring out what happened to Manny.

And now I have to deal with Ryan's friends. Two annoying girls—well, one doesn't talk and the other's rude—who Ryan hasn't talked about once since we got together. Not a Face-Time, call, or text, but somehow, they figured out she's back and want to see her? Ryan doesn't act the same way around them as she does with me or Nico. I don't even know if they mean that much to her anymore, but for some reason, she's letting them put her in harm's way. Away from me and closer to Javon and Ivan, since Ryan's old house is three houses from Hope's apartment.

So I take my time getting her there. I don't wake Ryan up on time, hoping she'll oversleep and decide to cancel, but she's ready to go when I get back from my workout. Then I make an excuse about needing a tea before dropping her off. She probably knows I'm stalling, but she doesn't call me out. We pull up in front of Hope's place twenty minutes after ten. Ryan doesn't seem mad about being late, but she's quiet in the front seat.

"You don't have to go." I turn off the car. It's not like she jumped out and waved me off, so maybe she doesn't want to go as much as I don't want her to. "Don't feel pressured to go if you don't want to."

She sighs and looks at me, revealing all her gorgeousness. Her hair's tied back in a ponytail and her face is natural. My practice T-shirt hangs loosely on her body over gray workout shorts. "I have to make some time for them. I shouldn't have come here and not told them."

"It's not like you're here to chill."

She nods. "I know, but still. It's been a long time, and we should catch up. They were all I had before you."

I won't fight her. I don't want to keep her from her friends or give them more of a reason to talk shit about me. "Just keep me updated, okay? If you get scared when you're out or even just get a bad feeling, call me. I'll get you as quick as I can."

"I will." She slides her hand across the console and entwines it with mine. "If you're not good, I'll be on edge, babe. Can you try to relax?"

I squeeze her hand, nodding. "I'll try." I lean over to kiss her cheek. "You know it's hard to be away from you."

Her laughter calms my nerves. She's the biggest worrier I know, so if she's feeling calm, maybe it's a good sign. "I get like that, too, but it's only a couple of hours."

"You don't want to wait till I'm close by? At least if I'm at my dad's, I'll get here faster if you want to leave."

"I'll be *fine*. Hope and Diana have always had my back." She leans in, her face centimeters from mine. "Kiss me so I can go. I'm already late thanks to you."

I pull her in immediately, making our first kiss of the day a passionate one, and unclick her seat belt to pull her onto my lap. "I love you."

She cups my face, smiling. "I love *you*." She leans in, tasting my lips. "Go see Manny so we can have some fun."

I think she's hinting at sex, but I can't tell. "Fun?"

She settles into my lap, smiling. "We only have two days left before we have to go back. We might as well enjoy it."

"What should we do?"

"Movies, shopping, museum . . . whatever will take our minds off all this shit." I love how Ryan's always trying to distract me from what's going on at home. Her presence here comforts me immensely. She's the calm support I need to get through this.

"A movie might help."

"We can take the little ones too," she suggests. "Make it an outing."

"I'll call you when I'm coming back if you're not ready before I'm done." I hug her close to me and kiss her again. "I mean it. Keep me updated."

"Promise." She grins. What's she so happy about? "I got to go." She kisses me before climbing over to her seat. She grabs her bag and gets out. "Love you!"

"Love you," I call as she closes the door behind her. I watch as she walks up the stairs to Hope's apartment, praying she'll be okay.

The hospital's pretty empty for late morning. A few people sit in the waiting room as doctors and nurses chat and do their work. I take the elevator to the seventh floor and go to Manny's room, where two nurses sit at the door gossiping. They turn to me as I approach.

"Morning." I smile politely at them.

"You're here to visit Emmanuel Flores, right?" one of the nurses asks. She looks at me through wide eyes, instantly alarming me.

"He's my brother." I nod. "Is he alright?"

"Emmanuel woke up this morning," the other nurse tells me. Without thinking, I move past them to see Manny. One of the nurses follows. "We've called your mother and sister, the emergency contacts, multiple times and no one's gotten back to us."

Manny's eyes are still closed, but the breathing tube's been removed. Is he really awake?

The nurse touches my shoulder. "He's resting," she whispers. "We've checked on him every thirty minutes since 4:00 a.m. He's in pain, but he's conscious and speaking. He's made a remarkable recovery."

"Thank you." I'm in shock. He looks like the same pale and lifeless man I saw yesterday. I step toward his bed and sit in the chair next to it. I'm afraid to wake him, but I need to see with my own eyes that he's okay.

I touch his arm gently, and his eyes flutter open. Instant relief floods my body for the first time in days. He's alive! I have to admit I didn't think he'd make it.

"About time somebody came to see me," he croaks, making me laugh. "Nurses said they been calling everyone."

"I haven't talked to your mom or Shae since yesterday," I tell him. "I'll call them, though, and make sure they get here as soon as possible."

"Nah." He shakes his head. "They probably asleep or something. Give them time to see the calls." He smiles at me. "It's good to see you, bro. They said I was out for a while . . . you on Thanksgiving break?"

"No, I came as soon as my dad told me. I couldn't stay out there knowing you were in bad shape."

"Look at me. I'm good. I'm alive."

"It wasn't easy, though." Manny used to be the only person I could come to with my thoughts, emotions, and anything else. I can't hide the tears as I talk to him. "You're lucky to be alive. Do you know who did this?" His face falls to the covers lying at his waist, and he's silent.

For the first time in our entire lives, I can tell Manny's keeping something from me. We've gone through the wars of life together since we were kids. What's he been doing since I left LA?

"Manny, you gotta help me." I wipe the tears from my eyes and pull myself together. I still need to be strong for my best friend. He's a long way from recovery. "The police know nothing . . . your mom and sister know nothing . . . my dad knows nothing. Niggas we grew up with go silent when I bring you up. What's going on? This involves more than just you."

"Who else got hurt?" Fear instantly comes across Manny's face. "Shae okay?"

"Everyone's good." He doesn't need to get worked up. "Is this about Shae?"

"Look, D, we're brothers. You know I'd do anything to keep y'all safe . . . your family and mine. But there ain't shit

I can tell you. The police came earlier, and I had nothing to tell them, either, so stop talking to them. All this will be handled once I get out of here."

"Manny, this shit needs to be handled *now*." He doesn't get how serious this is, and that it's more than just us. "You're not in a place to fight this. What can you do? You don't know when you're getting out of here."

Manny goes silent, rubbing his head to release pain or confusion or something else. But his eyes grow red. He doesn't cry, but after a minute, looks at me. "I'll tell you, but first, tell me everything that's went down since I got shot."

***

RYAN

"I have to find my own place." Hope says in between long sips of hot chocolate at the diner. A touch of whipped cream sits on the tip of her nose as she sets the cup down. "My mom went off on me yesterday about letting Nas spend the night—"

"Y'all have been together for three years." Diana laughs.

"Exactly! So, she needs to shut up. We're damn near married, and he's been spending the night for years. Now she's got a problem?"

I take a sip of my coffee before adding my input. "Did she know he was spending the night in high school? He used to climb through the window in the middle of the night."

"Not to mention you two used to only fuck at school because she was home during the day," Diana adds.

Hope lets out a long, exasperated sigh. "We're grown now!"

Hope's mother's a devout Christian, director of the choir, and hosts a weekly Bible study for women at their church.

I doubt she'll ever be cool with Nas sleeping over, but I keep quiet.

"What about going to his place?" I suggest as she and Diana go back and forth about how unfair Hope's mom is being.

Hope shakes her head. "That's sick! He shares a room with his little brothers."

I laugh. "I didn't know."

"Seeee," Hope drawls out her word to exaggerate her point. "We have no other option." She slouches in the chair, pouting.

"What'd Devyn say to his dad for him to let you stay there?"

I shrug. "He never told me. When Manny was shot, he just booked two tickets. I don't think he had to convince him; he's pretty cool about it."

"It's got to be because he lives with his dad . . . does he have a sister?"

"Yeah, but she's not having guys sleep over anytime soon. She's seven."

"You're really *living.*" Diana leans into the table. "Things are so different now. I never thought . . ." She pauses. "First, I didn't think you'd actually move, and then you left, and I knew you'd never come back. But you're here . . . and you're different."

I don't know how to respond. I'm happy I've changed. In the short couple months since I moved to New York, I've grown surer of myself and more confident and somehow found this great love. I can't admit to them I do plan to leave this place behind. "Is it that bad?'

"Well, are you happy?" Diana asks. "Really happy?"

I nod, smiling. "Yeah, things are just so different. Nothing's the same, but in like the best way."

"How?" Hope butts in.

"When you're at a university, living there and diving into the experience, you're so free. Like, there's no rules—no one telling you what you can't do. No one watching you. No one trying to control you. Every day, I do what I want. It's freeing." They heard the rumors about Javon and Ivan and even saw the signs. Just like everyone else in this town, they didn't ask. If they saw I was in pain or hurting, they never expressed concern. Instead, they'd offered movie nights or sleepovers with pizza when things got too hard for me to hide, and I welcomed the distraction. But I can't act like I wasn't happy to get out of here. Leaving them behind was sad, but I don't regret it at all. "Do you guys think about getting out of G-Heights or California or anything?"

Hope shakes her head. "I never had the grades y'all had. I applied to one university in San Francisco and didn't get in."

"You did?" Diana asks her. I'm surprised too. She never said anything.

"I was so sad. I knew it was a reach, but I saw Ry apply to all these schools and I figured I should try." I wish she would've told me, but I never pushed them to follow my lead. I was too focused on myself. "I never told anyone."

"You should apply to some more schools," I say. "There's *so* many colleges. I can help you look for some scholarships too."

"What would I do about Nas? Plus, my mom needs my check for half the rent. They docked her pay at the nursing home."

"You have to worry about you." Diana looks at Hope, both of their eyes glistening. We lost the connection of our trio, but their bond has strengthened. I'm not mad about it. "Maybe we can look at some schools together? If we like the same ones, maybe we can be roommates."

"I'd love that!" Hope exclaims.

Diana laughs. "I won't yell at you when Nas spends the night."

"That's good enough for me." Hope giggles. She looks at me. "I don't know if I can go out of state, but it'd be nice to get out of LA."

"That's definitely a start," I say as the waiter comes with our stacks of pancakes, eggs, and sausages.

"You know," Hope says as she stuffs her mouth with pancakes. She takes time to wipe her mouth and swallow before continuing. "We're really proud of you, Ry."

"And we'd love to be there for you more," Diana says. "If that's okay. We were talking last night, and we just miss you. I'm sorry for not reaching out more. We should have taken the time to stay in touch. We just thought you wanted to leave everything behind."

"Not you guys," I assure them. "You two are the only friends I have out here. You were there during the darkest time of my life, took me into your homes when my dad was doing everything but taking care of his daughter. God knows where I'd be without our friendship." I pause for a moment. "Who knows if I'd be alive."

My words bring all three of us to tears. I've never realized the way we fought to endure this place. A year ago, we were little girls, struggling to survive in this community. We overcame too much, raising each other while our parents worked or got consumed in their own addictions or took time to focus on younger siblings. We were all we had. We didn't share every tear together or every hard time, but when it mattered, we always came through. Now we're women trying to take control of our lives.

"We love you," Diana says, tears rolling down her high cheekbones. Hope wipes her tears before everyone starts noticing the three crying girls in the front of the restaurant. I scoot over to Hope and wrap my arms around her. Diana hugs the other side of her. "I love you, guys. Let's all promise to do better."

We sit there, wrapped up in the strong bond and love from a lifelong friendship before going back to our meals. The conversation gets lighter as we chat about boyfriends, they update me on people we went to school with, and we just enjoy our time together. It feels like we've reached a new height in our friendship.

We pay our bill and get ready to go. I'm full and happy I got to spend time with my girls, but I'm ready to get back to Devyn. I pull my phone out and text him to let him know I'm about ready to go.

"Ry." Diana grabs my wrist tight as we're about to exit the glass doors. She looks behind me in shock, and I turn to see Ivan leaning against her car. Our eyes lock and a bright smile reaches the corners of his chapped lips.

Neither she nor Hope know exactly what Ivan's done to me, but they've heard his sick jokes and the rumors. They also know how much I hate him. I look back at them. Their faces are covered in fear. They have no clue what to do.

"I'm going to talk to him." I walk ahead before they can stop me.

Ivan's smile widens the closer I get. "You decided to come home, baby girl? College got too hard for you?"

"Why are you here?" I step toward him but keep a safe distance. I need him to know I'm not afraid of him anymore. "You need to leave!"

"I'm not going anywhere till you get in the car." I hear the restaurant door open and don't need to turn around to know Hope and Diana are behind me. "I tried to make it easy for you and sent Daddy to get you, but you refused. I'm tired of being nice when you're not nice to me. So you got five seconds to get in this car or I'll snatch you by your ponytail."

"She's not going," Hope interrupts. "Everyone in there's watching you, Ivan. You really think you can get away with taking Ryan?"

"I can get away with any fucking thing!" he yells. "You forget who runs these streets? You think I give a fuck about any of them niggas seeing me? They can't do shit!" His eyes are wide and hysterical, his hair nappy, uncombed, and all over the place. He looks like he just escaped an insane asylum. His black, stretched-out tank top looks dirty and old, showing off the tattoo he got as a tribute to me. I shudder, reading the word *Eternity* in cursive on his chest. He'd call me that sick name when I was younger just to make me feel as degraded as the girls who work for him. "Let me show you bitches how much I don't give a fuck." He yanks open the door to Hope's previously locked car and pulls out the biggest gun I've ever seen.

Gasps come from all of us, and the door opens, probably with more people attempting to rescue us, but I'm too scared to take my eyes off him. He points the gun behind me, using both hands to grip it.

"I'll kill every mothafucka in that restaurant!" he screams. "Get your asses behind that door!" He gives them two seconds before squeezing the trigger and releasing a bullet. Hope, Diana, and I instantly hit the ground to cover ourselves. "GET YOUR ASSES BEHIND THAT DOOR!"

Tears fall from my eyes as Ivan turns back to me. He stalks past me and presses the gun against Diana's back. "Two seconds, baby girl, or I'll kill both your friends and still take you." Hope and Diana sob for their lives.

I know what to do. I don't have any other options. I slowly get up from the dirty parking lot surface. "Come on." My voice shakes as I reach out to him. "You don't have to hurt anyone. I'll go."

"Ry—" Diana protests, but Ivan shoves the gun deeper into her back, shutting her up.

"Please." I beg. "I'll do whatever you want, just don't hurt them. I promise, I'll do whatever you want me to do."

A smile creeps onto his sadistic face. "You're coming home with me."

It's not a question, but I nod.

"We have some making up to do."

I nod again.

"Where are her keys?"

"Hope's back pocket," I respond instantly. I need to get him to take that gun off of Diana. He stoops over to Hope and takes her keys, copping a slow and grimy feel of her ass before standing up.

"Get in the front seat." I shuffle toward the car with him following behind me. Ivan watches me get in and closes the door, his grip tight on the gun, and then goes to the driver's side. He sets the gun between his seat and the driver's side door.

Police sirens scream in the distance as Ivan turns on the car. He grabs my face hard and plants a soft kiss at the corner of my mouth. "We're gonna have some fun." He smiles at me. "I knew you'd come back. Eternity, baby girl."

Rivers of tears fall from my eyes. I worked too hard to become the woman I am, and he's about to take all of it away. I can't sit and let him do the things he used to do to me. I'd rather die than revert to that girl.

I close my eyes as he pulls out of the lot. After everything I've done to escape this town and this man, my life's about to end with Ivan by my side.

CHAPTER 22

DEVYN

Ryan: Waiting for you at Hope's!

The automatic glass doors open in front of me as I read Ryan's text. Relief floods my body. For the first time in days things look brighter—Manny's back, Ryan and my family are safe, I'm good. That's enough to be thankful for.

I get in the car and pull out of the hospital parking lot in less than a minute. My anxieties about Ryan evaporate. I want to give her a little extra time with her friends, but my natural instinct makes me want to get to her as fast as possible. It's only been a couple of hours, and I'm missing her. I want her to meet Manny, and I'm going to pick her up and come right back before we go off to have some "fun."

Twenty minutes later, I'm getting off the freeway when my phone rings. I answer to hear my dad's voice.

"Son, you still at the hospital?"

"I'm going to get Ryan. Manny's awake!"

"Wait, what?"

"Yes! You dressed? We're about to go back to the hospital, so I'll pick you up."

"Devyn, something happened to Ryan."

My heart slams against my chest, but I try to stay focused on the road. "What do you mean?" I hit the gas hard, speeding toward Hope's.

"Her friends just left; they said Ivan showed—"

"Fuck!" I yell over him. I can't take this. Ivan got to her the moment I turned my back, and now I don't know what to do.

"Relax, D. *Please.* I know you're scared." My dad rushes over the phone. "I'm texting you the number they left me. I've called the cops, and they're on their way to Javon's. You think she's there? I'll go now."

"I'm five minutes away." I hang up and call the number he sent. Hope answers immediately. "What happened to Ryan?"

She sobs over the phone. "I'm so sorry! We tried to protect her. Ivan had this gun—"

"A *gun*?" I gasp.

"He pressed it against Diana's back and threatened to kill all of us. He stole my car and took off with Ryan."

I'm nauseated with fear. My worst nightmare's happening. Ryan's worst nightmare is happening, and I need to save her. "Does she have her phone? Do you think he's taking her to Javon's?"

"I don't know." Hope sobs. "I'm so sorry Devyn, I—"

I hang up on her to call Ryan. The phone rings and rings and rings . . .

"Come on, baby, answer me. Let me know you're good." Let me know you're alive.

Please, please, please, let her be alive.

The phone goes to voicemail, so I call the only person left that can help me.

Shae's voice sounds light and happy when she answers. "Hello."

"Shae, give the phone to Manny."

"Everything okay?"

"GIVE THE PHONE TO MANNY!" I can't take any more small talk. I pull into Manny's driveway, right across from Javon's house, and get out of the car.

"What's up, D?"

"Listen. No questions, no small talk, no bullshit." I grab the key from under the welcome mat and let myself into the house. "That nigga Ivan kidnapped Ryan, and I need to know where they could be."

"What?" he breathes, shocked. "They're usually up in Javon's crib."

"He put her in a car, and there's no car here." I make my way to Manny's room and go to the closet to get his Glock from the Adidas shoebox on the top shelf. "Could they be anywhere else?"

"Not that I know. I've only ever messed with them there. They never leave, for real."

I open the box to see no gun. Fuck.

"Ask Shae. She's got to know something; she used to fuck around with them."

"D, I—"

"Yo, ask her!" I don't care how sick he is or what he feels he needs to hide. My question won't go unanswered. Ryan and her safety depend on it. Their voices lower as I rummage through Manny's closet.

"She said they take the girls to this apartment for work. It's at the end of G-Heights on King Boulevard."

"That apartment's closed."

"They've been running girls in and out of there for years." Shae's voice echoes through the phone. "If Ivan didn't take her to Javon's, he's there. Everyone thinks the place is abandoned, but they broke in. Go through the back. There's a fence with a broken door, so it's always open."

"Manny, where's your gun?"

"Dev—"

"This nigga is holding her at gunpoint!" I try to calm down. I can't save Ryan if I'm amped up on my own emotions. "I'll only use it if I have to."

"I hid the gun," Shae says. "I thought Manny would get in trouble if the police found it after the accident. Go into my room."

I rush across the hallway to Shae's bedroom.

"Look in the vent behind my desk. There's a little opening where you can pull it open . . ."

I cross over to her white wooden desk and push it to the side, find the hole, and open it to see a bunch of hidden shoeboxes.

" . . . it's the pink one, but Devyn . . ."

"Yeah?" I pull three boxes out of the vent until I find the sparkly pink one. I open it and the gun sits on top of a bunch of Polaroid pictures.

"Don't say anything about what's inside," Shae whispers. I flip a couple over to see a bunch of photos of her and Javon— kissing, lying in bed, even of him holding Jodeci as a little baby. What the fuck?

I don't have time for this. I grab the gun, put it in my back pocket, shove everything back into the vent, and leave.

"Thank you." I hang up.

***

RYAN

Ivan grips my arm tight and shoves me into an old apartment building I've never been to. He pushes open a gate and forces me ahead of him, his hold firm.

"Up the steps," he commands, forcing me to his left toward an old, broken-down staircase. He clutches his massive gun in the other hand. He's told me multiple times on the way here that he's not afraid to use it. He'd rather kill me than see me off "being someone you ain't with Devyn."

He promised himself he'd get me back to "me"—that shy, scared, broken girl I was when I lived here. He wants the version he can control, that's too weak to fight him, but I'll die fighting for the person I am now. He thinks he has me, that I will easily leave behind my new self. But I'm not going anywhere. I've grown since I left this hellhole, and I won't shrink down to the person I once was.

We walk to the fifth floor and past the first four apartments to a door marked 519. Ivan pulls me in hastily, and I can't believe my eyes. A row of large black dog cages is set up in the living room, buckets of bleach next to each one. Girls are trapped in two of them—their hair matted and falling off, their skin burned and discolored. One of them is in a black bra and orange shorts and another is completely naked. Both jump when we enter.

Ivan ignores the girls, dragging me down a short hallway to a bedroom in the back. He kicks the door open hard to reveal two more women, naked and asleep on an old mattress with filthy burgundy sheets. The floor's covered with empty alcohol bottles and food wrappers. Black trash bags are taped over the windows and chipped white flakes fall from the walls with any move we make. The girls wake up immediately.

"Get out!" Ivan yells. He throws me to the edge of the bed, and then wrenches one of the girls up by her hair. "Bitch, can you hear? Get out!"

The girl shrieks as he grips her hair harder. She doesn't say anything. Neither does the girl next to her, and neither do I. Ivan's out of his mind, and we all know it. Just like me, these girls have suffered from his torment. They know there's no stopping him.

Ivan heaves the girl to the door and kicks her out of the room, leaving the other one on the bed. He slams the door, leaving the girl at the other end of the door sobbing. The other one jerks up from the bed.

"I'm going." She tries to brush past him into the hallway, but Ivan moves, blocking her way. "I'm going," she repeats.

"Sit next to Ryan." He spins her around and pushes her beside me. Our legs rest against each other as she sits next to me with no clothes on. Ivan stands watching, a snide and vicious smile on his blistered lips. "My girls." He chuckles. The way he looks us up and down makes me want to vomit. The girl squirms next to me and tries to cover herself, crossing her arms over her chest and pressing her legs together tight.

"Baby girl," Ivan says to me. "Don't you think it'd be fun to add another person to our reunion?" He steps closer, towering over both of us, and brings his palm to the back of my neck. His damp, coarse skin makes goose bumps form all over my body as he rubs me. "Kiss her." He pushes my head toward the girl. Her lips part, ready to do whatever he tells her to do, but I tense.

"No."

Ivan slaps me hard across my face, and I fall back on to the bed. "What'd you say to me?" Tears spring from my eyes as he slaps me again and blood gushes from my nose. He takes the gun and holds it over my face before pressing it to my forehead. "You really don't think I'll kill you, little girl?" He looks over at the other girl. "Get on top of her," he yells. "Now!" The girl jumps on my waist, straddling me as Ivan jams the gun into my head. "Listen up. I don't care how long you were gone. You belong to me, and you will respect me. If I have to break you down in a cage, I fucking will." He slams the gun against my head, making me cry harder.

His eyes go from me to the girl. "Kiss her neck."

She doesn't hesitate or blink at his commands. She pushes my head to the side and begins sucking my neck, using her tongue and lips to form a dark hickey on my skin. I sob, feeling just as disgusted as I did all those times Ivan forced me to have sex with him. Except now he's watching, the gun still pressed to my head, one hand ready to pull the trigger as he rubs the bulge over his dirty cargo pants with the other. He doesn't take his eyes off me.

"Please, let me go." I plead to him. The girl continues to kiss me despite the blood gushing from my nose.

"Never, baby girl." His voice is quiet, and he moans. Nausea claws at my throat, and I swallow the bile-and-blood mixture. "Take her shirt off." The girl slides her hands under my shirt and pulls it over my head. It's the first time I'm really able to look at her. She has to be younger than me, her features not fully formed and her face still chubby with baby fat. Her light green eyes are dead as they lock with mine.

"Please—" I beg her to do something, but Ivan smashes the gun against my head. My vision blurs and my ears ring inside my skull. I can't move my hands with the girl's naked body on top of me.

"Didn't I tell you to shut the fuck up?" Ivan yells.

The gun moves from my head and the trigger goes off, making the ringing louder. The girl's body flies away from me, and a combination of screams and cries fill the room. The migraine and the ringing force me to keep my eyes shut. Ivan flips me over and jumps on top of me, taking the girl's place. He punches the back of my head and forces my face against the mattress so I can't breathe. He pushes down on the back of my neck, leveraging all his weight on me, his mouth close to my ear.

"I'll fucking kill—"

A crash echoes from somewhere else in the apartment, and his hold doesn't waiver as I try to fight him off. I push against him, but his grip only firms.

"Javon, get the fuck out!" Ivan screams in my ear. "Get the fuck out!"

I grow faint as footsteps get louder and louder, then another crash, then Ivan's body falls from mine.

"GET OFF HER!" Relief floods my body. I recognize the voice immediately, despite that piercing, high pitch. I grip my head, trying to pull myself together. Blots of red and orange and yellow and white fill my eyes as the room spins. Devyn's on top of Ivan, punching him. Ivan uses his teeth, arms, and legs to try to get him off.

I scrabble for the gun, patting around the bed to find it, despite the fact I have no idea how to use one. The pain in my head is unbearable, making me slow. I stagger up off the ground and instantly fall but try to stand back up.

Devyn is still beating up Ivan, his hands and the floor covered in blood, and I notice a gun in his back pocket. I need to grab it. I need to end this.

I stumble to Devyn and yank out the gun. He turns around, and Ivan hits him over the head with his gun. Devyn knocks his gun out of my hand, and it flies to the corner of the room. Ivan smashes his gun against my hip, making me fall on my face. Ivan grabs my legs, and Devyn wrestles him away from me.

"Get the gun!" Devyn yells as I struggle to escape Ivan and get to the corner of the room where Devyn's gun is. The room spins faster and faster.

And then the gun goes off twice, someone shrieks, a fire ignites in my back . . .

. . . and everything goes black.

CHAPTER 23

DEVYN

Five hours.

Five hours, and I still have no idea what's going on with Ryan. Five hours since anyone's been able to tell me if she's alive or injured or okay. Five hours since the police arrested me and put me in this interrogation room as Ryan and Ivan were taken away in an ambulance.

I can't believe he shot her.

I can't believe I shot him.

I've cried, I've pleaded, I've demanded, but no one will tell me anything. I even told the cops I'll pay them, that I'm willing to give them every cent I own, but they just laugh. For a man who's never gotten in any trouble with the police and doesn't have so much as a parking ticket, they treat me like I'm the one running women in and out of that apartment. The police don't even care who the real criminals are at the end of the day. They see a young black man and immediately assume the worst.

Like I would ever hurt a woman. Like I would ever force a woman to have sex with me. Like I would ever try to rape and kill my own girlfriend. They ask me every question about Ivan and Javon and even Manny, invent their own conspiracy that I manipulated Ryan into coming to Los Angeles so I could get her back to Ivan. They're even saying I'm the one who probably arranged for my own best friend to get shot in the head and I've been working for Ivan and Javon this whole time.

All I wanted to do was save my girl. I put the criminals in their hands, begged and pleaded for them to help me, but somehow, I'm the one they try to blame.

Fuck the police. They never cared about a man like me. They won't start today.

I'll never get those scenes out of my head. The girls in the cages. Ivan sitting on top of Ryan, her shirt on the floor, her face bruised, bloody, and beaten as she's pressed against the bed, struggling for her life. The naked girl with the giant hole through her body in the corner of the room. The shriek I'm almost sure was Ryan's soul escaping her body when Ivan shot the bullet through her back.

God can't do this to me. He can't do this to Ryan. He can't give us love so pure and consuming just to take it away. I've been praying since they threw me in the police car for her to be alive, but it doesn't matter how hard I fall to my knees, how tight I close my eyes, or how loud I pray, I still get nothing. I can't hear a thing and I don't see any signs. I'm helpless.

The iron door isolating the interrogation room from everything else creaks loudly. I force myself to take my eyes from the table I've been sitting at to the police officer walking in. He's different than the ones who keep coming in to ask me questions, and the first black officer they've let me talk to since I got here.

"I'm Detective Johnson."

I say nothing as he steps closer, our eyes locked on each other. He sets a small, individual-sized water bottle in front of me. It's the first drink I've been offered in the last five hours.

"You should drink something," he tells me. "All the crying is going to make you dehydrated."

"Will you tell me what's going on with Ryan?"

"We don't know," he replies, taking the seat on the chair across from me. "Your father just got here, though, and with the lack of evidence and your testimony, we have no choice but to release you."

I sigh in relief, trying hard not to cry even more. My dad needs to get me the fuck out of here and to Ryan.

"But, before you leave, I have some questions."

"I've told the police everything I know."

"I know, but we just want to double-check. That way, we won't have to bring you back."

I'd laugh if I didn't think it'd get me in more trouble. They think having another black man in here will make me more honest? I don't have shit to tell them.

"Go ahead."

"In your previous statement made with Officer Matthews, the officer who arrested you, you said Mr. Rutherford kidnapped your girlfriend, Ryan McKnight, from the IHOP on Crenshaw Boulevard. Is that correct?"

"Yes, and he held her at gunpoint."

"I saw that in your statement as well. You were there?"

"No, two of her friends told me."

"Can you give me the names of the two ladies that told you this information?"

"Hope and Diana."

He pauses for a moment, looking from the report in his hand to me. "Can you tell me their last names?"

I shake my head. "I told the other officer I don't know their last names. They're friends of Ryan's; I don't know them personally."

"And were they the ones who told you where he took her?"

"I went to Ryan's old house, where Ivan lives with her father. Hope told me that Ivan had stolen her car, but no car sat in the driveway when I pulled up. I called my friend Shae, and she was the one who told me where they might be."

"And how did she know where they'd be?"

The pictures of Javon and Shae flood my mind. I knew she was in love with him, but she was working for him too. How could she be in a relationship with a man like that? And why'd she ever let him hold Jodeci? Javon kicked her out of his life and his home the moment she got pregnant. "She's a close friend of Javon's."

"Was Shae also the friend who gave you the gun?"

I'll never rat them out for that. "Like I said, it was a friend of a friend. The man goes by the name Weights. He hangs out over by the swap meet next to that apartment building we were at," I lie.

Detective Johnson nods, confirming the information written down before him. I'm surprised he doesn't assure me they'll look into that like the other two had.

He places the pad of information gently on the table, crosses his arms over his chest, and leans toward me. "I want to believe you're telling the truth," he says. "But this *shit* you're telling us is fucked up, and damn near unheard of. If we find out you're lying—"

"I'm not," I interrupt him.

His eyes are glued to mine, and I can't tell if he believes me or not. I can't tell if he really wants to help me.

"Detective, this *shit*, as you call it, *is* fucked up. Why would a man sell his own daughter to someone just for some drugs and sex? Why would he try to stop her from getting an education, refuse to give her money so she's forced to work two jobs at eighteen just to survive, and even send this same man he let rape her for years all the way to the other side of the country to get her? That is unbelievable! But it happened! So, why did no one give a shit enough about her to do anything to help?

I wish I could have saved her. I wish I had taken the time to get to know her earlier. I hate myself for being like everyone else until now.

We all failed her. This community ignored her, knowing what kind of man Javon is, hearing the rumors about what was going on between her and Ivan. No one ever questioned it. No one ever pulled her aside and asked if she was okay. We turned our backs on probably the only woman who could put a bright light on this fucked-up community, demand change, and make it happen.

If Ryan's alive, I promise I'll spend the rest of my life making sure she never goes another second without being seen. She deserves people who care about her. How could someone so pure, so good, so loving be that way in a world that's done nothing but repeatedly fuck her over? It's insane.

"How could I lie about that, Detective? Ryan has gone through so much, and she's done it all alone. I love her. I vowed to always protect her; I'd do anything to keep that promise. You work in this community; you've heard what Javon and Ivan have been doing to these girls. You can't just believe I've made all this shit up and I'm the bad guy in this.

I've done nothing wrong." I'm done talking. I'm going crazy not knowing what's going on with her.

The detective nods. "I'm going to get your father. But first, I want to tell you Ivan Rutherford died in the ambulance on the way to the hospital."

For some reason, my heart drops. I shot him to protect Ryan, but he was still human. I didn't want to take anyone's life.

"Neither you nor Ryan have to worry about him any longer. And her father has been arrested and processed for a number of crimes, including prostitution and the trafficking of minors. He'll be away for a very long time."

"Do you really not know anything about how Ryan's doing?"

He shakes his head. "No. I'm sorry I don't have more information for you." The detective gets up and heads toward the door. "Devyn, I admire the way you stand up for the people you love. You're right about what you said. I grew up in this community, I'd watched Javon go downhill after high school, and I knew he had a daughter, but still, it never even crossed my mind how his life affected her." He opens the door, and my dad rushes in past the detective.

He immediately pulls me into his embrace. "You okay?"

I hold onto him tightly, nodding. Despite my relief, I won't let these cops see any more of my tears.

I let go of him. "How's Ryan?"

"She's in surgery. That's all I know, but we can head over now."

I nod and follow him toward the door where the detective stands, listening to our conversation. He and my dad exchange brief nods, and I shake his hand. We hurry out of there as fast as we can, jump in my car, and head to the hospital.

Dad is quiet the entire way there, knowing Ryan's the only thing on my mind. He drives quickly, getting to the emergency room in about seven minutes instead of the usual twenty. We pull up to the entrance, and I jump out of the car and rush to the waiting room to speak to a receptionist. "Good afternoon," says a female nurse. "How can I help you?"

"I'm here to see Ryan McKnight; she was brought here about five hours ago. She was shot in the back."

The lady nods, getting on the computer to search for information. "Are you family?"

"I'm her fiancé," I say without thinking about it. "I'm the only family she has. Is she okay?" My stomach cramps with the thought that something bad has happened to her.

"She just got out of surgery," the nurse says, the look on her face empathetic. She gets up from the table. "Would you like me to take you there?"

"Please." I follow her, practically running to find Ryan. We take the elevator six floors up, and then walk three minutes to her room. My eyes find her instantly. Her head's wrapped in a bandage, her left eye's swollen shut, a cast's on her right arm, and bruises cover her soft skin. I sprint into the room, relieved to see she doesn't have a huge breathing tube in her lungs like Manny had. A nurse is in the room adjusting her pain medicine.

"She'll be asleep for a while," the nurse says, her voice lax. "The bullet went through her shoulder, completely dislocating it. She has some nerve damage, but she should be able to recover fully with intense therapy."

"She's going to hate that." I bring the chair to her bedside and sit next to her. "She's a waitress; do you know how long she'll have to be away from work?"

"A couple months; it depends how well she does with therapy. She won't be able to start for about three weeks."

"How's her head?"

"She has a severe concussion, so we're monitoring her closely. We've given her a strong painkiller to help with the discomfort and give her some time to rest. She's going to be a little foggy, but we have no way to tell how severe the trauma is until she's coherent. The blows to her head caused some severe bruising to her skull."

We could get through the hard stuff and the healing as long as she's okay. I take her hand, content just to be touching her again.

Just this morning, she was in my arms, trying to take away my stress and worry. We didn't expect the day's events, but I'm thankful we got through it. When we're together, we really can take on the world.

Dreams of gunshots and Ryan's screams wake me out of a deep sleep. The room's pitch black, except for the dim white streetlights peeking through closed blinds and the yellow light coming from the hallway, reminding me I'm in a hospital.

More groans force me to lift my head from my hands. I'd fallen asleep, my upper body toppled over the edge of Ryan's bed. Another round of groans meets my ears before I realize Ryan's crying. I look up instantly. She's sitting up, holding her head in her palms, weeping in pain. I shoot up, running to the hallway to call for help.

"Nurse!" I call. One jumps from the front desk. "It's Ryan."

She strides past me. Ryan's still crying, holding her head.

"I woke up, and she was like this."

"Sweetie, I need you to lean back." The nurse takes Ryan's hand in hers and carefully pushes her onto the bed. Ryan weeps, begging the nurse to please help her, which only tears me apart. I walk over to the other side of her as the nurse shines a light in her eyes. "I know it hurts," she whispers. "Just try to relax while I give you more medicine." I take Ryan's hand in mine and squeeze it. Our eyes lock for the first time since this morning. "I'm right here," I say quietly to avoid making her pain worse. I bring her hand to mine and kiss it. It won't ease her pain, but her eyes do soften as tears fall. I look to the nurse. "Will it help if she closes her eyes?"

The nurse nods. "Her vision's probably still blurry, and her sensitivity to light won't make it better." Ryan closes her eyes and her hand clenches tightly as she tries to shift the pain. I ache to do something to ease her—to run my fingers through her hair or rub her head the way I do to get her to sleep. But I can do nothing with the large bandage over her head.

The nurse fills the tap with more medicine in thirty seconds, subsiding Ryan's tears. The crinkles around her eyes disappear and her body relaxes as the medicine works its magic.

"There we go," the nurse whispers, a satisfied smile on her face. "I'm going to monitor this every hour, instead of every three, and schedule you for another head CT scan first thing in the morning."

"What time is it?" she croaks.

"A little after ten," the nurse tells us. "I'm going to get the doctor. Do you have any recollection of what happened today, Ryan?"

"Ivan took me to an apartment." She looks down at her lap, brushing more tears from her face. "He kept hitting me over the head with his gun."

"Do you remember being shot?" the nurse asks.

"No." Ryan wipes more tears from under her chin.

"You've had an awful few hours, so just give yourself time. You've survived a miracle, and it's going to take some time to recover. Your shoulder is dislocated, and you've got a concussion. You're lucky to be alive."

Ryan says nothing, her only response to blink in bewilderment.

"Do you think you could give us some time alone?" I ask the nurse. "This is a lot for her to take in right now."

"Of course," she replies. "I'll be outside if you need anything and back in an hour." She leaves the room silently, closing the door behind her.

Ryan scoots over as far to the left as she can and tries to pull me into bed with her.

"Your arm, baby."

Her eyes are glued to mine. "Please."

As much as I want, I can't deny Ryan anything right now, especially her need to be close to me. I get in the bed as cautiously as I can, careful not to mess with any of her IV tubes or touch her until I'm fully in the bed, and slowly pull her into my arms. She buries her face in my neck, holding on to me tighter than she ever has before, and my neck instantly dampens from her tears.

"I thought he was going to kill me," she confesses for only my ears.

I can't even hold back my own tears. I hold on to her a little tighter and say, "I thought he did."

Ryan moves her face, her nose rubbing up my neck to my chin to my lips, and then pulls me into her, pressing our lips together slowly. She's too fragile, so I let her lead, not sure what she can handle.

"How'd you find me?" she asks, kissing me again.

"Baby, I'd blow up all of G-Heights just to find you." I chuckle, careful not to raise my tone to an octave that will make her head hurt. "Shae told me about the apartment, and how your dad and Ivan run girls through there. We figured he didn't have many options for places to take you, and once I heard the gunshots, I knew exactly where you were."

"That's when he shot me?"

I shake my head. "Another girl was in the room. She was dead when I got there. Ivan had your face pressed to the bed."

She gasps. Visions must run through her mind as she recollects what happened before she blacked out. "She was so young." She covers her mouth with her hands. "He was going to force us to . . ."

More tears fall from her eyes, so I shush her. We can go over what happened later. All that matters is we're together now.

"Let's talk about that later." I take her left hand and entwine it with mine, looking at her.

"I love you." She touches her head to mine slowly and carefully, her eyes shining holes into mine as she speaks. "You saved my life, Devyn. No one has ever loved me the way you do."

I bend down, pressing my lips to hers. "I love you." As much as I don't want to relive today's tragic events, the fear of Ryan hating me for killing someone overwhelms my thoughts. Ryan only knows the best parts of me, but I can't hide this from her. "I have something to tell you."

"Okay," she whispers, her hands still entwined with mine.

"I killed Ivan," I whisper. "Everything happened so fast— he shot his gun, I shot mine. The next thing I knew, the ambulance was taking everyone, and I was thrown in a police car for what they said could be three murders—"

"Police car?"

I nod. "I just want you to know I'm not another monster. I—"

"I'd never think that," she assures me. More tears fall from her eyes, and I wipe them away. "Do you know what this means?" I shake my head. "I have nothing to be afraid of anymore. No more looking over my shoulder or worrying about what's going to happen to you or your family. This ends here . . . because of you, Devyn."

"It wasn't my job to kill him, though."

Ryan's fingers trace my jawline. "You regret saving my life?"

"You know the answer. How could I regret that?"

"Then don't look at it like this," she whispers. "He *murdered* that girl because I told him no."

"What?"

"You saved so many more lives than you know." I can tell she's starting to get sleepy, but I let her fight her rest. I selfishly don't want to stop talking. Her body gets heavier as she gets more comfortable. "What happened to my dad?"

"He was arrested," I reply. "I don't know anything other than that."

"Will you be here when I wake up?"

I kiss her temple. "I don't plan on letting you out of my sight."

Her giggles make her recoil, touching her head in pain. "Ow." She pouts. "Don't make me laugh. My head is throbbing."

"I'm not being funny." With her arm and the rehab she'll have to do on top of tutoring, I don't plan to leave Ryan alone until she's fully healed.

Ryan cuddles into me, wrapping her uninjured arm around my waist, the other one resting on her stomach, so

I let her sleep. We're back together, in each other's arms and in the safest place possible.

CHAPTER 24

RYAN

Sunlight coming through the blinds wakes me up this morning, the light shining in my eyes. Devyn sleeps silently next to me, his neck fully extended as he rests on the wall behind us. I can't believe everything that happened yesterday. Ivan and the women in that old apartment. The girl Ivan killed and Devyn killing Ivan. My dad in jail . . .

Just yesterday, life was completely different. But thanks to Devyn, who's now saved my life in more ways than one, I no longer have to live in fear. Even with my injuries and throbbing headache, I feel so much relief.

A light knock on the door takes me out of my thoughts as I watch my nurse from last night walk into the room. "Hospital beds are for patients," she scolds, but is quiet enough not to wake Devyn. "Did you get any sleep?"

I nod as she examines my IV. "Yes, but only because he's here. Can we let him rest? Yesterday was just as bad for him as it was for me."

She looks at me through long lashes. "I don't see a bullet wound on him." I'm not sure if she really has a problem or is messing with me. "How're you feeling?"

"Sore," I tell her. "And tired."

"As you should be," the nurse replies. "I'm going to take you up to X-rays to get a head CT. It'll take thirty minutes, but your fiancé won't be allowed to come. He can stay in here or the waiting room."

Fiancé?

She goes to get the wheelchair from the corner of the room while I pull the covers from my body, careful not to wake Devyn. Hopefully he's still asleep when I get back.

The nurse helps me out of bed and into the chair. Devyn stirs once I get settled but doesn't wake up.

"I better not get in trouble for this." She sighs, rolling me out of the room.

I come back fifty minutes later, my pleasant morning mood shifted. I'm tired, and all the moving around only made me sorer and more irritable. I don't know how I'll be able to lift trays and clean up plates when I get back to New York.

The new nurse, an older white woman with heavy hands and terrible breath, takes me to my room with hastened steps. Unlike the night nurse, she makes no effort to start small talk or even maintain a bedside manner. So I'm relieved to find Devyn out of the bed and back in the chair when we come in. He stands as we enter.

"Good morning." His smile makes me want to melt into a puddle in my seat. Doesn't matter the time of day or my mood, my attraction to him goes beyond my body's capabilities. I'd jump out of this chair and into his arms if I could muster the strength.

"Morning," I respond, watching him glide toward me. He bends down to press a kiss to my lips.

"Do you need help getting her into bed?" Devyn straightens up.

"No. If you get out of the way, I'll be fine." Her comment's rude, but I don't say anything. The smile on Devyn's face tells me he finds her amusing, though. He steps out of her way and goes back to his seat, watching carefully as she helps me onto the bed. I'm happy I can finally rest. My shoulder is aching and itchy in this cast.

"I'll be back with your breakfast and to re-up your pain meds," she tells me. "The doctor gets in around seven-thirty. He'll discuss your X-ray results and the extent of your injuries." She turns around and walks out of the room, not giving me time to say thank you.

"The nurses in this place are awful," I say.

Devyn laughs, leaning into the bed and resting his arm on my leg.

"Did they say anything about when I can go home?"

He shakes his head, "I don't know, baby. I'm sure we'll know more after we talk to the doctor." Devyn reaches over and takes my hand in his, rubbing his fingers over my knuckles. I don't know if he knows I'm irritated and in pain, but he sure knows the right way to calm me down. "Does your head hurt?"

"Kind of." I sigh. "My shoulder hurts more."

Devyn nods. "Good. Hopefully that means your concussion is healing."

"How long have you been up?"

"I opened my eyes as they were wheeling you out."

I take a moment to analyze him. The bags under his eyes are heavy and his beard is overgrown and disheveled. "You should've woken me up. I could've gone with you."

"The nurse said no one else could be in the room." I'm not going to mention the nurse's lecture about him being in the bed. If I have to stay here tonight, I can't have him chicken out of sleeping with me. I retract my hand from his and cup his face. "You're tired. You should go home and rest."

Devyn shakes his head. "I'm not leaving you here alone."

His protectiveness makes me smile. "So if I'm here for another night, you're not going to change your clothes or shower or brush your teeth?"

"I'll have my dad bring me stuff."

"Devyn—"

"I'm good." He pulls his chair as close to my bed as possible. "You want me to leave?" A smile sits at the tip of his lips, telling me he knows the answer.

"I don't want you to be uncomfortable. You're going to have to go home and get yourself together a little bit."

"How about I take care of you?" Devyn brings our hands to his lips and plants a kiss on my wrist. "You look tired too."

"I am." I pout. "And my shoulder hurts."

"Lie down." Devyn moves to adjust my position and pillows with careful precision. I'm too tired to resist. Devyn takes the blanket and pulls it up to my chest.

"I miss you lying next to me." Hospitals are the least homey environments, and I'd much rather be healing in a big, comfortable bed with him.

Devyn laughs, leaning in to kiss me. "That's why we have to get you better." He plants another kiss on my mouth and cheek.

"I don't like it here."

"I know." He leans up. "Another reason we need to get you home."

***

After hours of questioning the doctor, discussing pros and cons, and then being convinced to allow Hope and Diana to watch me, Devyn reluctantly agrees to get his things from his house. I know being in a hospital is wearing him down. He needs to get outside, shower, and recoup. He's been by my side all day, sitting in the chair and tending to my every need.

My concussion's so severe, I have to spend a couple more days in the hospital to watch for bleeding, but the swelling has gone down. I'm to be back in four days to get another CT scan, and to immediately come back if I start having bad migraines. We'll have to go to New York a couple of days later than we thought, but the doctor says I'll be good as long as I'm careful.

Devyn asks how long it could be till I'm able to work, and the doctor says a month, which makes me burst into tears. I've saved enough, but even coming here for a week makes my paycheck smaller. Devyn keeps quiet, but I know he's happy I'll have more time to be by his side when we're back at school.

It's mid-afternoon, and I'm drowsy from the medicine-induced nap I just woke up from. I've been in and out of sleep for the last couple of hours but I know Hope and Diana have been here for at least thirty minutes. I briefly heard Devyn instruct them to let him know when I wake up, if they do any more tests, or if I'm in any pain at all.

"Hey." Diana speaks softly as my eyes open. She and Hope sit in chairs at my bedside. They both look tired but keep sympathetic smiles on their faces as they look at me with concern. "How are you feeling?"

"Just tired." I use my free arm to lift myself up and lean against the headboard. They watch me carefully as I take my time getting comfortable. "I'm so sorry about what happened with Ivan. Are you guys okay?"

Both of them open their mouths to speak, but Hope goes first. "Are *you*?" Her eyes instantly water and tears fall. "Did he do anything to you?"

I shake my head. "Devyn got there before he could." I lean over and take her hand in mine. "Neither of you deserved what happened yesterday. Ivan had no right to touch you guys or hold you at gunpoint. I should have told you what was going on so we could all be aware, but I—"

"Ryan, I thought he was going to kill you!" Hope sobs, burying her face in her hands. Tears fall from Diana next, but she stays silent. "We should've went with you. I was just so scared; I didn't know what to do."

"It's okay—"

"It's not," she cries. "He shot you and he hit you, and you're sitting here apologizing to us about how *we* didn't deserve that? We're sorry. I'm sorry for all the times when I could see something was wrong and never tried to do anything about it."

I don't know what to say. For the first time in forever, I don't have to hide my pain. My truth has finally been set free and my burdens are gone.

"I love you guys." I wipe the tears off my face as they get up to hug me. I feel like they're finally seeing all of me for the first time. None of us can avoid what happened or what we've been through. All we can do is move on, support each other, and grow from this. Maybe this situation was the slap in the face we all needed.

"We love you," Diana responds as we hold each other. Hope's still crying, which surprises me. She's never emotional. A knock on the door interrupts our intimate moment, making us all release our embrace and turn to the two men at the door.

"Good afternoon," a handsome black man in a navy suit says as he steps inside the room.

"Good afternoon." Hope straightens up and wipes her tears, her face hardening. She's taking Devyn's orders to watch over me seriously. Diana keeps her hands on my upper back, comforting me.

"I'm Detective Karim Johnson, and this is Officer Jason Matthews, the officer at the crime scene yesterday." He keeps his eyes on me as he speaks while the redheaded white man in the police uniform stands behind him silently. "We'd like to talk to you about the things that went on last night."

"You don't think Devyn should be here for this?" Hope says to me.

"We'd like to speak to Ms. McKnight alone," Detective Johnson interrupts.

"They need to stay." I'm not about to be alone with the officers who arrested Devyn when he was only protecting me. I don't want to be alone with the police, period. I turn my attention toward Hope again. "Can you call Devyn?"

She nods and quickly exits. Diana stays by my side.

"First, I'm glad you're okay. My condolences for what's happened to you. We have some questions, and then hopefully we'll be done. Your boyfriend, Devyn, gave us a lot of information."

I nod.

"First, can you tell us what you remember?"

"I know everything until Ivan shot me," I tell him, "I was getting breakfast with Hope and Diana. Ivan was waiting outside. I don't know how he knew I was there."

The detective nods. "It's a small neighborhood, and you weren't too far from where he and your father lived. I'm sure he'd been watching you since you got to LA."

I won't ask how.

"Had Ivan contacted you while you were in New York?"

I nod. "He had my father call me and offer money to spend time with him."

"Your father, Javon McKnight."

I snort. "If you can call him that."

"Do you know why Ivan went to New York?"

"My dad said to pick up some girls. I never saw them, but he threatened to put me in the car with them." I look down at my hands. "Maybe he planned to take me back all along. Devyn was with me, and I think he got scared."

"When Ivan threatened to take you, did he use force or have a weapon?"

I shake my head. "He was just talking."

The redhead officer speaks next. "Do you know if Ivan and Devyn had any previous relationship before his relationship to you?"

"What do you mean?"

"Did he work for them or have friends who did?"

If he's talking about Manny, he won't get any information out of me. Devyn has no connection to this.

"Not that I know of."

"What's this about?" Diana asks.

"We have evidence that Devyn could have worked with Ivan and Javon."

I laugh. "That's impossible."

"No one's seen any interaction between the three of them, but for some reason, both Ivan and Javon seem to fear him. Ivan comes to get you from New York, and he has to know you won't be willing to go back with him. He didn't bring any weapons or try to touch you, but when he saw Devyn, he just let you go. Suddenly, Devyn's back in LA—"

"His best friend was shot."

"As we've heard." The detective speaks up. "Your father has already admitted to shooting Emmanuel."

"What?" I gasp.

"You didn't know?"

Tears fall down my face, making me angry. Javon doesn't deserve my tears. He tried to kill Manny, and for what? To get me here? To set this up? "I have barely talked to that man since I left for school."

Hope enters the room and walks over to me.

"You're trying to convince yourselves Devyn dating me was a plot to get me back to LA so he could . . ." I have to force the words out of my mouth. "*Sell* me to Ivan and Javon? How does that even make sense?"

"Please calm down, ma'am. We're just exploring all possibilities," Officer Matthews says. His attempt to soothe me only makes me want to punch him in the face.

I brush the tears away, still not clear on why I'm crying. "All Devyn has ever done is protect me. He came here to protect Manny and to make sure his family's good. I came back to LA to support him. He didn't have anything to do with this."

Detective Johnson nods. "Devyn was cooperative with us, and it looks like your stories do align. I'm going to put both statements on record and make sure the case is closed."

"Will Devyn be okay?" I ask, relief brimming in my psyche. The detective nods. "Yes. I'm going to rule Ivan's death as self-defense. We cannot determine Ivan's intentions with you, but I'll assume he wanted you back to either sell you, have you for himself, or both."

"What'll happen to my dad?"

"Because of his admission to the attempted murder of Emmanuel, he'll be charged for that as well as kidnapping, pimping, and pandering, and the trafficking of minors. Your father will not be a problem for you any longer."

"Will I have to testify?"

"No. We have more than enough evidence, but should we find out further information, would you like us to give you a call?"

I shake my head. I'm ready to leave my father behind. Our relationship has gone far beyond its boundaries and breaking points. He'd be an unfillable void, but I'm better off without him.

I can finally put my past to rest. I've laid down my burdens and can now walk in a new light, a light I can shine on myself instead of using it to keep others warm. I feel safe and protected. I feel optimistic and healed, despite my physical injuries. I'm ready to get out of this hospital and step into new beginnings.

All eyes go to the door as Devyn rushes in, looking like he sprinted all the way here from the parking lot. His chest rises and falls as he struggles to catch his breath, his eyes on me.

"Everything okay, officers?" Devyn asks the men.

"We're fine," I say as he quickly kisses my cheek to greet me.

"We're just asking Ms. McKnight some follow-up questions."

"I'll let her give me the details." Devyn stands up straight, growing tense as he talks with the policemen. Officer

Matthews keeps his eyes on Devyn, saying nothing. Devyn doesn't even look his way.

"Sounds good. We'll be out of your way then." The detective nods. "I'll do everything in my power to make sure this case doesn't inconvenience you any longer."

"Thank you," Devyn says sternly, but his steady exhale tells me he's relieved.

"Of course." Detective Johnson motions for the officer to lead them out of the room. He does so without a word, but I notice the weird glance he gives Devyn as he exits the room. The detective waits for Officer Matthews to fully exit before stopping and facing all of us. "You know, I've been in this neighborhood my whole life, and it fails us—every kid raised here is failed." He looks at me. "You did not deserve what happened to you, and I'm so sorry that it did. But thank you for fighting to get out of here, and for fighting against the sickness that's diseased this community for generations. Hopefully, actions like yours can make G-Heights better."

CHAPTER 25

RYAN

THREE WEEKS LATER

"You're the only person in this world who tries to hide the fact that they have a cast just for pictures," Devyn says as he helps me slip my black leather trench coat over my shoulder brace. We've been in his room all morning and into the early afternoon, Devyn helping me get dressed like he does every day. Just putting on clothes can be excruciatingly painful and takes careful precision, so it's not a job I can do myself.

"When we look back at pictures, I'd like to forget being shot." I smile as he adjusts my outfit so it's as perfect as can be. He knows how important a good outfit is to me, and the caution he takes in helping me look my best is cute. He even helped me put on makeup (something he swears to deny if I tell anyone). "No cast, no memory."

"I hope it's that easy." Devyn backs up to assess my outfit, so I take the time to assess him. He looks so handsome. His long black button-down and black jeans are identical to the black turtleneck and leggings I have on, and I'm loving that we're matching.

It's been three weeks since my accident, my father's arrest, and Ivan's death. We managed to get back to New York in time for Devyn to play his last game for the season and to meet with our teachers before heading back to LA for Thanksgiving. We originally planned to stay in New York to save money, but with everything that's happened, we both decided it's best to spend the holiday with family and friends.

I keep silent, letting Devyn finish getting me together. When he's done, he helps me up and twirls me around to admire his work.

"Damn." He pulls me closer. "I did a good job."

I wrap my good arm around his neck and press my lips to his.

"Love you," I say in between kisses.

Devyn cups my face in his, the pad of his thumb rubbing back and forth along my jaw. "I love you too." He kisses me again. "I don't think we should try to forget."

"Yeah?"

"Yeah." He nods. "We went through a lot, but I think some good things came out of the situation."

I laugh. "Like what? Injury and—"

"Like love," he says, shutting me up. "And new appreciation for family."

His sentimentality makes my heart flutter. "What else?"

"We're more solid than we've ever been." He smiles gently and his eyes shine as he speaks. "Maybe we can shift the meaning of all this trauma and think of the good things that came from it."

"You heal people in more ways than one, baby." I get on my tippy-toes to kiss him again. "I'm so thankful to have you as my partner."

Devyn laughs and pulls me into him, devouring me with kisses until silly giggles escape my lips. "We're in this till the wheels fall off." He kisses me again. "Come on. Dinner should be ready in a little bit."

Thanksgiving dinner with the Bakers consists of the twins, Devyn, his father, and Manny and his family. Manny, who was just released from the hospital two days ago, sits with his sister, the twins, and my newfound half-brother, Jodeci. All of them talk over the Rams versus Seahawks game playing on TV, and the mouthwatering scents of a Thanksgiving feast prepared by Devyn's dad and Manny's mom wafts through the house. We greet them all with hugs and "Happy Thanksgivings."

"Why didn't you tell me we were matching today?" Cara says as I hug her last. She just finished setting the table, which is decorated with a burgundy tablecloth, candles, and colored cutouts of leaves.

"I can't have one day to myself?" Devyn teases. He picks her up and kisses her cheek. "Go grab everyone. We're about to eat." He places her on the ground, and she runs to grab the rest of the family.

We all gather around the table, trays of turkey, mac and cheese, yams, greens, and more filling the table. The smell alone is enhancing my desire to eat and making my stomach growl. Devyn's dad sits at the head of the table, Devyn to the left of him and Cara to the right, me and the rest of the family filing in next to them. We all take our seats before joining hands.

"It's been a hard few weeks." Devyn's father's voice booms through the kitchen. "But through every tribulation, we've shown that family is what gets you through. There's no love greater than this one, and nothing we can't do together." My eyes lock with his as he speaks, and he winks at me. "So let's be thankful for that. Family—both new, old, and extended."

My heart feels so full. I lost my father but gained so much in such a short period of time. I'm now around people who I know have my back and will be there for me. They all accepted me into their hearts and home, and I'm so grateful.

"In Baker tradition, we'd like everyone to say what they're thankful for."

"My family!" Cara says.

"My brother and sister," Cory says next.

"Happy Tanksgiving!" Jodeci says next, making everyone laugh.

Shae wipes her falling tears with her napkin. "My son and my brother."

"My children," her mother says next.

"Life," Manny says, his face also a mixture of smiles and tears.

I have so much to be thankful for, I find it hard to say just one. "All of you."

"The greatest love," Devyn says last, his eyes on me.

"Happy Thanksgiving. I love you all." Devyn's dad holds up a glass of iced tea in cheers. "Let's eat."

"Finally!" Shae exclaims, reaching for the mac and cheese. A ring at the door makes Cara jump from her seat.

"I'll get it!"

Devyn's dad gets up to run after her. "Ask who it is first!"

Devyn leans into me. "You make me feel like I can do anything, so I'm most thankful for you. I love you."

I lean in and kiss him. "I love you."

He smiles at me, but something above me instantly takes the color out his face. "What the fu—"

I turn around as Devyn's dad walks into the room, the look on his face mirroring his son's. Next to him, Cara holds the hand of a disheveled, almost gray woman in raggedy, ripped jeans, a turquoise tank top, and overgrown cornrows in her hair.

"This is the best Thanksgiving ever!" Cara jumps. "Mommy's finally home!"

ACKNOWLEDGMENTS

—

I would like to thank anyone and everyone who contributed to making my dreams of publishing my first book possible! The love and support I have received during this process has been far more than I could have ever imagined. I am so grateful to Eric Koester and all those at NDP who assisted in helping create this book. With every step and question, you all were so kind, caring, and helpful. Coming across this program was one of the best things to happen to me in 2020. You've exceeded my expectations and made the process of coming out with this book an amazing experience.

To all the family and friends who took the time to get interviewed, read sample material, and give feedback: Part of my goal in writing this book was to create characters people could not only enjoy but identify with. I could not have done it without help from all of you.

And a special thank-you to all of my lovely beta readers!

Alexis Shettleroe
Aline and Danny
    Bakewell Sr.
Allen Moret

Anastasia Christos
Ansley Benton
Antoinette Brown
Arnolda Lewis

Avis Bell
Bethanee Boggs
Blair Blackwell
Brandi Bakewell
Brandi Bakewell
Brandon and Bria
 Brooks
Briana Barnes
Bryan Bloomfield
Bryce Bakewell
Candace Moret
Candy Torres
Caroline McCreary
Carrie Mathews
Chanel Lake
Charleen Blache
Chloé Lewis
Chrissa Gaines
Christopher Nola
Courtni Hill
Cynthia Pollard
Daniel Pollard
Daniel Pollard
Danny Bakewell III
Danny Bakewell Jr.
Denee Stokes
Denver Mackey
Diana Andrews
Dylan Neil
Eddie Gorton
Edward Morales
Eric Bradley

Eric Koester
Fatima Elswify
Georgia Simpson
Giselle Sorial
Hanna Hedberg
Ia Brown
James A. Bolton
Jamie Pascal
Janae Washington
Jannie McKinney
Jenna Gulick
Jillian Taboada
Joi Harris
Joni Folse
Jonie Thomas
Joya Mills
Joyce Jones-Ivey
Julia Ayala
Julissa Lagune
Kai Bakewell
Kamryn Rabb
Kanani Hartage
Karen Jones Jordan
Kennedy Shirley
Khylah Everage
Kraig Golden
Kristina Smith
Lauren Barnes
Linda DeCuir
Loreal Carter
Lupita Lopez
Naima Stepheson

Nichelle Holliday
Pamela Bakewell
Quentin Collier
Rickey Ivie
Riley Benjamin
Rodney Mathews
Santana Lewis
Sarah Jordan
Sashanie Keise
Sunna Brooks
Sydnie Johnson
Taelor Bakewell

Tamela Motchell
Tana Tate-Bakewell
Tiffany Menendez
Tracy Mitchell
Tricia Elam Walker
Tyler Shadrach
Vanessa Clarke
Wanda Lewis
Wendell Youkins
Yolanda Sanders
Zoe Lavallie

This book would not have happened if it weren't for you. Thank you for believing in my dream and taking this journey with me. Thank you for embracing Ryan and Devyn's story and the love they share! I hope I've made you all proud with this novel. This is only the beginning!

ABOUT THE AUTHOR

Devyn Bakewell wrote this book because she believes that black people need to be better represented in literary canon. They deserve to give firsthand accounts of their stories and to read about them. Black life and love also need to be discussed more and celebrated in literature. Devyn currently studies English and African Studies at Howard University.

Her passion is that all black people, young and old, find a way to share their stories and ideas with the world, and that they connect with the black community as a source of encouragement. She believes that if we all come together as one in love and support, the opportunities of this life are endless.

For more information, you can connect with Devyn Bakewell at *greaterlovenovel@gmail.com* or on all social media platforms *@dgirl2221.*